THE LAST ANGEL

THE ACCOUNT TRILOGY: BOOK ONE

SARAH PJ WHITE

White
Heart
Publishing

First published in the UK
by White Heart Publishing, 2013

Copyright Sarah PJ White, 2013
(Cover change & grammatical edits, 2018)

A copy of the British Library Cataloguing in Publication Data is available from the British Library

eBook edition ISBN: 978-0-9573679-1-3
Print edition ISBN: 978-0-9573679-2-0

Cover Design: Sophie-Louise White - White Spark Creations

For those friends & family members
who supported me – no matter what came our way

ACKNOWLEDGEMENTS

My thanks go to those people who have helped to bring this novel into existence. To my mum for the love and support she's provided, and to my talented daughter, Sophie-Louise White at White Spark Creations – not only for her amazing graphic design skills on the cover, but also for her help, support and faith in me. To Katie and Jon for their support – and letting me talk for hours about a book that, in that moment, didn't exist. And finally, to Alan, my husband and best friend, for grounding me when it was needed – and letting me fly when the time arose. Without his unwavering love and support, this book would never have happened.

BONUS CONTENT

Get your bonus gift of my 'Behind The Scenes' pack, when you join my free Readers VIP List.

To get started, simply head over to:

sarahpjwhite.com/bonus-content/

1

Crystal pulled her coat collar closer. The evening had turned cold and breezy. She was glad to be heading for the pub – and just as grateful for the warmth her red wool coat provided. Her mother had wanted to have a chat but, after the day Crystal had had, she needed a drink, a laugh, and time to let her hair down, before yet another dream-fuelled, unsettling night ensued. A few stray strands of black and red hair freed themselves from her beige scarf, whipping her across the face. She tucked them, rather pointlessly, behind her ear as she turned the corner into Turpin Street and again, as she crossed the road. She nodded at Father Javier as he passed her, before heading towards the end of the street.

She'd lived in Thatcham all her life and Father Javier had been a regular feature for the past two years, since he'd taken on the role of parish priest of St Barnabas Roman Catholic church and the pastoral care of the community. Thatcham was a pretty little town – quiet, with nothing much of interest ever happening. Its main claim to fame however, was its mention in the Guinness Book of Records as the oldest continually inhabited place in Britain. Its other saving grace was the Duke of Earl pub, where Crystal and her friends met on a regular basis.

As she neared the Duke of Earl, she spotted the small group of her friends to the side of the pub, huddled around the patio heater that had been thoughtfully provided for the smoking patrons.

'Bloody weather,' she could hear Amy grumbling. 'Bloody smoking ban.' Amy dragged on the remnants of her roll up, before angrily stamping on it with her purple, four-inch stiletto. 'God, Crystal. I'm glad you're finally here, I'm freezing my bloody tits off.' Amy briefly hugged her friend, before turning on her heels and hurrying inside. Chris, Mark and Emily followed her through the pine double doors. Amy, all wiggle and bouncy raven black hair, walked straight over to the bar and banged on the counter.

'Oi, Russell. When you get a second?'

Russell, the barman, put down the cloth he was drying the glasses with and walked, grinning towards Amy.

'All right Amy? Want the usual?'

Amy grinned back at him before nodding her head and leaning forward to give him a kiss and affectionately tousle his brown mop of hair.

'You know you're my favourite barman.' She flashed him another show-stopping smile. 'I love the fact you know exactly what I need to make me happy.' Her eyes wandered to the guy walking past the bar.

'Hi Justin.' She flicked her hair behind her shoulders and jutted her chest out. The guy looked away and hurriedly walked past.

'Someone you know?' Russell asked as she turned back to face him.

'Not anymore.' Amy quickly replaced the hurt look on her face with a dazzling smile. 'Do you know what will make me happy then?'

'Yeah, vodka and cola... Unless you've changed your mind and wanna hook up with me?' Russell flashed a hopeful look in Amy's direction, before looking past her, assessing the rest of the group and continuing, 'Let me make that two vodka and colas, one white wine and two pints of cider.'

Whilst Amy flirted with Russell and got the round in, the others wandered across the old, wooden floor to the corner booth. Crystal took off her coat and scarf, hanging them on the wall hooks behind the booth, hugged Chris and Mark and sat down next to blonde, angel-faced Emily. After they had all exchanged pleasantries, they agreed it had been a shit Tuesday and, with Amy being the rowdiest one of the group and still at the bar, they all lapsed into their own little worlds.

Crystal loved this pub. It was always well lit, warm and clean. She looked around at the other red leather seated booths. Obviously it was a quiet evening, as most of the booths were empty. A group of women were having a whispered conversation in the next booth, whilst a couple of men played pool in the corner to Crystal's left. The click of the cue against the pool balls was intermingled with Snow Patrol's' 'Chasing Cars' playing softly over the speaker system. Apart from this, the bar was quiet. She looked over the far side of the room, glancing past Amy at the bar and towards a scruffy middle-aged man in the opposite corner of the room. Their eyes met, ever so briefly, before Amy, returning with the drinks got in the way. Crystal leant back so Amy could put the tray of drinks down on the table, before gratefully accepting her own vodka and cola.

After two more rounds of drinks, Amy had roused the group from their thoughts and woke everyone up. They had placed their money on the pool table, ready for when the men had finished their last game and began making unsubtle comments about Crystal getting the next round in. Five minutes later Crystal finished her drink and, deciding the others had waited long enough, got up and headed towards Russell.

The middle-aged man in the opposite corner of the bar was watching Crystal walk closer. He stood up, rather unsteadily and worked his way from his corner of the room, around the counter towards her, before collapsing exhausted on the nearest stool. Crystal cast a glance at him, whilst she waited to order the round of drinks.

He was early 40s, she guessed, with really dark blue, almost black eyes. She couldn't help but notice them, as he was staring straight at her. He was also pissed as a fart – judging by how his body was swaying from left to right on the stool he was sat on, even with both of his army-boot clad feet on the ground. His tatty, long brown, oilskin jacket smelt like damp tent and was obviously much loved, as it had been repaired in places with bits of finger strip plasters. She wrinkled her nose in disdain. She wasn't sure if it was his breath or his grubby black t-shirt and jeans that stank of Jack Daniels. Crystal broke eye contact and willed Russell to hurry up with the customer he was serving.

'All right?' the man slurred.

Oh crap, he's talking to me, Crystal thought. She rubbed her arms as a slight breeze made her shiver, then gave him a half smile in acknowledgement, but stayed quiet.

'Hey – are you alright?' he asked again. He was persistent, she'd give him that.

'Oi, I'm talking to you!' Even his scruffy dirty-blond hair

4

bounced back and forth with annoyance. He leant towards her, at an alarming angle, in danger of sliding off the stool and onto the floor.

Crystal gave in and replied. 'I'm fine thanks, you?' She really didn't want to talk to him, especially as he was obviously off his face and smelt as if he had bathed in his drink, but Russell was still caught up with the other person's drinks order – and the drunk man was only going to get louder if she didn't respond.

'I'm good, nothing another J.D wouldn't solve,' he hinted, smiling unsubtly.

Oh God, Crystal thought, indignantly, I'm getting chatted up by a geriatric, pissed, stinky alcoholic.

'I'll get you another drink if you like, once the barman gets here – and if you'll then leave me alone.' She thought it was worth a shot, just to get rid of him. He didn't respond.

Crystal watched as another group of people walked into the pub, straight up to the bar where Russell was stood. She felt the gentle breeze created by the closing bar door. Her shoulders drooped in despair as Russell began to take their drinks order. Bugger, if I'd been Amy he'd have noticed me stood here straight away, she thought despondently. She looked back at the booth. Her friends were all deep in conversation. Well, at least they're not noticing how long it's taking for me to get served, she thought, before looking back round again. Her eyes met with the eyes of the drunken man. He must have been quite handsome, once. He leant forward, beckoning her to come closer.

'I want to tell you a secret.'

Oh God, she thought, I don't think I wanna know. Crystal leant forward, if only to prevent him from sliding off his stool and onto the floor.

'I want to tell you a secret,' he repeated.

'Ok, what's this big secret?'

He was close now; exhaling alcohol-fuelled breath in her face. He leant close enough to whisper in her ear.

'God didn't create the world,' he whispered. 'People like us did.'

2

Crystal stared at the man. 'Pardon?'

He stared back at her, leant across and repeated his comment. 'God didn't create the world,' he whispered. 'People like us did.'

Before Crystal could comment, Amy interrupted by shouting across the room at her.

'Hey, slow coach, hurry up with those drinks!'

'I'm waiting for Russell to finish serving.' She turned back to the man. He was still staring at her, waiting for some sort of reaction.

Crystal looked around at her friends. Amy had rejoined the conversation, wildly throwing her arms around as she spoke, whilst the others were laughing at her efforts. Guess there was no help coming from that direction, she thought ironically. Her gaze turned back to the man, as he tapped her on the arm. She looked straight into his piercing eyes – although they seemed bluer than she remembered and lighter.

'I'm not mad you know.' He looked around. 'I'm not that drunk either. Although, to be fair, I have had a few drinks.'

No shit Sherlock, she thought, but didn't dare say it out loud. Because, to be honest, he did suddenly seem quite sober.

She looked over in Russell's direction. Luckily, he was coming over to her. He gave her an apologetic look before asking if she wanted the same order again. She was grateful for the intervention, as she really didn't know what to say to the drunk sat next to her. But he, unfortunately, wanted to continue the conversation.

'We're alike, you know.' He tapped his nose, indicating the supposedly shared secret, but Crystal had absolutely no idea what he was on about. She looked at Russell for inspiration.

'Look mate. She's not interested,' Russell stated before looking at Crystal and saying, 'Ignore him, love. He's off his face and doesn't know what he's saying.'

The man leant over the bar and said quietly, 'Piss off, mate. We were having a private conversation.' He turned, beckoning Crystal nearer again. Russell shrugged his shoulders and continued pouring the pints. Crystal tried to ignore the man and looked over instead to where her friends should be. Unfortunately, they had given up on the delayed drinks and had started on the first of many games of pool.

He took a swig of his drink and continued. 'We're alike, you and me. Not the same, but alike. We're special ya know.'

Crystal stifled the laugh that threatened to come out of her throat before replying. 'Yeah, we're *really* special.' She looked him up and down whilst raising an eyebrow to indicate the sarcasm she felt over that comment.

He ignored the sarcasm, although he had noticed it. 'I told you. People like us are special. We're involved.' He seemed so serious. So sober.

Sitting back on the stool, he continued. 'We're involved

in the big picture. That's why we're different' He jabbed his finger in her direction. 'You know it's true. You can see it.'

The man was starting to really piss her off now. Russell placed the tray of drinks in front of her, thankfully interrupting the rather one-sided conversation. Crystal paid for the drinks and looked at the drunk, whilst she waited for her change.

'OK mate. Whatever you say.' She pulled a confused face, indicating she was trying to end the conversation and then turned to walk away.

He sat on the stool, looked shocked and then actually laughed. 'Oh, jeez! You *don't* know, do you?' He grabbed her arm, making her jump and causing the cider to slosh out of the pint glasses and over the tray.

'How old are you? Have the dreams started yet?' he asked urgently.

Now he'd got her full attention. She hadn't talked about the dreams to anyone, other than her mother, so how the hell could he know about her dreams? Crystal shivered. He still had a tight hold of her arm, his fingers digging into her skin. She looked over at her friends. They were still concentrating on the game of pool. 'So much for their help and support,' she muttered to herself. Crystal looked toward Russell – he was serving customers in the suddenly busy bar. If she moved away and pulled from the drunk's grip now, the tray of drinks she'd waited so long for would go everywhere.

He swigged from his never-ending drink with one hand and hung onto her arm with the other, while muttering about the dreams. All Crystal could do was stand and wait either for him to let go, or someone to rescue her.

She stood there, trying to calm her breathing and heart rate. She hadn't told him anything of interest or anything personal, she reminded herself. He hadn't actually hurt her – present vice-like grip excluded. She felt her sheer panic falling to an almost normal apprehensive level and half-listened to his mutterings. 'After all,' she reasoned, 'I want a good look at this guy so I can describe him to the police, when I report him for bloody assault – or at least creepiness.' She edged round to face him, in an attempt to see more of his facial details, as well as to enable her to get into a position that would be nearer the counter and enable her to put the tray down.

He had a faraway look in his eyes as he muttered to himself about dreams. It was as if he was remembering dreams of his own. His eyes seemed dark again, like they had seemed when she'd first looked at him. She couldn't really hear much of what he was saying, but her ears pricked up – her heart rate sped up too – when she heard him mention flying. He was still in his own little world, so Crystal placed the tray on the bar counter and tried to gently prise his fingers from her arm.

'I was so scared when those dreams started.' His gaze flashed back to her, her efforts to remove his fingers from her arm jolting him back to the present moment. She had his full attention again.

He stared intently at her. 'You are having the dreams aren't you.' This time it was more of a statement, rather than a question.'Have the dark shadows started appearing yet?'

Crystal's eyes widened in fear. She couldn't release his grip and now he was just plain freaking her out.

She was really scared now. She opened her mouth and hollered as loud as she could, 'Russell!'

Russell came rushing round the end of the bar counter, placing one hand firmly on the man's shoulder.

'Hey, mate. Leave the girl alone.' He emphasised each word, to drive them home.

'*Mate*, you know nothing. So piss off and let me finish talking to the lady.' He drank the dregs from the bottom of his glass and slammed it on the table. 'So do me a favour and do your job. Fill up my empty glass.' He stared at Russell, waiting for a reaction.

Russell stepped round the end of the bar, grabbed Crystal's arm in one hand, the drunk's wrist in his other hand, and pulled the two of them apart.

'She doesn't want to talk to you. Now, take the hint.'

Crystal rubbed the sore finger marks on her arm that his tight grip had made. But she made no real effort to move back to her friends. She rubbed her eyes and stared at the man.

He was protesting to Russell that he was only trying to help her. He then asked Russell to get another drink – before lurching forward in an attempt to make another grab at Crystal.

Crystal stepped backwards out of harm's way, looking towards the pool table. Finally, her friends had noticed the commotion that was going on around her.

So had everyone else in the bar.

Emily came over with the others and put her arm around Crystal, fielding her towards the pool table and asking if she was OK. Bless quietly maternal Emily, Crystal thought, as she gratefully let herself be led away. Amy grabbed the tray of drinks before telling Chris and Mark to leave the pisshead to Russell – he would sort it. From the safety of the pool table area, they all watched Russell wrestling the drunk off his stool, resorting to a semi head-lock – all the while the drunk was protesting loudly about how he was trying to help her.

As Russell finally made it to the main entrance doors, Crystal watched as he unceremoniously shoved the man outside. When the door closed, Crystal planted a false smile on her face and turned back to her friends.

'I must be more tired than I thought; my vision is going all funny.'

Amy picked up her drink, took a swig and rather nonchalantly replied, 'Nah, he probably spiked your drink with some shit when you weren't looking. Decoy tactics and all that.'

'Thanks for your concern *mate*,' Crystal bit back sarcastically.

3

'Are you sure you're ok, Crystal?'

Crystal broke out of her trance and managed a weak smile in Emily's direction.

'I'm fine, honest. See – I'm smiling!'

'Do you want to play the next game of pool?' Emily looked towards Amy and the boys, watching Amy unsubtly leaning over the table, flashing her ample cleavage for them – and Russell. I'm sure they won't mind?' She was never very good at lying.

'Come here and let me hug you.' Crystal beckoned her friend closer, before wrapping her arms around her.

'You are the sweetest, best friend I could ever have.' Crystal pushed her friend back to arms length before continuing, 'but please, stop worrying about me.'

'But you still look really unsettled...'

'Em, I've known you since forever – and longer than any of them,' she added, glancing over at the pool table. 'Now you should know me well enough to know – when I say I'm fine; I really AM fine!'

Emily shrugged and looked at the floor. 'I'm worried

about you. First those dreams and now the weirdo – you've not been yourself lately either.'

'God, Emily!' Emily jumped and stared wide-eyed at her friend. Crystal softened her tone and hugged her again. 'Sorry. You know I hate fuss, but honestly, I'm fine. Would I lie to you?' Crystal tried to make her smile genuine.

'Hmm. Okay.' Emily wasn't convinced but knew when to leave it. 'Look, hasn't Amy got more front than Blackpool!' She was relieved when Crystal laughed. It lightened the mood and she knew she was forgiven.

Understandably, the pool table champion wasn't content with winning by a small margin. Amy insisted on playing several more games with the boys. They'd all clearly gotten over the earlier ruckus with the drunk – and they certainly had given up paying any attention to Crystal and Emily – both were sat in silence, with their own respective thoughts. Crystal loved Amy but you had to be in the right frame of mind to handle her 'over the top' attitude and character. And after tonight's happenings – she really wasn't.

She wondered if it was still too early to go home, without causing suspicion. She desperately wanted to have a moment to herself, to think. She glanced at the clock, before getting to her feet and giving an exaggerated stretch.

'I think I'm going to make a move home, Em. Do you want to walk with me?' She didn't wait for an answer, just took it as a done deal and started putting on her coat.

'Okay.' Emily stood and picked up her bag. 'Shall we let them know we're going?' She turned towards the pool table, glancing in Mark's direction.

'Night Guys!' Crystal hollered, as she headed towards the door.

Trudging down the road in mutual silence, Crystal could sense Emily giving her sideways glances every couple of minutes. She waited until they got to get to Turpin Street, before breaking the silence.

'You didn't mind leaving did you?'

'Nah, it's fine.' Emily replied.

The silence returned, as they walked down Turpin Street. Crystal knew her friend wouldn't start a conversation, due to the slight atmosphere. She'd wait for Crystal to make the first move, for risk of getting shouted at or starting an argument. Emily's mobile phone beeped to signal she'd received a text, breaking the silence. Glancing over at Emily, Crystal could see the colour rise in her cheeks.

'Come on then, who's that from?' Crystal turned and grinned at her. 'Judging by the colour you've gone... I'm betting it's from Mark?'

'He wanted to check whether we were all right, that's all.'

'You've liked each other for ages, everyone knows it.' Crystal continued before Emily could interject, 'We all know it and you both know it... so why don't you just ask him out?'

'It's not down to the girl to ask. I'm waiting for him to ask me.' Emily typed a quick reply before putting her phone back in her pocket. 'Anyway, I've let him know we're fine and I'll call him later.'

Crystal linked her arm through Emily's.

'You can be so old fashioned at times. Just ask him out! Did he think it was weird – us leaving and the stuff with that drunk guy?'

'He didn't mention it. I'm sure if he's got anything to say about it, he'll say it when we talk later. He just asked if we were all right and said he was going to Chris's flat with Amy, as she doesn't have to get back because her mum's at bible study with my dad, at church – again.'

'Sorry.' Crystal squeezed Emily's arm.

'Don't worry about it. I wouldn't have gone to Chris's

anyway. Let Amy have some more of the attention. I over-heard her talking to Chris, saying her mother was at church with my dad again. So I'm sure she'll have lots to say about that.'

'I know I, for one, cannot stand it when Amy gets on her soapbox about religion.' She looked across at Emily. 'I noticed you got a plaster on your finger. Did you do that at work?'

Emily glanced down at her index finger. 'Yeah, cut it with a craft knife whilst showing the school children how to safely use it.' She held her finger up in the air. 'Some health and safety lesson that turned out to be!'

'Let me have a look.' Crystal gently pulled the plaster off Emily's finger, before cupping it gently in her hands. A brief glow emanated from her cupped hands, briefly lighting the area, as if someone had lit a match, before fading away to darkness again.

'You didn't have to, you know.' Emily looked at her healed finger, then at her friend. 'Someone could have seen you do that.' She looked around to check no one was around.

'I know, but I wanted to. Take it as an apology. I'm sorry about snapping at you earlier. In the pub.'

'Do you want to talk about it yet?'

'No.' Crystal squeezed her arm again. 'Maybe tomorrow.'

They walked, arm in arm, down the road in a more agreeable silence until they reached the crossroads where they had to go their separate ways. They hugged each other goodbye, before walking down their respective paths – Emily to her house on Buttercup Crescent and Crystal to hers.

As she walked down the road towards her home, Crystal gazed at the other homes on the cul-de-sac. They were mostly three-bedroom homes, like the one Crystal and her mother lived in and theirs was one of only a few that had a conservatory built onto the back, but what really made their house stand out was the garden. Nestled at the end of the cul-de-sac, their brick house had a small, fenced off, front garden. The black iron fence protected Izzy's haven. She loved flowers and their garden had plenty of them in various colours and shapes.

As Crystal walked through the iron gate and followed the path to the front door, she brushed past the beautifully scented lavender bushes that sat in front of the rose bushes. She glanced over at the fragrant rose bushes and could see several tall plants growing steadily and healthily behind them, including stocks, with their heady evening scent. A small heavily cropping apple tree grew to the right of the path and, as she reached the front door, she was met with the wonderful smell of white jasmine, from the established plant that climbed up the side of the house. Crystal reached up to smell the flowers, a ritual she never grew tired of completing, before unlocking the door and going inside.

4

Upon waking Wednesday morning, the first thing Crystal became aware of was the fact that her nose was pressed against the ceiling – again. She opened her eyes and let out a strangled shriek before falling back down to her bed.

'God! That hurt!'

She gave herself a few seconds to catch her breath and, feeling slightly childish, tried at the same time to quieten it enough to listen for any sign that her mother might have heard the contact crash and come to investigate. Satisfied there were no tell-tale footsteps coming up the stairs, nor a concerned face appearing around the door, she gingerly swung her legs over the edge of her bed and sat up.

The second thing she noticed was how tired she felt.

Unbelievable, she thought, slept for nigh on ten hours and I'm still bloody knackered.

She rested her head in her hands for a few minutes, allowing her brain time to connect with her consciousness, time to register the details of the latest bizarre dream.

Dragging her fingers through her black & red tangled

hair, Crystal mulled over the details. This was the fifth time in two weeks that she had dreamt about flying. It was also the fifth time she had woken up with her nose squashed against the ceiling. Needless to say, it was also the fifth time she had woken up feeling equally crabby and knackered after sleeping a supposedly 'decent' amount of time.

So much for turning twenty-one, Crystal thought as she hauled herself to a standing position.

Crystal glanced in the mirror, moving the flourishing Prayer Plant out of the way to get a better view of the depressing black lines that had appeared under her normally bright blue eyes. Grumpily picking up her hair-brush, she finished unknotting her shoulder-length hair. Satisfied the knots had gone, she made a mental note to remember to get hair dye and redo her rapidly growing out red streaks, before wrapping her slender figure in an over-sized cotton fluffy dressing gown and heading downstairs.

The smell of cooking bacon reached her nasal passages before she was even halfway down the stairs. She allowed herself a little smirk, before rounding the corner at the bottom of the stairs and spying her mum standing in front of the cooker, at the far end of the kitchen.

Izzy had been steadying her breathing to a normal rate since she had heard the crash upstairs. She now planted a smile on her face before turning to face Crystal.

'Morning Princess, how'd you sleep?'

Crystal dragged a beech coloured wooden dining chair across the tiled kitchen floor, before collapsing on it and leaning her head on the table.

'Bloody awful,' she moaned. 'Yet another hectic, dream-filled night. That's five on the trot now!'

'Oh, sweetheart – that's not good.' Her mum walked over and kissed Crystal's forehead tenderly. 'Have you tried drinking a nice warm drink before bedtime? Maybe going down the pub on a work night, and drinking alcohol before bed was a bad combination.'

She returned back to cooker, to deal with the sizzling bacon that was demanding her attention. 'Maybe you should try visualising grounding yourself before going to sleep?' Izzy's voice sounded a little clipped to Crystal, but she wasn't sure why.

'It's stupid having to do that just for some stupid bloody dreams. Anyway, the pub has nothing to do with it.' Crystal banged her head lightly on the table. She didn't want to think about the fiasco at the pub last night. 'God! It's just so irritating, knowing I won't be able to concentrate at work today – again! They all think I've been constantly partying since my birthday, two weeks ago!'

Izzy laughed – a pleasant, contagious sound that made Crystal fight back a smile – before placing a plate of bacon, eggs and tomatoes in front of her daughter.

'It's not funny!' Crystal moaned. 'I wouldn't mind so much, but I'm too tired to even go out to party and it won't do me any favours with my new boss either.'

Crystal watched her mother walk across to the toaster. It didn't matter what the weather, or mood, her mother always had a glow about her. Her blonde hair seemed to have a halo of its' own. Sometimes Crystal would get so peed off over the fact her mother had a permanent cheery and positive attitude, no matter what the circumstances. Some people seemed to carry their own black raincloud around with them – her mother seemed to carry her own personal sunray – twenty-four seven.

Izzy settled opposite Crystal at the wooden table, before tucking into her breakfast.

'So, tell me about this latest dream.'

'Well, it's not much different from the other ones.' Crystal finished chewing on bacon, before continuing.

'I always seem to be flying around outside, looking down at houses below.' She sat back in the chair, munching on her toast.

'I go in through someone's' bedroom window and see them asleep in bed.'

'Go on,' Izzy encouraged, before continuing with her breakfast in silence.

'I fly over to them and gently set down on the floor next to the bed. I lean across and see an elderly face, eyes closed, fast asleep.' Crystal swallowed a mouthful of bacon.

'I place my hands on the elderly woman's face and she kinda glows slightly.' Crystal glanced across at her mother. 'I kind of heal her with energy – like reiki healing – as she's ill and dying. But it's more than reiki – it's like I am actually really instantly healing her.'

'Then what?' Izzy swallowed nervously.

'I fly out of the window.' Crystal frowned and looked at her mother 'But I don't see any wings. I don't seem to have any.'

Izzy got up and walked around the table to hug her daughter. Crystal loved being hugged by her mother: it was like being drawn into sunshine. She felt herself calming in her mother's warmth.

'They're only dreams, sweetheart.' Izzy tried to sound reassuring, but failed miserably.

Crystal reluctantly pulled out of their embrace, before continuing.

'I fly to another house and again, fly in through the bedroom window.' She frowned as she remembered the details.

'I fly over to the bed and, as I did before, I set down on

the floor next to the sleeping figure.' Crystal looked into the concerned blue eyes of her mother before deciding to continue.

'I pull back the covers and see the peaceful sleeping face of a little girl. I place my hands on her, you know, to heal her.' Crystal swallowed before continuing.

'But Instead of her glowing, I feel the room going cold and dark. I look at the little girl's face and she seems to age right before my eyes. She seems to draw the light out of me.' Crystal kept her head down, refusing to look at her mother.

'I feel cold and heavy. She then opens her eyes and with a raspy deep voice, struggling with her dying breath says, 'You did this to me – this is your fault.' I break away from her and struggle to fly to the window. It's like I've lost the ability to fly; like I feel too heavy and dark. As I drop to the floor, I wake up.'

Izzy leant back against her chair and willed herself to breathe normally. The dreams her daughter was having terrified Izzy. She forced herself to calm down, to banish the rising panic and fear inside.

'Dreams are just dreams, sweetheart.' She hugged Crystal tightly again, drawing her back into the warmth.

'Remember, when I taught you Reiki, the energy healing therapy?' she continued without waiting for confirmation. 'And I taught you the extra strong way to tie your conscious and subconscious to the ground – like you're actually grounding yourself? Maybe, you should make more of an effort to practice that grounding technique before you go to sleep.'

Izzy placed her hand on Crystal's forehead, willing the healing Reiki energy to work faster. She wanted to do what she could to soothe her daughter's unease, soothe her pain.

But she had to be careful. She didn't want to do too much at a time.

Izzy continued until she felt Crystal go calm, until her breathing had slowed. She kept her healing energy in check – kept it just a little above reiki levels; enough to heal Crystal's chakras and calm her, but not enough to make it too obvious. There was so much Crystal had to learn, but the dreams had started to already show glimpses of her potential. And Izzy needed to make sure Crystal was ready before she told her too much. Not that Izzy had all the answers.

Izzy reluctantly let go of Crystal and began clearing breakfast things from the table.

'Sweetheart, do you feel better now you've talked about it?'

'Yeah, thanks Mum.' Crystal smiled at Izzy and stood up. 'A hug from you always makes me feel better.' She glanced over at the clock before heading for the stairs. 'Shit, I'd better get a shift on, or I'm going to be late – again!'

As Crystal ran up the stairs, she wondered why she hadn't told her mum about constantly waking up with her nose against the ceiling – or the rest of the dream. Or, for that matter, about the drunk at the pub on the previous evening.

s her daughter headed upstairs, Izzy wondered why she was so reluctant to have that all too inevitable conversation with her daughter.

5
——————

Crystal shut the bedroom door and walked over to her en-suite. She undressed and stepped into the shower. The hot water pummelled her, giving her pale skin a rosy glow. As she shampooed her hair, Crystal let her mind replay the latest dream again.

She replayed the entire scene involving the little girl. It was similar to the previous time she had dreamt it; however, this dream had gone that bit further. It still started the same as the last one, but this one had shown more darkness, more intense heaviness around her. It had also felt more real than the last time.

Crystal lathered soap over her body and let her mind wander to the other dreams. She remembered seeing other people flying, others seemingly warm and friendly. All without wings.

She also remembered the light changing, as a dark shadow seemed to spread across the sun, cutting off the warmth and light – the shadow caused by a couple of dark people flying past. Crystal shuddered as she remembered the cold feeling this created. She turned off the shower and stepped out.

As she dried herself with a towel, Crystal mulled over what these dreams meant. They were all based around her local area, but the locality had a different feel about it. It seemed more intimidating; threatening almost.

Crystal looked at the silver clock on her apricot coloured wall, before putting on her underwear and upping her speed in an attempt to be ready on time. She pulled on a grey and black pleated mini skirt, black knitted sweater and grey over the knee socks. She then applied dark kohl pencil around her blue eyes, followed by a couple of coats of black mascara and swiftly applied a pink lip gloss before running the brush through her hair.

She peered at herself in the mirror. God, even with makeup on, I look a state! She fluffed up the sides of her hair. Well, at least it won't be busy at work today. Wednesday's are always quiet, she thought. She'd worked at Cosmos Carriers for the past two years, and it had never changed: Mondays dragged, Wednesdays were quiet – the lull before the storm – and Fridays were always manic. Needless to say, the weekends were her favourite days.

Sitting on the edge of her bed to fasten her shoe straps, Crystal allowed herself a few moments to mull over what the dreams could mean. She knew from her dream dictionary that flying dreams signified gaining a new and different perspective on things. She also knew that losing control, being unable to fly or finding obstacles in your way could symbolise a situation in your life that you were struggling with.

That's it! Crystal thought, trying to convince herself. These dreams are showing my struggle adapting to the new boss and the new atmosphere at work. She stood up and smiled at herself in the mirror.

Sorted, she thought, as she checked her appearance in the mirror. All sorted. Dreams interpreted and I'm ready for work, and all with ten minutes to spare before I have to leave.

Crystal turned and headed for the stairs. Refusing to listen to the nagging little voice in her head that kept taunting her with 'So, if it's all sorted, why do you still feel unsettled? Why do you feel scared? And why won't you talk about the levitation to your mum?'

6

Izzy was washing up the breakfast things while mulling over Crystal's latest dream. She had been warned about the changes that would happen to Crystal once she hit twenty-one. Unfortunately, there was nothing she could do to prevent them from happening.

As she washed down the cooker splash-back, she caught sight of her reflection in the glass.

Hmm, she thought, I don't look bad for forty-two. Izzy took note of the healthy sheen of her shoulder-length blonde hair, along with the ever present sparkle of her blue eyes. She also noticed the lack of any real signs of ageing and, as she stood back a bit, gave her trim figure the once over. Izzy also tried to shut off the slight glow that emanated from her. The yellow-gold light radiated out by about an inch around her entire body and it had a slight shimmer to it, like the brushed stainless steel of the range cooker had when the light hit it.

As she turned back to the sink, Izzy sighed. She would really have to work on shutting off, or at least cloaking her light. Luckily, Crystal had always seen Izzy's glow as a natural part of her radiance; almost seen it as part of the 'happiness aura' her mother gave off as part of the reiki she practiced. Until now. Now the dreams had started, trouble was coming and they had to be careful, they had to stay hidden – especially Crystal. She looked around the cream and beech coloured kitchen, noticing all the thriving, healthy plants. Crystal would have to know her mother was a healah and that reiki was only a small, very small part of what she could do. And Crystal would have to know that she was a half-breed, a reject, trouble as far as the others were concerned.

Izzy folded the tea towel over the radiator and turned on the kitchen radio, just as Crystal entered the room.

'See? I'm getting used to getting ready in record time.' Crystal smiled at her mother. She pulled open the fridge door and grabbed a can of cola and a Red Bull. 'And on time! All I have to do now is drink one to give me a quick sugar rush and the other to give me enough energy to get through the morning without being accused of burning the candle at both ends. Then I'm set for the day.'

'I wish you wouldn't drink all that rubbish.' Izzy frowned at her daughter. 'It would be much better if you ate fruit and got a grip on your sleep patterns.' Izzy sighed as Crystal opened the first can. 'Especially if you practiced grounding yourself,' she added as an afterthought.

'Fruit doesn't work as quickly as a can of cola and you know what they say about Red Bull.' She grinned at her mother before continuing. 'Red Bull gives you wiings – and maybe I need some for my dreams!' She laughed to herself.

Izzy decided to stay silent. Now was not the time to have that conversation.

Crystal sat at the table, taking swigs from the cola can.

The newscaster was stating that the time was eight-thirty, before commencing with the latest news headlines.

'And the top news story for this hour. A local girl has gone missing in the Castle Gate area of Newbury. Tanya Headlington is the third girl to go missing in that area of Newbury in as many months.'

Abruptly Izzy found the nearest chair to sit on. The newscaster continued, 'Tanya is described as 5' 6" with blue eyes and blonde hair. She was reported missing by her mother, after failing to come home from work two days ago.'

As the newscaster continued with the remaining headlines, Crystal gulped the remaining mouthfuls from her can. She stood up and placed the empty can into the recycling bin, before putting the Red Bull in her handbag – ready to drink on the bus to work. She walked over to her mother.

'Mum, are you ok?'

Izzy was sat on the chair, staring into space, with her hand to her mouth.

'Mum?' Crystal touched Izzy's arm, jolting her back to the present.

'Sorry sweetheart, I was miles away. Are you off now?' She looked at the clock before continuing, 'You'd better get a shift on, or you'll miss your bus. Don't worry about that poor missing girl. I'm sure she'll be ok.' Izzy hugged her daughter and escorted her, rather forcefully, to the door.

'I'll see you later. Love you.' Crystal just managed to kiss her mother goodbye before being almost shoved out the back door.

As the door shut behind her, Crystal couldn't help but wonder why her mother had seemed so shocked about the girl going missing. She decided to mull it over whilst she was on the bus to work and made a mental note to ask her mother later, when she wasn't acting so weird.

As she leant against the closed back door, Izzy thought about the latest missing girl and what it signified. She knew the troubles were coming and resolved to work on cloaking her light before it was too late – along with having that long overdue conversation with Crystal.

7

___

Crystal kicked her shoes off and collapsed on the sofa. 'What a day.' She leant back into the sofa cushions; head hanging off one end – feet off the other. Closing her eyes, she allowed herself a deep breath. Her shoulders relaxed, just enough to allow the tightness in her neck to relax slightly. Her neck let out a few protesting cracks as she rolled her head slowly left to right, then back again.

'Anyone in?' Emily's voice could just be heard through the kitchen and over the sound of the washing machine.

'Come in. I'm in here, dying on the sofa. Please don't make me move.'

'I picked up a takeaway – got the usual Thursday special; Chinese – so clear a space on the coffee table.'

Crystal groaned before hauling herself to a seated position. She deposited the magazines from the coffee table onto the floor.

'You look knackered. Is the new boss putting you through your paces?' Emily placed the tray of food on the coffee table and started opening the plastic cartons.

'He's all right, thinks I need some more sales training.

Ooh is that spicy smoked chicken? You're a star! Thanks for getting the food. How's your week been?' Crystal leant forward and started piling up her plate.

Emily put the DVD into the player before picking up the remote control and settling on the sofa next to Crystal.

'Kids at school were all loud and hyper as usual – but I'm loving the chance to open up their creativity.' She ran her hand through her blonde hair. 'I'm sure I still have purple paint in my hair somewhere. Can you see it?'

'Nope, can't see any. Are you actually going to put any of this food on your plate?'

Emily bent down and helped herself. 'I couldn't decide which DVD to get this time, so I settled on 'Avengers Assemble.' It's got Robert Downey Jr and the rather yummy Chris Hemsworth in it.' She turned on the TV. 'I love our girly nights, especially when it's just you and me. Mum's been busy cooking something special for their night in. I left just as your mum turned up – Kitty was already there.'

'Shush a minute and turn up the TV – is that another missing person?'

Emily turned up the TV and they both watched the evening news report.

'Patrick Roberts was last seen in the Templedon area at 5.30pm last Tuesday evening. His wife made this emotional appeal for help...'

Emily turned the channel over to DVD.

'I don't want to listen to yet another emotional appeal. That's the fifth one in the past week! It's so upsetting seeing their distraught partners plead for their return. Chances are he's run off with the cleaner or something.'

'Don't you think it's odd that these people are going missing?'

'Crystal, people go missing all the time. Look at Amy's dad; my uncle Kevin and there's your dad too.' She turned to face Crystal. 'Sometimes people just don't want to be found. Maybe they just get tired of their old lives. Okay, bad example – of course that doesn't apply to your dad – he loved you. But look at Amy's dad.'

'Yeah, well he's been missing for sixteen years – that's so obviously down to not liking his life. But then, look at Amy's mum – wouldn't you want to run away from her. I know she's your aunt and all that, but she's a bitch. And a religious nutcase. Let's face it, Amy can be one too. Bitch, that is – not nutcase.'

Emily raised her eyebrow then shrugged her shoulders in agreement. 'Yeah, point made. My relatives are fun. Let's just watch the film now.'

The smell of roasting beef filled the kitchen. Melanie Williams loved preparing for their regular girls' Thursday night. She liked the thought that her daughter Emily and Izzy's daughter Crystal were continuing the tradition and hosting their own regular nights in too. She chopped the vegetables and placed them in a bowl, ready for steaming later. Glancing up at the clock above the kitchen doorway, she smiled before heading towards the back door.

'Am I really that predictable?' Catherine called out from the end of the garden path. 'I haven't even opened the gate yet!' Her freshly-washed brown and blonde streaked shoulder length hair swung in time with her steps down the garden path towards Melanie. She reached the back door and hugged her.

'Kitty, early as ever – and with a bottle of wine! This is why I love you! Come in and I'll find the bottle opener.'

'Good idea, Mel. I'm in need of a glass of this.' Kitty handed Mel the bottle, leant back and looked through the kitchen doorway and towards the living area. 'I take it we're safe to drink?'

'Yes, Frank left for church about an hour ago. He's meeting his sister-in-law at church for extra Bible study.' She pursed her lips in disdain.

'I don't know how you cope with those two. Hi Emily, how you doing, hun?' Kitty got up and hugged Emily. 'Mark says 'Hi'. When are you two going to get your act together?' She grinned at Mel and they both watched in childish delight, as Emily reddened at the mention of Kitty's son, Mark.

'Oh look, Izzy's here. Don't worry; I'll let her in on my way out.' Emily ducked past Kitty to open the door and whispered, in passing 'Thanks for the good timing, Izzy.'

'Don't mess my house up too much!' Izzy replied with a smile, before walking into the kitchen and throwing a confused look at Mel and Kitty. 'What did I miss?'

'Oh, we were just winding up Emily over her crush on Mark.' Mel grinned at Izzy before hugging her best friend. 'Don't worry. I'm sure Kitty is ensuring Mark is being pushed in the right direction too. Aren't you Kitty?'

Kitty looked up from pouring Izzy a glass of wine. She smiled. 'Oh yes, don't worry, we know what's best for them.' She handed Izzy the glass of wine.

Izzy took the glass and looked towards the living room. 'I guess we're safe to drink this?'

'Do you honestly think I'd be popping the wine cork if

Frank was around? Don't worry, he won't be back for hours – he's with Mandy. Again.' Mel led them into the living room and slumped back on the sofa. 'So we can all relax for a while.'

'I don't know how you can live with the man. You're a stronger person than I am.' Kitty put her feet up on the coffee table and took a swig from her glass. 'I mean, I know you need to, but God, he'd do my head in.'

'You know I need the stress. It keeps me sane. You need love –and your lovely Peter gives you all of his; I need the stress. It's the only way I can get enough of it.' Mel twiddled a strand of brown hair around her finger. 'We all have to make sacrifices.'

'Don't I know it,' Izzy replied solemnly.

Mel got up and sat next to Izzy. 'I know it's hard for you hun, but I'm sure you'll see Sam again soon. You have to be strong.'

'Group hug!' Kitty launched herself at her two friends and wrapped her arms around them. 'Come on. It's a girly evening in. Both of your girls are round Izzy's house having fun, your husband is the other side of town, Peter is at home, hopefully conning the boys into doing my housework and I'm getting some female company! Let's lighten up!'

'You're right as ever Kitty. I'll get the food sorted; you can turn on the TV.' Mel got up and disappeared into the kitchen.

Kitty picked up the TV remote and turned on the TV, just as the news came on.

Izzy sat forward and dejectedly ran her hands through her blonde hair. 'We might not get a chance to lighten up,' she said, with her voice loud enough for Mel to hear. 'Another local person's gone missing.'

8

Mandy pulled her baggy cardigan close. The autumn evening had developed an extra bite over the last few weeks. She pulled her cardigan collar up around her neck and tucked her curly red ponytail inside. Putting her head down, she braced herself against the icy breeze that always greeted you as you turned this particular corner into Church Lane. One hundred and twenty-three steps once you turned the corner. She knew it off by heart. One hundred and twenty-three steps she would have to walk until she reached the gateway to the graveyard. Until she could look up and see the welcoming, warm, beckoning lights emitting from the Roman Catholic church and the statue of Christ watching from the top of the tower, arms outstretched, as if beckoning everyone to enter and be saved.

'Ninety-nine, one hundred.' Counting was Kevin's fault of course. Him and his obsessive compulsive behaviour. 'One hundred and six, one hundred and seven.' She hated him with a passion, a passion so deep it knotted her stomach and threatened to rot her very core. 'Get a grip,

Mandy. Calm yourself. You'll be safe soon.' He'd been gone for sixteen years – yet he still had the ability to scare her. Every time she walked this route to church. It was the small flutter of hope she felt inside, the hope and guilt in equal measure. '

Steps counted, she looked up, grateful to be through the gateway and into the graveyard. She felt her shoulders relax, just a bit. She walked up to the church entrance, hoping she could calm the butterflies in her stomach – the butterflies that flew so strong for her brother-in-law. The same butterflies that had to constantly fly against the guilt that threatened to keep them heavily laden. She couldn't help herself though; she loved him so much – as a person and for his beliefs. And at least he could lighten her burden by sharing the guilt. She lived for these Thursday meetings.

'My dear Amanda. How are you this cold, cold evening?' Frank was the only one who called her by her entire first name. He walked down the nave towards Amanda before placing a protective arm around her. 'You're so cold; here come stand by the candles.' He led her to the vigil candles that stood next to the altar, staring sternly at Father Javier, defying him to come near – or to comment on the close proximity he was currently enjoying.

She leant into his concerned embrace and let him lead her towards the front of the church. 'I bought my Bible, Frank.' She watched Father Javier disappear through the door to the vestry before rummaging in her bag and pulling out the small, brown, well-thumbed book.

'That's great! Let's take a seat over here.' He led her to the pew nearest the candles and patted the seat next to him. 'It's so good to see you. How have you been?'

'You know me, Frank. Never one to complain. We all

have our burdens. The path Amy is leading weighs heavily on my soul.' She bowed her head in shame.

He tenderly placed a finger under her chin and raised her head. 'I may not be a priest Amanda, but I know a good person when I see one. You are so God-fearing and selfless. Things like this are sent to test us, to make us stronger. God's will will be done.'

'I know, but she has no father to guide her. I feel so much shame.' She picked up her Bible in both hands and offered it up to him. 'I need to find a scripture in here that will release my shame; the shame I feel for having his offspring.' She looked up at Frank with water-filled eyes. 'My past ungodly ways led me down this path, I know.' Head in hands she continued. 'You are my salvation, Frank. I've been let down by all my so-called friends – they let me marry him so Melanie could have you. Globules of spit showered the Bible in her hand. She looked up at Frank, her tears had vanished, her eyes stony cold jade. 'But I feel no shame for feeling how I feel for you. Or for what we did to him.'

Frank cleared his throat before slowly prising the Bible from her hands and waving it in her face. 'My brother was evil and the Bible is full of examples of good overcoming evil. This book holds all the answers we seek. It holds our forgiveness and our salvation.' He placed it next to his Bible on the pew between them. 'If we look hard enough, we will find both.' He reached out and touched her hand. 'Together.'

9

The weekend had passed by far too fast for Crystal's liking. Sat fiddling with papers on her desk, she couldn't believe it was Wednesday already. She didn't even have Amy to talk to, as she'd disappeared ages ago to get a cup of coffee.

Amy must be picking her own bloody coffee beans, the amount of time she's been gone, Crystal thought ruefully.

The telephones had been quiet all morning. So far this afternoon, her phone had rung twice – once for a customer query on a delivery timescale, which had taken all of two minutes to sort, and the second call was from an IT geek, wanting to know what time she went home, as he needed to update something on her computer. Crystal had shuffled papers around her desk, fiddled with the papers in her filing trays, gone back and actually filed them and had now resorted to counting the paperclips in the silver mesh dish.

'Fifty-three.' She dropped the final one into the dish and placed it back in its place to the right of her screen. She peered over the top of her cubicle and past the five other tables, before spying Amy by the drinks dispenser in the far corner. Picking another victim, I shouldn't wonder, she thought. She looked up at the clock before letting her head fall backwards and groaning aloud. Is it really only 3.35? She rolled her eyes before stretching and leaning forward and resting her head on her hands. She looked at the empty cola can sat at the bottom of her dustbin. Maybe I should get up and get a drink? Can't really be bothered. She imagined the answer as soon as she'd asked the question. She found herself thinking back to the drunk man from the pub last weekend. "People like us did, people like us created the world." That's what he'd said – but what did it mean? She'd hidden it quite well, but he'd really unsettled her – especially when he mentioned the dreams.

She remembered the feeling of weightlessness as she floated towards the building in her dream. Her shoulder blades moving rhythmically in and out; the pressure of the non-existent wings pressing heavy on her back. When she entered the darkened room, she felt the heavy atmosphere, could smell something akin to damp soil and could just make out the small figure outlined under the bed covers. Once Crystal got to the bed she could see the little girl looking so peaceful – her blonde hair fanned out on the pillow around her head like a halo. After placing her hands on the girl's face, Crystal could hear the rasping breaths getting louder; the little girl's skin getting greyer & her eyes, so black, boring into Crystal's soul. Even when Crystal broke contact, every step she took away from the bed was getting harder and harder to take. The darkness enveloping her, her limbs getting heavy, the girl saying...

'Wednesdays are always quiet, aren't they?' The statement made by her boss, Anthony, pulled her back into the present with a jolt. 'You see, people are bored with the working week dragging on, and yet it's too early for them to be panicking about the last minute things they have to do before the weekend.' He stood in front of her, hands in suit trouser pockets and grinning down at her.

Crystal felt the flush of red working its way up her neck and to her cheeks. Damn him for catching her being bored – and for looking even better with that wry grin on his face, she thought.

'I was just organising my desk.' She looked around for some papers to grab – but there weren't any.

'I thought you'd finished tidying, once you'd put the paperclips back.' He grinned at her again. 'Don't worry about it. Wednesdays are always quiet – even at Head Office in New York.' He wheeled the office chair from the desk behind him and sat down next to her.

'So, Crystal. What's good to do around here at the weekends? I've been here over a month now, and not had a chance to go exploring.' The word 'exploring' was said in a long drawn out American twang –while his eyes worked their way from her feet to her eyes, before holding her gaze for a split second longer than necessary.

Crystal managed to break the gaze and looked over to the coffee machine. That cup of coffee Amy was having must be the longest cup ever, she thought, as she looked around at the other empty desks, before finally looking back at Anthony.

He was waiting patiently for an answer. Even his blue eyes had a flash of humour in them. 'So, I'll leave you alone to get on with something.' He stood up. She watched him wheel the chair back to the desk behind him, before he turned and leant past her to pick up a stray paperclip, half-hidden under her desk diary. His chest was inches away from her face. The smell of Fahrenheit filled her nostrils.

'I think that makes fifty-four.' He handed it to her but

kept hold of it. She didn't want to be the first to move her fingers, so she kept them there – touching his – and looked up to let their eyes meet again. Seconds passed, before he let go of the paperclip, but held her gaze. 'Let me know when you think of something good to do at the weekend.' Gaze broken, he walked away.

Crystal collapsed back against her chair and let the smell of his aftershave linger a bit longer, before letting her breath out in a gentle 'whoosh'. Her heart returned to a normal rate as her breathing settled back down. He got to her every time. He was what she considered a stereotypical all American man. Blond, tanned, good-looking with pearly white teeth and an incredibly sexy accent. And he was definitely flirting. With her. She grinned at the paperclip still in her fingers, before clipping it to today's page of the desk diary.

She was bumped back to the present by Amy knocking her chair back against hers. She had yet another cup of coffee in her hand.

'You can go and have your tea break if you like. There's no one at the drinks machine now.' Amy swung her chair round so she could face Crystal. 'Anyway, what are you sat there grinning to yourself for?' She frowned suspiciously at Crystal.

Crystal grabbed her mug and stood up. She glanced down at the paper clip on her diary before responding. 'I've decided I quite like Wednesdays.'

10

Crystal entered the Duke of Earl Saturday evening at precisely 7.15 pm. She wanted to be there first, so she could be calm and composed when Anthony arrived. She shoved her empty chocolate bar wrapper into her coat pocket, undid the buttons of her red wool coat, before unwinding the scarf from around her neck and heading for the nearest booth. Sliding her bag along the seat, she placed her coat and scarf on top of it, before going to the bar.

'Hi Russell.' She smiled, grateful to see a familiar face. 'You working again? Don't you have a night off?'

'Hi. Crystal, right? He looked past her and failed to hide the disappointment in his eyes. 'It's unusual to see you in here on your own.'

'Amy and the others will be in later, at about 8.30. I'm here on a date. A date with my boss, would you believe it?' She was still trying to wrap her own head around the fact – voicing it to someone else just made it sound weirder.

'Good for you! Will make life at work a bit easier, I should think. What can I get you?'

'Oh, I'll have a vodka and cola please. Need to steady my

nerves. She glanced at the clock again. 'Got here fifteen minutes early just to make sure I could get a seat. And to calm down. You know how it is.'

Russell flashed her a smile before bending down to get a glass. He really was quite nice. Too nice for Amy to ruin. She watched him as he reached up to the optics hanging at the back of the bar. He had nice hands. And muscular arms. With just a hint of a tattoo peeking out from under his t-shirt sleeve. He turned round to fill her glass with cola from the dispenser in front of her. He looked up and smiled as he handed her the glass.

'That'll be £3.20 please.'

Crystal handed him a £5 note and took a sip whilst waiting for her change.

'£1.80 change. Have a lovely date, Kristen.' He smiled, looking straight into her eyes, before flicking his direction to the right of the bar. 'Don't worry; I'll make sure he doesn't bother you.'

Crystal ignored the slip-up in her name and followed the direction of his gaze. Her eyes came to a stop at a scruffy, taped up army coat and a bright blue pair of eyes in a silhouette haloed by sunlight.

'Oh, God,' she groaned to herself.

He raised a glass of what she suspected was JD and cola in her direction.

'Evening Crystal. Fancy bumping into you when you're on your own.'

Crystal pocketed her change and picked up her drink. She didn't remember telling him her name the other night. She took a couple of steps towards him.

'It's my local, so I'm in here a lot.' She continued quickly, 'I won't be on my own for long. I'm meeting someone.'

'Oh, on a date then?' He smiled and actually seemed

sober, so Crystal took another couple of steps to stand just within arm's reach of him.

'Yes, a date. I don't remember giving you my name.'

'I listen. I hear a lot.' He took a sip from his glass. 'I'm actually glad I have you on your own. I wanted to apologise for the other night.'

'You don't have to.' She wanted to appear polite, like it hadn't really bothered her.

'Yeah, I do. I don't want you thinking all Americans are wankers.' He grinned at her and continued. 'I drink a lot. Sometimes too much. But hey, we all need a vice, don't we?'

Crystal glanced at the clock behind the bar. She still had ten minutes to spare before Anthony got there. Assuming he wasn't early. She looked across to the booth where she had left her bag and coat. There wasn't anyone else around so she took a chance and sat down on the stool next to him.

'Okay. Apology accepted. Actually I'm meeting an American for my date.' She took a sip of her drink and continued. 'So, shall we start afresh? As you already know, I'm Crystal. How do you do?' She held out her hand.

'Nice to meet you, Crystal. I'm Nathan. Nathan Fielding.' He took her hand to shake it.

'Ouch!' A bolt of electricity rushed through when their hands met and shot up her arm.

Laughing, they both let go of the other's hand and shook their arm to release the surge.

'So Crystal Meadows, apart from shocking me, what other talents do you have?' He smirked at her before sipping his drink.

She laughed. 'None that I know of.'

'Everyone has a talent of their own. You must have at least one!'

'I'm always being told I have a vivid imagination. Does that count?' She looked up at the clock –five more minutes.

'A vivid imagination? I guess that depends if what you imagine is real or not.'

'Oh, purely imaginary.' She nodded and grinned

'He looked at her, his blue eyes flashing darker. 'When you're awake or asleep? Daydreaming or dreaming?'

She found his gaze a bit unsettling, his eyes a bit too intense and the conversation seemed to have suddenly taken a detour down a dark alley. She glanced back up at the clock then got up from her stool.

He reached out to grab her arm. 'You've got a couple more minutes yet. Stay a bit longer. We can talk about the dreams.'

'It's been nice to get acquainted, Nathan.' The smile didn't reach her eyes. 'You're making quite a habit of grabbing my arm, aren't you?'

They both looked up as the cold breeze from the front entrance door signalled the arrival of Anthony. Crystal smiled at him across the room and nodded towards the booth that housed her bag and coat. She picked her drink up from the bar and went to move away.

Nathan half raised himself off his stool to whisper in her ear. 'I told you the other day, we're different. You need to heed the dreams, they're warnings.' He glanced across at the booth where Anthony was currently taking off his coat. 'You'll need me. I'll be coming in here every day, so you know where to find me when you finally decide to discuss them.'

Crystal pulled her arm away. 'Not a chance,' she retorted and took a few steps towards Anthony.

'If not me, speak to your mother,' he hissed, loud enough for her to hear, the urgency echoing in his voice.

She hesitated mid-step, then with renewed determination, continued to walk across the room.

'I got competition?' Anthony leant to see past her

'Not a chance, Anthony. He's too old for me.' She slid into the booth opposite him. 'I wouldn't mind another vodka and cola though.' She smiled and passed him her glass.

'Whatever the lady wants.' He stood up 'And please, call me Tony.' He flashed her a pearly white smile and headed for the bar.

Crystal watched his spiky blond hair bounce as he walked towards the bar. It was the first time she'd had a chance to really study him, without the threat of ridicule from other work colleagues. His rear view was almost as impressive as the front view. His jeans clung rather pleasingly around his backside; the polo shirt fitted enough to show off his slim, muscular torso. Over six feet of toned, athletic hunkiness, she grinned smugly to herself.

Crystal wasn't the only one watching him. She noticed Nathan was staring at him through narrowed eyes. Tony nodded in his direction, before turning and returning to the booth with the drinks. He slid into the booth, gave her her drink and then took a large gulp from his pint glass.

'That's better! I'll be honest; I was a bit nervous about meeting you tonight. Me being your boss and all.' He held her gaze and fiddled with the ring on his right little finger.

Crystal blushed. 'I know, I was too. Nervous about meeting you that is, not me!'

They both laughed, the ice broken.

'Well, at least my competition has gone.' He looked over towards the swinging entrance doors.

'He's not competition, just some drunk who thinks he knows me.'

Nathan leant forward, resting his arms on the table. 'Oh, how so?'

'Oh, it's nothing, honestly. Just the random ramblings of a drunken guy.' She looked up and met his concerned gaze. 'Honestly, it's nothing to worry about.'

'As long as you're fine and he isn't bothering you.' He leant back into his chair and fiddled with his signet ring.

'So, now we're out of the work environment, what shall we talk about?' Crystal smiled at him before looking down at his hands. 'Was that ring a gift? I noticed you always wear it.'

'Oh you have, have you?' He looked down at it, spinning it back until it faced the right direction.'

'Yes, I have. I noticed you fiddle with it when you're nervous or if you're thinking. Which one is it this time?'

'Neither. It's just a habit I have. It's a graduation ring, from Harvard.' He leant forward to show her the detailing. 'See, it says 'Harvard Business School' around the plain black stone. Do you have college rings in this country?'

'It is really pretty. What did you study at Harvard?'

'I was there for five years, getting my business economics PhD.' He leant back again in his seat. 'My father wanted me to go into the family business.'

'You didn't want to then? Did you not like the family business? Is that why you moved to England?'

Tony grinned at her. 'No, I did go into the family business for a year, to learn the ropes. My family own a couple of international businesses. Then I moved – with my dad's blessing – to the head office of Cosmos Carriers in New York, and within eight months was asked to run the Newbury office in the UK.'

'Eight months, that was quick!' She sounded shocked.

'I earned it fair and square. Although my father's influence would have reached into the office if I wanted it to.' He laughed. 'Anyway, they were desperate for a new CEO, after the last one disappeared.'

Crystal nodded and frowned slightly. 'I didn't know Mr Wilkinson personally, but it was on the news. His family looked devastated.'

Nathan took a sip from his glass. 'Well, I guess that's understandable.'

'So your father is quite a big fish is he? Do you miss New York and your family?' Crystal asked, wanting to change the subject to a happier one.

'Enough about me – I'd rather not talk about my family or my father too much. What about you? How do you get on with your dad?'

'I don't see him. In fact, I haven't ever seen him.' She paused for a minute, 'Well, not when I was at an age to remember him. Apparently he was around when I was born, but when we moved, we moved on our own.'

'So, where were you born?'

'I've lived here for as long as I can remember! I think I was born in this area anyway. My mum runs her own florist shop called *Inspired Flowers*. She loves any kind of plant and is brilliant at making bouquets and all that stuff. A natural talent.'

'You must get on really well with her – your face lights up when you talk about her. Maybe I'll be able to make you do that one day.'

Crystal looked down, embarrassed. 'You'll have to see more of me for that to happen.' Before realising, too late, how that could be taken two ways.

'Mmm. We'll have to work on that.'

She hid behind her drink and flushed beetroot red. 'Bloody hell, you're a bit forward aren't you?'

'I'm an American!' Tony bowed as best he could from his seated position. 'I'm sorry, m' lady, I'll do my best to behave,' he responded, in his best fake English accent. 'You appear to have finished that drink – let me get you another.'

Crystal gratefully handed him the glass. 'Can I have a vodka and Red Bull this time please?' *I need the energy kick,* she thought.

Tony returned with the drinks a couple of minutes later and slid back into the booth. 'I believe it is an English custom to propose a toast.' He raised his glass. 'So, I propose a toast, to the start of a potentially beautiful relationship – if that isn't considered too forward?'

'I'm more than happy with that.' Crystal chinked her glass with his. 'To a potentially beautiful relationship!'

'Obviously, I'd like to see more of you – date-wise' he added hastily. 'I'm guessing you'd like to too.' He took Crystal's hand and looked into her eyes. 'I really like you, Crystal. I want to know everything about you. Are you up for that?'

Crystal nodded, not wishing to say anything to break this moment. She liked the feel of his hand, warm against hers. She loved the way his thumb was gently rubbing back and forth across the side of her wrist – and the butterflies it was producing in her stomach. Finally, she allowed a rather squeaky 'Yes' to emerge from her mouth. She coughed to clear her throat, reminded herself to actually stop holding her breath and to take a breath of air in and, in a stronger voice repeated 'Yes, I'd like that, very much.'

The background sounds of the bar had disappeared. The other patrons seemingly silenced – it was just she and him, in their own silent, still, charged bubble. Tony kept hold of her hand, gently, slowly and rhythmically rubbing his thumb back and forth, back and forth. His voice hypnotically enchanting, slow and deep. 'I want to know what you like, and what you don't like; who your friends are and what your wishes and dreams are.' He glanced up at her face, his blue eyes holding her gaze, his lazy grin setting the butterflies in her stomach off into full flight. They seemed to have taken flight with the lid to her soul, for she had the overwhelming urge to pour her heart and soul out to him. To share her fears and desires, her hopes and wishes. She wanted to actually tell him about everything.

Crystal blinked and broke the moment. The buzz of people talking, chinking glasses and tap of pool cue on ball swarmed into her ears, surrounding her with the noises of reality and life. It felt as though those soaring butterflies had just crash-landed in the bottom of her stomach with a heavy 'thud'. She stopped holding her breath and let it go with a 'whoosh'.

'I have the strangest of dreams – they'd make your head hurt.' She rather shakily picked up her drink, took a sip and continued in a rather lighter tone. 'But you'll be able to meet my friends. I invited them to meet us.' She looked up at the clock behind the bar, surprised at how quickly the time had moved on. 'They'll be here in twenty minutes or so.'

Tony reached and took a big gulp of his pint with his left hand, then stretched, removing his other hand from hers, before leaning back against his seat.

'I'd love to meet your friends, but maybe another time.' He looked down at his watch before continuing. 'I've got another meeting to get to.' He saw the disappointment cross her face. 'Before I go though, how are you fixed for next Wednesday evening?'

'I'm free.' A big smile spread across her face. 'Did you want to meet in here again?'

'Hmmm, no. I'm thinking dinner, wine, maybe a movie? Why don't I pick you up from your house – say about 7pm?'

He stood, put his jacket on and leant down to kiss her on the cheek.

Crystal closed her eyes and inhaled the heady scent of his aftershave. 'Seven would be great. Do you want my address?'

'Nah, I already have it.' He gave an exaggerated look around the pub before continuing 'Being the boss, I have access to the personnel files.' He winked at her then slid his business card across the table. 'Here's my card. I've already written my personal mobile number on the back. I'm always up for a call – as long as it's not while we're at work!'

Crystal took the card and turned it over, just to check he really had written his number on it. She looked up as he was headed for the door. Slightly panicked she raised her voice. 'But I haven't given you my ...'

'I already have it,' he replied before she could finish.

11

Crystal threw open the back door. Walking into the kitchen, she tossed her handbag on the table, put her empty cola can in the bin and pulled out a dining chair to sit down on.

'God, what a day!' She grabbed a chocolate bar out of the fridge, ripped off the wrapper and started to munch on the chocolate.

Chocolate finished, she stood up and walked over to the kettle, filled it with water and switched it on.

'Do you want a cuppa?' she asked, as her mum walked into the kitchen.

That would be lovely, thanks hun.' Izzy sat down on the dining chair. 'Did you have a better day at work today?'

'It's still odd, but at least Tony was actually in work today.' Crystal frowned as she poured water into the two mugs she'd put on the side. 'He wasn't at work on Monday, and both today and yesterday he's been acting really odd.'

'Odd, how?'

'Well, he's not spoken to me at all. In fact, he seems to be avoiding me.'

'Maybe he wants to keep his business life separate? You could be being a bit sensitive, as you had a disturbed night again last night, don't forget. Did you hear from him about your date tonight?'

Crystal handed her mother a cup of tea and sat down opposite her.

'I suppose you're right. He did text to check I was still okay for 7pm.' She shrugged. 'I just replied with a 'Yes, see you then.'

'Well, there you go then.'

'How's your day been then? Lots of orders?'

'Yes, I had the floral arrangements and bouquets to do for a wedding today. Not a problem though, they're all finished and ready to collect now.'

'Ooh, I'll tell you what did happen today.' Crystal's eyes lit up and she blew on her mug of tea to cool it down. 'I think Amy slept with the bloke from IT.'

'Crystal, you don't know that!'

'Well. She must've. Last week they were all flirty around the coffee machine and now he's blanking her. The common symptoms of after-shag-itis. You know what she's like. She attracts them, sleeps with them and then they end up hating her. It's the law of reciprocity.'

'Don't be so mean!' Izzy took a sip of her tea. 'Anyway, she can't help it. She's deeply insecure. She's has an unhappy home life.'

'So she might, but she should have a bit more respect. I mean, Chris sleeps with anything with a pulse, and he still manages to stay decent with them afterwards. In fact, all his exes still adore him!'

'Well, he is a bit less, well, prickly.' Izzy tried to stay diplomatic. 'But it's still not a free ticket to sleep with lots of people.'

'Mum, times change you know.'

'I know, let's just change the subject now. What are you wearing for your dinner date tonight?'

Crystal leant her elbows on the table and sighed. 'I have absolutely no idea. Do you think I should go really smart, or smart-casual?'

'You don't know where he's taking you, do you?'

'No. I think I'll play it safe and go for trousers with heels and a smart top.'

'Sounds like a plan.' Izzy looked up at the clock. It was just coming up to 6pm. 'Can you lean over and grab the TV remote – I'd like to catch up with the news.'

'Do you think I should stick to black trousers, or would I be okay to wear colour? I was actually thinking about my cropped red trousers.'

'Mmm, you'll be fine with whatever.' Izzy was only half-listening as she was watching out for the news headlines.

'I could wear just my underwear.'

'Yes, that's an idea.'

'Mum, you're not listening!'

Izzy swung her head round to face her daughter. 'Sorry, hun, I wanted to catch the news headlines to see if there were any further developments on those missing people.'

'Why the interest?'

'Well they're getting closer to us.' She smiled reassuringly at Crystal. 'It's nothing for you to worry about. I'm just being a typical mother and worrying about my daughter's safety.'

A picture of a blonde female filled the TV screen. Izzy grabbed the remote and turned the volume up. She nervously bit the tip of her thumb nail, whilst she listened.

Felicity was last seen walking home from work at

approximately 8.25pm on Monday evening. She's a nurse from
Newbury Community hospital. We're now going to our reporter
outside the hospital for the latest...'

'You okay mum?'

'Shush.' Izzy held her finger up to signal Crystal to stop talking.

'Felicity is 23 years old, blonde, 5ft 4 inches tall. She is also 28
weeks pregnant. If anyone has any information, please can
they contact the hotline number displayed below. Alternatively,
they can contact the local police in Newbury. The telephone
number is displayed below.'

Izzy grabbed the remote and turned off the TV. Crystal saw the deep worry furrows across her mother's forehead.

'Are you okay, Mum? She isn't someone you know, is she?' Crystal put her hand on her mother's arm to comfort her.

Izzy attempted to smile at her daughter. 'No, I don't know her.' She looked directly at Crystal. 'But I do worry. I worry for that poor girl's family. I worry about all the missing girls' families.' She looked down at the table. 'It's terrible not knowing what's happened to someone.'

'Does it remind you of Dad?'

Izzy placed her hand over Crystals' hand. 'Your father had to leave, to keep us safe. You know that.'

'Did he go into witness protection? Is that what you mean?'

Izzy pulled her hand away from Crystal's. 'I've told you before; we will not talk about it. Ever!'

Crystal's chair scrapped violently across the tiled kitchen floor. 'Why not? You expect me to believe my father loves me, but I never see him, am not allowed to talk about him or ask where he went and how.'

'He does love you! You don't know how difficult it was for him to leave us.' Izzy stood and walked towards Crystal.

'If that's the case, why did he leave?'

'He had to.'

'Why?' Crystal shouted at her mother.

'He just did.' Izzy closed her eyes and took a few calming breaths. She continued in a calmer voice. 'You just need to remember he loves us, wanted to protect us and gave up everything for us.'

'Like what? What do we *actually* need protecting from?' Crystal was standing with her hands on her hips, her head held defiantly up.

Izzy sat back down again. Her shoulders slumped in defeat. 'Don't you have a date to get ready for?'

'Don't change the subject!' Crystal yelled at her mother.

'I'm not. We just don't really have time to go into this all now.' Izzy looked beseechingly at her daughter, willing her to understand.

Crystal looked at the clock. Torn between wanting answers and wanting to get ready, she hesitated before responding.

'When then? When will we be able to talk about it?' she pleaded with her mother.

Izzy looked down at the table. 'Maybe we can talk about it tomorrow.'

'It's always tomorrow with you!' Crystal turned to walk away before turning back again. 'Maybe I should ask the drunken guy down the pub.'

Izzy's head shot upwards. 'What drunken guy?' Her gaze held Crystal's intently.

Crystal shifted her stance and lowered her voice slightly.

'The one down the Duke of Earl.' She looked defiantly into her mother's eyes. 'He wants to talk to me about my dreams.'

Izzy's eyes widened and the colour drained from her face. 'He wanted to what?'

'He wanted to talk to me about my dreams. He also said he knew you.' She looked hesitantly at her mother, suddenly unsure of how high this metaphorical high ground she was stood on actually was.

'What's his name!' Izzy shouted at her.

'Nathan. He said it was Nathan Fielding.'

Izzy's hand shot to her mouth. Crystal could see her mother's whole body was shaking slightly.

'Is he always down there?'

'So you do know him then? He said I should speak to you about my dreams and that.' She stared at her mother. 'How long have you known him? More importantly, what do you know about what is happening to me?'

Izzy held up a shaky hand. Her voice had a slight tremor to it. 'Please can you get ready for your date.' She looked at Crystal through watery eyes. 'I'm not putting you off; I just need to get my thoughts in order. Please Crystal.'

'I'm sorry Mum.' Crystal walked over and placed an arm around her mother. She hugged her tightly. 'I didn't mean to upset you, but I've been waiting for answers for so long.' She leant her head against her mothers.

'And you'll get them, I promise.' Izzy gently tapped her daughters arm. 'Just please can we just have one more normal day.'

'What do you mean by normal? What's going to change?'

'I'm tired, Crystal. Please can we do this tomorrow?'

'But...'

'Please Crystal, I promise we'll talk about it tomorrow.'

'Okay. But I will hold you to that.' Crystal let go of her mother and walked towards the stairs.

'I didn't mean to upset you, Mum.' She hesitated at the foot of the stairs.

Izzy managed a slight smile. 'It's okay. I understand.' She nodded slightly. 'You'll get your answers. I promise. Go get ready for your date.'

12

I zzy waited ten minutes after Crystal left, before grabbing her coat and heading out. As she walked, she took her mobile out of her coat pocket and dialled.

'Hi Mel, it's me. I'm heading to the Duke of Earl.' She listened for a few seconds before replying.

'No, it's fine. I'll be okay on my own. I said I wouldn't go back into that pub until he returned. And, I think he has.' Her voice was shaking at the possibility.

'I'll catch up with you later, once I've had time to check it out.'

She put the phone back into her pocket and strode purposefully towards the pub. She kept her pace steady, but not too fast, as she didn't want to arrive all flustered and out of breath. Her heart was already racing. The blood pumping around her body was making her tingle, whilst keeping her warm.

'Don't get your hopes up, Izzy!' She spoke to herself sternly. But she couldn't help it. It had been fifteen long years and, contrary to appearances, she'd really missed him. There had been times where her heart was so full of love for him, but it was intermingled with the pain of having to stay apart. Times when she thought her heart would break into a million pieces, shattering through the weight of both.

Once she had turned the corner and crossed the road, she stood outside the pub, closed her eyes and steadied her breathing for a couple of seconds. On her next breath out she opened her eyes and strode through the doors.

She could see the man with scruffy blonde hair from across the room. He was sat with his back to her. Her steps quickened as she headed towards him. He sensed her behind him and began to turn on the stool. Their eyes met as she got within two feet of him.

Oh my God! It's not him! Her eyes widened and her mouth fell open in shock and disbelief. Her heart double-skipped and she almost crumbled under the pain of the realisation.

He reached out and grabbed her arm, pulling her gently to the empty stool beside him. 'I'm so sorry, Izzy,' he placed his drink in her hands. 'Drink this. It must have been a terrible shock for you. I'm so sorry.' He helped her lift the glass to her mouth and tilted it, just enough to ensure she could reach the liquid inside.

'He couldn't risk coming himself, so I offered.' He watched her swallow, then cough as the Jack Daniels warmed her insides.

'Nathan, why didn't you warn me? I thought he was using your name to stay safe.' She looked at him, her eyes filling with tears, her voice full of disappointment.

'I couldn't risk it. Not now Crystal has just turned twenty-one.' He looked around. 'They're looking for her, you know. That's why it had to be me that came.' He offered her another sip of his drink.

'No, thanks.' She pushed the glass away. 'Get me a

double vodka.' She slumped against the bar counter, disappointed and defeated.

Nathan signalled to the bar tender for service. He ordered the drinks, paid for them and slid Izzy's drink towards her. He waited for the bartender to go back to the other end of the bar before turning back to Izzy.

'Samuel really wanted to come. You gotta know that, Izzy. But when we got wind of a story that Crystal may be being watched, well he just couldn't risk it.'

'I know it would've been silly for him to come back under those conditions. I've taught her to ground herself and I'm always careful not to give myself away.' She took a swig from her glass and let the vodka warm its way down her throat. 'I just thought he would've been the one to help me have the conversation with Crystal.'

'And he would have, if he could found a way to come without causing you more problems.'

'I know.' She put a hand on his arm. 'Thanks for coming. I know it wasn't easy for you either.'

Nathan raised his glass to her. 'This stuff sure does help though! I've found I can stay around, undetected. It kinda helps me to stay grounded. Literally!' He chuckled to himself before downing his drink. 'By the way, your daughter is just as feisty as you were at that age.' He grinned across at her.

'I know.' Izzy smiled, and then sighed. 'That's why I've been putting off giving her all the details. It's not easy telling your daughter she's an angel.' She finished her drink and stood up. 'Well, you'd better come with me back to mine.' She stood up and walked towards the door. 'We've got a few hours to get the facts in order before Crystal gets home.'

13

The car pulled to a stop outside her house. Crystal glanced down at the clock on the car dashboard. It was 10.30 pm.

'Thank you so much for this evening. The dinner was lovely.' She glanced at Tony, before reaching down to undo her seatbelt.

'Are you sure you're okay? You've been kinda quiet.'

'It's fine. I'm fine.' She smiled to reassure him. 'I'm sorry. I've just been a bit distracted.' She glanced towards her house. 'I just hate falling out with my mum.'

Tony touched her arm, causing her to look back in his direction. 'It doesn't matter. I'm sure she'll be fine with you now.' He rubbed her arm gently. 'You're more than welcome to talk to me about whatever it was.'

'No. I don't want to bother you with it.' She patted his hand reassuringly. 'It's all a storm in a teacup, I'm sure.'

'Okay, well thanks for your company this evening. It's been a pleasure.' He pulled her towards him and kissed her, slowly on the lips. She opened her mouth slightly and allowed his tongue to explore. Closing her eyes, she allowed her arms to wind around his neck and responded to his kiss, before reluctantly pulling away to breathe.

'Phew. I don't really know what to say now!' She looked down at the floor, so he couldn't see her embarrassment. Tony placed a finger under her chin and gently lifted her head.

'Honey, you have nothing to be embarrassed about.' He leant forward and kissed the tip of her nose. 'Let's do this again next week. I'll text you.'

'I know. You want to make sure this is kept separate from work. So I promise not to flirt with you or text you during work hours.' She grinned at him before stepping out of the car.

'Bye honey. Until then.' He waited for Crystal to shut the car door before driving away.

Crystal turned and walked down the pathway to the front door. She enjoyed the warm tingling feeling that was currently buzzing through her body. She could still smell his aftershave on her clothing, so she closed her eyes slightly and breathed in deeply, reliving their kiss, the warmth emanating from his body, his tongue causing her entire body to tingle. Allowing herself a moment to stand and relish this ecstatic moment of happiness, she realised she hadn't felt this alive and happy for the past several weeks. Opening her eyes, she took the key out of her coat pocket and let herself into the house.

'Mum, are you still up?' She took off her coat, hung it on the coat rack and headed towards the kitchen. 'I had an amazing time tonight. I'm sorry we argued earlier.' She rounded the kitchen door and stopped dead in her tracks.

'What the hell is he doing here?' She looked in surprise at Nathan, who was sat at the kitchen table, with a cup of coffee in his hands.

'Now, Crystal. I want you to calm down and have a seat.' Izzy pushed the dining chair that was opposite her slightly with her foot. 'You wanted answers. Well, Nathan's here to help give them to you.'

Crystal walked over to the fridge and grabbed herself a can of cola, before doing as requested. She pulled at the ring pull of her can, took a swig and placed it carefully on the table. 'So, you know each other then?'

'We go way back.' Nathan started to explain.

'I'm not talking to you, just yet.' She glared at him before looking back to Izzy.

'Mum?'

'Nathan's right. We've known each other since before you were born.' Her eyes darted towards Nathan for reassurance. 'He knows your father too.'

'So is he in witness protection too?'

Nathan laughed out loud. 'Who told you your pop was in witness protection?'

Crystal shot him a look of pure disdain. 'Don't laugh at me! I had to come to some conclusion as to why I never get to see my dad, let alone talk about him! I figured either he, or we, were in some kind of witness protection or something. After all,' she scowled at her mother, 'you kept saying he stayed away to protect us! What else was I supposed to think?'

Nathan held his hands up in surrender. 'I'm sorry. I didn't mean to upset you. I'll try not to do it again.'

Izzy leant across and placed her hand on Crystal's. 'Nathan knows things. Things that can help you control your dreams.' She glanced at Nathan. 'He can explain your dreams.'

'Why couldn't you have just told me when you first met

me that you knew my mum and dad?' She glared straight into his icy blue eyes.

'I couldn't take the risk. They could be watching you and I didn't want to put you and your mom in danger.'

Crystal slammed her cola can on the table. 'For God's sake! Can we please stop with all this secret shit. Just tell me what is going on, without all the dramatics.'

Nathan slumped back against his chair. 'Okay. You want it straight, so here it is. Your mom's a healer, your dad and I are both flyahs and you're an angel so you can do both.'

'I know my mum can heal, but that's down to the Reiki. And I know you're a drunk, so maybe you're just a tad delusional.' She screwed her face up in disdain at him.

Izzy leant across the table and touched her daughter's hand. 'Crystal, true healing is way more powerful than Reiki. Reiki uses external energy, but when we heal, we can *create* that energy. He's right. I know you can heal, as I've seen you do it, so you know he's telling the truth on that point.' She glanced across at Nathan before continuing. 'You started having the dreams when you hit twenty-one. If you were a full-blood like Nathan or me, or your father for that matter, you'd have been born with your ability and, as long as you had a mentor, you'd learn how to use it from an early age. As you are a half-blood, you're born with your dominant ability but don't get your other ability until you reach adulthood.'

Crystal stared at them both, her mouth agape, before shaking her head slightly and gulping from her cola can. 'Are you winding me up?'

'Crystal, that's why you've been having your dreams, it's your ability coming out in your sleep.' Izzy pointed at the cola can. 'And that is why you have to drink so much cola and eat so much chocolate. You need it for energy, as you're burning all your energy up during the night, whilst you are flying in your sleep. That's why you're so tired when you wake up.'

'I don't believe you. Ah, but I don't fly in my sleep!' Crystal retorted.

'But you do. That's why I hear you crash back onto your bed each morning. And you can't deny *that*.'

Crystal looked at the floor, embarrassed. 'But I don't leave my room, I just levitate slightly. Anyway, people can't fly.'

'Nathan, show her.'

Nathan pushed his chair back and held his arms out. His eyes turned a really dark blue and he slowly rose from the floor. He levitated from one side of the kitchen to the other, before setting himself back on the floor and calmly sitting back down on his chair. Crystal held a shaky hand over her mouth. Nathan stared at Crystal, his eyes back to their icy-blue colour. Izzy was watching her daughter, unsure what to say. A few minutes passed before Crystal finally spoke.

'Holy shit! And you're saying I can do *that*?'

'You sure can.' Nathan continued staring straight at her.

'Why? How?'

'You just have to think it.'

'It's that simple?'

'Yep.'

'So why am I not doing it now, if all I have to do is think it?'

'Because you don't *know* it, you're just wishing it could happen.'

'This is ridiculous.' Crystal looked across the table to her mother for support.

'But why? Why am I an angel? I really don't understand.'

'Crystal, we have these special abilities because we *are*

special.' Izzy held her daughter's hand tightly. 'We're special because we can use the capacity of our brain in a different way to other humans. Most people only use small amounts of their brain at any one time. When *you* hit twenty-one, your brain kind of unlocked the limits The Others placed on it. That awakened your second ability, along with an ability to fire electrical pulses around faster than usual – so your senses improve, your ability to learn speeds up and you *know* you can do whatever you put your mind to. Do you understand?'

'But angels have wings.' She turned to Nathan. 'And what did you mean when you said we made the world?'

Izzy scraped her chair back and stood up. 'I think you've had quite enough information for one night. It must've been quite a shock for you and you need time to process it all.' She pulled her daughter to a standing position and hugged her tightly. 'We'll talk some more tomorrow. Nathan's staying in the spare room for a few days and, between us, we can answer any question you may have, but for now you need to get some sleep. You have work in the morning.'

'Yep, your mom is right. After all, you'll need a clear head to process the rest of what we've got to tell you.' Izzy shot Nathan a stern look before gently pushing her daughter towards the stairs.

'You mean there's more?' Crystal stared at her mother.

'It's really nothing for you to worry about. Go on, go to bed.'

'You expect me to actually go to *sleep* now?'

Nathan chuckled to himself and poured himself another drink.

Izzy waited for Crystal to finally go up the stairs before she turned back to Nathan.

'Go easy on her, Nathan.' She glanced at the glass in his hand. 'And go easy on the booze.'

Nathan raised his glass in her direction. 'This is the only thing that can stop me being detected and the only thing stopping them from following me to you.'

Izzy sat down opposite him. 'I know, but I don't want any drunken ramblings going on in front of Crystal.'

'You're frightened, I get that. But you've gotta realise that she has to know the whole story. About her father and our beginnings.'

'I just don't want you filling her head with the politics of it all.' She closed her eyes for a second then opened them to look directly at him. 'I don't want to lose her. She is all I have.'

'You have Samuel and you have me. Maybe it's time Mel came out of retirement? We could do with some insights.'

'This is what I am on about! You cannot expect everyone to take up your cause, just because you say so!' She slammed her fist on the table. 'I'm not going to put my family and friends in danger. I won't do it!'

'Sweetheart, you don't have much of a say in that. It's coming, whether you're for it or not. It's unavoidable now Crystal's abilities have woken.'

14

Izzy had to almost shoehorn Crystal out of the front door to get her to go to work. She sighed to herself. She couldn't blame her daughter, of course, as she'd had a lot to take on board after last night's conversation. She set about putting the breakfast bowls into the dishwasher and tidying up the kitchen in readiness for her visitors. Nathan had disappeared in the early hours – Izzy had heard the front door close at just after 5am. She decided he had made the decision to stay out of the way until this evening, when they could talk some more to Crystal.

She glanced up at the kitchen clock – 9.30am – she had fifteen minutes to get herself looking presentable before Mel and Kitty were due to arrive. She rushed upstairs to put on her makeup and brush her hair.

At exactly 9.45am the back door opened as Kitty let herself in. 'Hi Izzy, it's only me!' She took off her black coat and hung it on the coat rack, before walking over and filling up the kettle. 'Don't mind if I make a cuppa do you? The boys didn't give me a look in this morning.'

'I'll be down in a minute Kitty; I'm just finishing my mascara. I'd love a tea if you're making one.'

Kitty took three mugs from the cabinet and was filling the third mug with coffee when Izzy came down.

'Blimey, it must be serious; you're not wearing denim *and* you've shut the shop.' She grinned at Izzy, who had put on a pair of black trousers, a silver-grey silk blouse and pearl drop earrings.

Izzy hugged her friend and gratefully accepted the cup of tea that was offered to her. 'I just felt the need for a change, a need to ...'

'Come out of the shadows?' Kitty offered helpfully.

Izzy sighed, and then turned as Mel walked in.

'Morning hun, is that coffee I smell? I got your text last night, luckily Frank was already asleep, so he didn't hear my phone go off.' Mel took the cup of coffee that Kitty gave her and sat down opposite Izzy.

'What did he have to say then?'

'Sam couldn't make it; it wasn't safe for him.'

Mel reached across the table and held Izzy's hand. 'I'm so sorry hun. You must've been disappointed.'

'I was, especially when Nathan had to be the one to sit here and tell Crystal she was an angel!'

Kitty's eyes widened 'Ooh, how did she take *that*?'

'She was quite calm, considering.' Izzy took a sip of her tea and continued. 'It was such a shame, as she'd had a good evening prior to that. She was out for a dinner date with her boss.'

'Really? What's he like?' Mel chipped in.

'I don't know. I didn't get to meet him. Anyway, we have more important things to talk about.' She glanced at Kitty. 'I know you've been working on getting Mark and Emily together, how's it going?'

Kitty and Mel looked at each other and laughed. 'My daughter is playing the old-fashioned game of waiting,' she nodded in Kitty's direction, 'for her son to actually ask her out. You know what she's like; her heads so in the fifties!'

'And Mark is waiting for the 'right moment', whenever that is!'

Izzy put her mug down. 'We really need to get them sorted, sooner rather than later.' She placed her hand on Kitty's arm. 'Nathan confirmed that Crystal is being watched somehow, so she's going to need her friends more than ever. Mark needs to make a move on Emily now, to give her somewhere to relax and kick start her ability.'

'There's no way I can relax the stress enough at our house, especially with Frank around.' Mel looked at them both. 'He's gotten so cosy with Mandy, it's making him really anxious, and he gets so het up and focused on religion when he's anxious.'

'So you're keeping stressed at yours then?' Izzy quizzed Mel.

'Yes. I can't function totally under the stress, so there's no way Emily will be able to.'

'Nathan thinks it's about time you came out from the stress and started using your ability.' Izzy put her head down.

'Does he have any idea what I have to put up with?' Mel slammed her mug down on the table and looked around. 'Where is he? I mean, he's been back one night and expects everyone to just 'wake up' for no real reason?'

Kitty, ever the peacemaker, reached over and took Mel's hand. 'I don't pretend to know what it's like having your abilities, either of you. But we all knew what we were getting into, when Izzy fell pregnant and escaped with Sam. There's no way *they* would willingly let an angel live. They knew, as well as we did, that she would show up on their radar when she turned 21. And then you'd all be in danger.'

Mel squeezed her hand in response. 'I know it's been a huge learning curve for you, dealing with all of this, learning about us and our abilities. But I married a religious fanatic like Frank so I could stay hidden, buried under the stress.'

Izzy reached over and placed her hand on top of theirs. 'We're in this together; we have been for the last 21 years. We knew this time would come and we have to be ready for what's coming.' She looked at the both. 'I'm not talking about the war Nathan wants to start, just the bit about keeping us all safe.' She turned to Mel. 'And for that, we need your insights to give us advance warnings of what's due to happen.'

Mel nodded and let her shoulders slump. 'Okay, I'll spend more time away from home and in a more peaceful environment. But I can't change the stress levels in our house, as Frank's the one radiating those heavier energies.' She turned to Kitty. 'Can you push Mark to ask Emily out, or do I need 'modernise' my daughter?'

Kitty smiled. 'Leave it to me. I'll sort it.'

15

Mandy had the day off. She waited for the sound of the front door closing to signal Amy's departure for work before she got out of bed. She threw the covers off and had a quick shower before pulling on her clothes – a long brown skirt, cream t-shirt and the customary baggy grey cardigan. She sat in front of her dressing table mirror and started to brush her long red hair.

As she brushed, she examined her face in the mirror. 'I look tired. No, correct that, I look wrung out, squashed.' She put the brush down and picked up the cleanser fluid. Squeezing some onto a cotton pad, she dragged it quickly around her face, followed by a quick dab of moisturiser. Letting out a sigh, she looked into the green eyes of her reflection.

I'm not a bad person, she thought. She heard Kevin's voice echo in her head. 'You're a slut. A whore. You trapped me with your good looks, led me on and let me down.' She grabbed her Bible off the dressing table and clasping it tightly, closed her eyes to pray. 'Dear God, forgive me for all my sins. I beg for your forgiveness and ask your light to shine, to show me the way for my true path. Amen.' She kept her eyes closed for a few more minutes, before the buzz of her mobile caught her attention. Picking it up, she read the text message before placing her hands together and looking upwards. 'Thank you!'

It was a message from Frank, saying he'd meet her at church at 10 am.

F rank sat patiently on the pew at the front of the church. His hand rested lightly on the Bible at his side. He had his eyes closed, as in deep prayer, however he wasn't praying – he was trying to listen in on the conversation between Father Javier and the scruffy stranger.

He wasn't usually nosy, he liked to tell himself, but he'd been watching Father Javier over the last few weeks and something wasn't quite right with him. He seemed preoccupied lately, and there was nothing Frank liked less than a man of the Church who wasn't committed to his calling.

Frank opened his eyes and watched them both. The blond scruffy-looking man wore a long brown oilskin coat and dark jeans. He looked like a tramp. Someone who, in Frank's opinion, shouldn't be welcomed into this church. The man seemed to be getting short tempered with Father Javier. Frank watched as the man seemed to be using his 6 foot plus height to its full effect by leaning over Father Javier's short stocky frame. Frank smoothed his tie and looked down at the immaculate front crease of his navy blue trousers. Not like me, he thought. I'm earning my way into heaven. He smiled smugly to himself.

They finished talking and the blond man strode purposefully out of the church. Frank looked at his watch – it was 9.55 am.

≈

'Fifty-eight, fifty-nine...' Mandy jumped as a tall blond man in an army coat knocked into her and carried on past her.

'Apology accepted!' she yelled indignantly at his retreating figure. Damn! I've lost track of the number. She sighed to herself and stood debating whether to go back to the corner to start again or to continue without counting, risking the potential panic it would bring. She decided on the latter and took a couple of steps forward.

'One, two...' She clenched her fists and clamped her jaw tight. Stop it! You're being ridiculous! she thought as she rubbed a clenched fist along her cheek. He's not even here anymore, so don't be stupid! Taking a deep breath, she hastened her steps and almost ran through the graveyard to the safety of the church. She almost fell through the doorway in her haste to get inside. She saw Frank sat on the front pew and rushed towards him.

'Are you okay Amanda?' His face was full of concern as he stood up.

Mandy held her hand to her chest and exaggeratedly caught her breath. 'Yes, thank you Frank. There was some ruffian outside that knocked me clean off my feet!'

'Here, have a seat.'

She loved that he was protective of her, and the feel of his warm hand on her arm. She missed the touch of a man on her body. She let him lead her to the pew and sat just a bit closer than he may think was appropriate in a church – but she wanted to feel his thigh against hers.

'Was it a tall blond man in a dark coat?' She nodded in response. 'Mmm, quite interesting.' He rubbed his chin with his right hand. Mandy touched his left hand gently.

'What is it, Frank?'

'That man was in here just now, talking to Father Javier.' He leant forward slightly and lowered his voice. 'They looked like they knew each other. Deep in conversation, they were.'

'Huh, I bet they were up to no good.' She pursed her lips in disdain. 'You said Father Javier was trouble, didn't you Frank?'

He nodded. 'I think it's our godly duty to keep an eye on him. For the sake of the congregation, of course.'

'I don't know what the church was thinking, letting someone so young be our priest. He's got to only be in his 30's.'

'They must've had their reasons. God does work in mysterious ways.'

'I know, but he's a distraction for the young girls.' She looked around before continuing. 'I'm sure he's had a bad past. He looks like an ex-convict with that short hair. I've seen him you know, walking around in jeans and a vest top! Not very priest-like you know.'

They watched Father Javier walking around near the back of the church, as he briefly disappeared into the sacristy before coming back out and heading out of the church.

She squeezed Frank's hand. 'You know you have my support.' She looked into his eyes. 'You know you have my support in everything you do.'

'I appreciate everything you do for me, Amanda. We

have to be vigilant and observe what is happening around us in our little corner of the world.' Frank gently took her hand and placed it on her lap. 'Let's not forget where we are though, shall we.'

She bowed her head. 'Sorry, Frank.'

16

'I'm home!' Crystal threw her bag on the floor and kicked off her shoes. 'Mum?' She started to walk towards the kitchen but, as she walked past the sitting room, she saw Nathan sat on the sofa watching TV.

'Where's Mum?' She hesitated in the doorway, unsure whether to go in or not.

'She had to get milk.' He held his mug up. 'I finished it off.'

'Hmm, that was polite of you. Why didn't you go get some then?' She sat down on the single seater opposite him.

'I'm a guest.' He grinned at her. 'Anyway, I wanted to catch you on your own.'

'Why's that then?'

He switched off the TV and turned to face her. 'I wanted to have a chat with you, without your mom here.'

'Well, here I am. So what did you want to talk about?'

'You turning twenty-one is a big thing, ya know.'

'Yeah, I know, you said yesterday. I get my abilities and can do weird shit.' She threw her hands up and collapsed back into the seat.

'No, I'm serious. There's a bigger game at stake. When I said to you God didn't create the world, I meant it. There is no God, there's just The Others.'

'Who are these mysterious 'The Others?' She said in a sarcastically dramatic tone.

'No one knows.' He sighed. 'But they are who you have to watch out for. Them and their disciples.'

'Well, how can I watch out for them if no one knows who they are?' She laughed.

'It's serious! You have to try to stay hidden. Each time you use an ability you give off a hint of that.'

'Like at the pub, when your eyes changed to a dark blue, almost black?'

'Yeah, and you let off a glow or a shimmer. Each type of full-blood gives off a slightly different 'tell'.'

'I saw you kind of shimmer, when your eyes changed colour and when you were in the kitchen yesterday.'

'Yep. Flyahs also create a slight breeze. Healahs glow and digahs, well digahs just seem to have a heaviness about them.' He ran a hand through his hair, messing up his already dishevelled look. 'You have to learn to hide those 'tells', to stay safe and stop other full-bloods, and The Others from finding you.'

'Like how?'

'Your mother and other healahs, ground themselves and your mother limits her healing to small tasks, like the flowers and plants she sells. I don't know about other flyahs, but I found alcohol works well for me.'

'So, you're basically saying I need to ground myself and stay half-cut all the time?'

'You're different, because you're a half-blood.'

'So what do other half-bloods do to stay hidden?'

He leant forward in his chair. 'You don't get it do you?

You're not *supposed* to be here. Full-bloods have a strict hierarchy, set by The Others, and they're not supposed to interbreed. Any half-bloods are found and killed at birth. *That's* why your mom and dad *had* to stay apart. So The Others couldn't find out about you.'

'Why?' She looked at him, confused.

'Because it's a half-blood that The Others are scared of! It's a half-blood that is destined to upset the balance they have created.'

'How do they know that, are they psychic or something?' She shivered slightly.

'It's foretold in The Account.'

Crystal let out a huge sigh. 'So, what's The Account and what balance is supposed to be upset? God, it's like trying to get blood out of a stone!'

'The Account is the real story of how the world was created. It's the *real* Bible, if you like. The Others don't want the world to know about full-bloods. They want humans to stay ignorant of their true abilities. The Bible was written to satisfy curiosity about how humans, and the world, came to be. It's like a half-truth'.

'So what balance are they worried about being upset?'

'A half-blood is destined to uncover the truth and enlighten the world at large. It would be catastrophic for The Others if this came out, as they'd lose all control they have.'

'So what did they do with the real story, The Account?' She leant forward in her chair.

'Before The Others could destroy it, it was hidden safely away, by someone known only as The Guardian.'

'So, where is this Guardian and The Account now?'

'No one knows. But if you're the one, The Account will find you.'

'So what am I supposed to do now?'

He gestured at her seat. 'Maybe it would be a good idea to actually come down and sit on your seat. You're currently hovering six inches above it.'

Crystal looked down then shrieked, as she fell back onto the chair.

He grinned at her. 'Think yourself lucky you're old enough to understand what's going on. Being born with the ability to fly can be a real pain in the ass!'

She looked down, embarrassed. 'I'm sorry, I must look really incompetent.' She smoothed her skirt down over her legs. 'I'd better start grounding myself more often.' She looked across at him. 'What do you mean it's a pain in the ass?'

'Imagine a mischievous small child who knows they can fly. You can't keep them in their beds if they don't want to stay put. Babies are a nightmare! They have loads of energy and can't stay still. That's why flyah parents have to tie them to their beds with a rope attached to their ankles. Where'd you think the idea of cherubs came from?'

'Is that what your parents had to do to you?'

Nathan stood up. 'I don't want to talk about my family.'

'I'm sorry, I was just interested.'

'Well don't be,' he replied abruptly.

'I said I was sorry!'

Izzy walked into the sitting room. 'What's going on?'

'Hi Mum. Nathan's just been telling me about The Others and The Account.'

Izzy smiled at Crystal and handed her the milk. 'Be a darling and make me a cup of tea, please.'

Crystal took the milk and headed for the kitchen. Izzy waited for her to leave before turning to Nathan and glaring at him. 'You should've waited for me before you told her any of that!'

'She was interested.'

'I don't care!' She lowered her voice slightly. 'I don't want her getting dragged into this so called war you keep on about.'

'Well you kinda make that decision when you chose to have her.'

'I wasn't going to get rid of my baby!' She took a step closer to him and looked him square in the face. 'Samuel and I protected her then and we will protect her now. May I remind you that you also played a part in our escape. You chose your side when you helped us.'

'And I'm here now aren't I?' I have to live with the consequences of that decision too, ya know!'

'I know.' She touched his arm. 'And I'm grateful, but I just want to keep her safe. We don't necessarily know that Crystal's the half-blood talked about in The Account.'

'Well we'll find out soon enough, if the Guardian contacts her.' He looked round as Crystal walked into the sitting room carrying three mugs of steaming hot tea. 'And I'm betting he will. Soon.'

17

It was 7pm and Crystal was waiting for Emily to arrive. Her mother had gone over to Kitty's for their girl's night in, and Nathan had disappeared down the Duke of Earl. Crystal curled her legs up on the single seater and closed her eyes.

'What a day!' she groaned aloud to herself. Her head was buzzing with questions. Who were The Others? Where could she find The Account? Crystal opened her eyes and sat forward in her chair. Would her Dad come back now she knew what was going on?

'Hi Crystal, it's only me!' Emily closed the back door and walked into the sitting room. 'I've got our usual.' She placed the Chinese containers on the table and started peeling off the lids. 'How's your day been?'

Crystal laughed, she couldn't help it. 'It's been interesting.'

'Interesting, How?' Emily paused and looked at her friend. 'Everything okay?'

Crystal wrinkled up her nose. 'Yeah, it's nothing really. I'm starving!'

Emily handed her a plate. 'You'd tell me if there was something bothering you, wouldn't you?'

'Honest, it's fine.' Crystal started piling rice on her plate. 'Anyway, it'll keep.'

'Oh, okay. You know where I am when you want to talk.' Emily knew not to push Crystal if she didn't want to talk. 'I got a DVD. I bought series five of the TV series 'Supernatural' over. I thought we could watch it again. I fancy drooling over the Winchester brothers again.'

'That sounds like a plan. Give me the DVD and I'll load it into the player.' Crystal took the DVD from Emily and turned on the TV. She wasn't too eager to watch a series based on hunters, angels and demons – but it was better than talking.

They settled down to eat their food and Crystal let Emily talk. Crystal was only really half listening to Emily, as she was wittering on about how Mark had asked her over to his house on Friday evening for dinner. Crystal couldn't even settle with eyeing up Sam & Dean Winchester on the TV screen. An hour into the DVD, during the second episode, Crystal finally spoke. 'Do you believe any of this is real?'

'Well, if I ever have to face any supernatural being, I am going to make sure I have a huge supply of salt and matches!' Emily laughed and carried on watching. 'If in doubt, salt and burn, right?'

Crystal hit the pause button and turned to her friend. 'No, I'm serious. I mean, do you believe in angels, demons, God and everything?'

'Oh, like do I believe if people like this exist?'

'Yeah. Take Castiel, he's supposed to be an angel with no visible wings, and then there's Crowley who's supposed to be a demon. Do you believe in the supernatural?'

Emily twiddled a strand of her hair and thought about it

for a minute, before replying. 'I guess I do. I mean, you can heal and that's not 'normal', so I guess I believe that other things are possible. Why'd you ask?'

Crystal bit her lip, unsure whether to confide in her or not. She took a moment to stack the Chinese containers in a pile before coming to her decision and turning to face Emily. 'If I tell you something, do you swear not to tell anyone?'

'Sure.'

'No, I really want you to swear that you won't. This is really big.'

'Okay. I swear.' Emily leant forward in her chair. 'What is it?'

'You know that drunken man that was at the bar, the one who was harassing me? Well, he knows my mum. And my dad. He's called Nathan.' She looked at Emily and continued, 'My dad had to go away to keep us safe.'

'Safe from what?' Emily stared at her friend through wide eyes.

'Safe from people called 'The Others'.'

'Who are they? What do they want with you and your mum?'

'I don't know who they are.' Crystal sighed and fell back into her chair. 'But I know what they want. Me.'

Emily's hand flew to her mouth. 'Why an earth would they want you? Is it because you can heal people?'

'Apparently I'm a bit of a freak.' Crystal agitatedly ran her hand through her hair.

'You're not a freak! Healing people is a good thing.' She leant forward and took hold of Crystal's hand. 'You can do so much good with that.'

'Especially if I can fly into their open windows and heal them whilst they're asleep.' Crystal replied sarcastically.

Emily let go of her friend's hand. 'You being serious?'

'See, even you think it's weird. I told you I was a freak!' Crystal stood up, grabbed the pile of Chinese containers and walked into the kitchen. Emily leapt up to follow her.

'You're not a freak, you're my best friend!' She grabbed Crystal's shoulder, turning to face her. 'You're my best friend who has an amazing ability that can help a lot of people. There's nothing freakish about that.' She opened the bin for Crystal to put the empty cartons inside. 'So, how does the flying part work?'

'I'm still working on it. At the moment, it mainly happens when I'm asleep. It's only happened once whilst I've been awake. I didn't even know how I did it, but I do know that it tires me out.'

'So you can't do it that much then. I mean, it's not like you can just whizz off whenever you like?'

'No. But I do like your idea of using it for good and healing sick people.' Crystal walked back to the sitting room and turned on the floor standing lamp. Emily pulled the curtains closed, pausing only to wave at Father Javier who was walking past.

'Amy and Chris are good with people. We could get them to find out who's sick in our area.'

Crystal turned and grabbed her friend by the arms. 'You can't tell them about this! You can't tell anyone!'

'Ouch! You're hurting me! I promised I wouldn't tell anyone, and I won't. We could tell them it's for something I'm doing with my class at school.'

They both sat down. Crystal leant over and turned the TV off. Emily sat twiddling with her hair. She suddenly let out a giggle. 'You'd be like a superhero. Would we have to think of a name for you and make a costume?'

Crystal relaxed and smiled. 'No costumes or names. I'm aiming not to be seen, remember?'

'What if they wake when you're in their room?'

'Then they'll assume I'm an angel. And they wouldn't be wrong.'

18

They were walking along Alpine Way, five minutes from Emily's home in Yew Tree Lane, in an amicable silence. Crystal had offered to walk Emily home, as she wanted the fresh air to blow the cobwebs away and knew Emily wasn't that keen on the dark. This time, Crystal was the first to break the silence.

'Is your mum happy that you're going to Mark's on Friday?'

'Yeah, she's actually been quite interested in it all. I guess it's because he's Kitty's son.' She shrugged her shoulders.

'Does your dad know?'

'No. I'm not going to tell him. I'll only get another lecture about how boys are "only after one thing".' She sighed. 'It's bad enough that he's always going on about Chris and Amy's behaviour with the opposite sex! He's so worried that I'll be led astray.'

Crystal linked her arm through Emily's. 'Don't worry about it. All parents are a bit like that. My mum keeps asking to meet Tony, but I've managed to keep them apart, so far.'

'Well I can understand why your mum would be protective of you. Especially with what you said about 'The Others'.'

'Shush!' Crystal looked around to make sure there was no one else around. 'Remember, not to say anything.'

'I won't. I promised didn't I?'

Crystal squeezed her friends arm tightly. 'I know, I'm sorry. You can understand why I'm a bit nervous about it all though.'

'I know.' Emily turned and unlatched her front gate. 'Will you be okay walking home on your own?'

Yeah. I'll be fine. Go on in and, if I don't see you before Friday, have a lovely evening and let me know how it goes.' They hugged each other and Crystal watched Emily walk to her front door and quietly let herself in. Crystal didn't go in with her as she could do without bumping into Frank, Emily's father. She waited for the front door to close and turned to retrace her steps back home, turning the corner at Alpine Way.

'Shit you scared me!' She put one hand to her chest and the other on Father Javier's arm. 'Sorry Father, I didn't mean to swear at you. I didn't see you stood there.'

Father Javier walked forward, out of the shadow of the trees and into the beam of the street light. 'Sorry Crystal, I didn't mean to scare you.'

'Are you walking back to church?'

He nodded. 'Want to walk with me?'

'Uh, sure.' She fell into step with him. 'Have you been out visiting parishioners?'

'I've been keeping an eye on them, yes.' He dug his hands deeper into his brown coat pockets.

'You must be really busy at the moment; I've seen you around quite a bit lately.' She glanced at him in the darkness. She could just make out that he was in casual clothes.

'I have indeed been really busy – what with services, visiting parishioners and running the homeless hostel attached to the church.' He smiled. 'God's work is never-ending.'

They walked towards Church Lane and he turned to face her. 'Actually, have you got a few minutes spare? I'd appreciate your help with something.'

Crystal hesitated and looked at her watch. 'Well, my mum's probably going to be back at any minute.'

'It's really rather important. You can always send your mother a text to let her know where you are.'

She shook her head. 'No, It's okay.'

Father Javier ushered her in the direction of the St Barnabas' church and into the graveyard.

'What did you want my help with?' They walked past one of the floodlights that lit the church and it stretched their shadows to twice their usual length, adding to the eeriness of the graveyard.

'I'd rather wait until we are inside, then I can talk freely.' He ushered Crystal inside and she followed him between the pews and along the nave, until they reached the doors leading to the sacristy. Father Javier was looking around to make sure they were alone, while Crystal was hoping there was someone else there to make this feel less bizarre.

Crystal stopped outside the sacristy, unwilling to go any further until she had some answers. 'Father Javier, I don't mean to be rude, but I'd really like to know what it is you want my help with, before I go in there with you.' She held her hands up to stop him from protesting. 'I'm not implying anything and wouldn't dream of even thinking that you would be up to no good, but a girl can't be too careful.'

Father Javier stopped in the doorway and turned to face her. 'Especially someone like you.'

'What's that supposed to mean?'

'A girl like you cannot be too careful. You're exposed, so to speak, at the moment because you haven't learnt to harness your gifts.' He turned away and walked into the sacristy. 'You need to learn and learn fast to stay safe.'

'I really don't know what...'

'You have nothing to fear from me. Your secret is safe. I will tell no one. I'm here to help you.'

Crystal followed him inside.

He walked across to a large covered chest in the corner of the room. He threw off the maroon coloured velvet cover and opened the chest. Rummaging inside, he retrieved a small wooden box then, from inside this box he took out a small key about two centimetres long. He turned to face Crystal and handed her the key. 'I need your help for this part. If you could follow me, please.'

They walked back down the nave to the other end of the church and through a plain oak door, next to the confessional. They went up a stone set of steps that opened up into a room high in the church tower. Father Javier walked over to an old, thick wooden bookcase and started counting the books – first from the bottom upwards, then across the shelf. Finally, he reached out and removed three of the books. Crystal craned her neck to see what he was doing. She could just make out that he was removing a small section of the wooden back panelling to reveal a small compartment. He removed another wooden box from this compartment. He placed it on the table to the left of the bookcase and beckoned her forward.

'This box is made from the Acacia tree – the same wood that was used to make the Ark of the Covenant that housed the Ten Commandments.' He gently placed a hand on the box and continued. 'As is mentioned in Exodus chapter 25, verse 10. It was an ideal wood to use to house something important, due to its hardness and durability. It is naturally resinous, so relatively resistant to both odour and moisture.' He picked it up and let the sunlight dance off the grain. 'See? It also has a chatoyancy about it – which means it appears to change colour, depending on the lighting conditions.'

Crystal ran a finger over the ornate carvings that covered the heavy oak coloured box. She could make out an eye, what looked like flames, and a sun. It also had two small gold inlaid keyholes.

'Is this what you needed my help with?' She held up the key. He nodded and pulled his cross out from under his t-shirt. He pushed down on the loop that the chain went through, whilst simultaneously sliding the overlaid platinum cross across the larger wooden one. Inside was an identical key to the one Crystal was holding.

'My father passed this to me when I turned of age. Like you, twenty-one is a milestone for Guardians like me, as we are usually given The Account when we reach our twenty-first birthday. Due to outside circumstances I was given it at a younger age. Your abilities, or gifts as I prefer to call them, awaken when you reach twenty-one.' He gestured to the box on the table. 'Alas, I have no gifts but I became the guardian of this. I've been protecting it for the last twenty-three years.'

'So, why are you showing whatever it is to me?'

He raised an eyebrow at her in disbelief. 'You're really going to ask me that?'

She shuffled from one foot to another, looking at the ground.

'I've spoken to Nathan to clarify it, but I know you're an

angel. Actually, you're *the* angel that I'm supposed to pass this on to.' He sighed. 'I understand that this is all a bit much for you to take in, but you have no choice. How long do you think you can stay hidden from them?'

'We've managed this far,' Crystal mumbled at the floor, fiddling with the small gold key in her hand.

'But that was before your second ability awakened. The one that you need to learn to control.' He raised his eyes upwards. 'This hasn't been easy for me either you know. I'm a man of the church, who believes something different to what I have to preach!' He stared back at Crystal. 'Do you think it was just coincidental that you kept seeing me around lately? I've been watching you and, if I can see the glow you're emitting, it won't be long before others do. The Others will send someone for you.'

Crystal stepped forward and held out her key. 'What do you want me to do?'

'We have to turn the keys to the right at the same time. On the count of three. One, two, three.' There was a small clicking sound and the box swung open. Inside was an old brown, leather bound journal. It was roughly twenty centimetres long by fifteen wide and had a brown leather string wrapped around it to keep it sealed. Father Javier unwound the string and opened the cover. Inside, the yellowed pages had sepia brown writing on them.

'What language is that written in?' Crystal touched the pages. They certainly weren't made of paper. 'What paper did they use?' She looked up at him.

'They're written in Hebrew,' Father Javier replied. 'You will pick it up soon enough. The paper is actually vellum – from the Latin word *'vitulinum'* which means 'of calf'.' He turned the book back to the light. 'See? You can still see the veins showing against the white animal skin.'

'That's disgusting!' Crystal took her hand off the book. 'And I'll quickly learn Hebrew, will I?'

Father Javier sat down on a dusty chair and beckoned her to sit next to him. 'When you turned twenty-one, your gifts were unlocked. But your brain was too. It's like having a partition taken down inside your mind. Most of the normal human population can only use small amounts of their brain at any one time – they're wired differently. You can now use *all* of yours. You can now do whatever you put your mind to. Knowledge is the key.'

'Like learning Hebrew?'

'Yes, and learning how to use, and hide, your gifts. *Everything* will be that much quicker for you. The world will seem more *alive*. Your senses will be heightened, as will your sixth sense. And *that* is what you have in your favour. You'll be able to sense when others like you are around.'

'So why do I have to stay hidden if I'll know when others are around or coming for me?'

'Because you're not ready yet. Rather than flooding you with all those heightened feelings at once, your brain is still processing it all. The partition is coming down in sections, rather than all at once. Does that make sense?'

'Yeah, I guess.'

He stood and held the book out for her to take. 'This is now yours to read and learn about the true origins of man and Earth. You are the angel destined to bring enlightenment to the world.'

'Not too big a job then!' The sarcasm was evident in her voice. 'Can I come to you if I have any questions?'

'It's not a good idea – they are probably watching you as we speak.' He put the book down and pulled a business card from his jeans back pocket. 'This has my private mobile number on it. Call or text me, but don't come here again to see me.'

She looked at the card. Apart from a phone number, it was blank.

He picked up the book and forcefully shoved it towards her.

'Take it.' She took the book from him as he continued, 'You *must* keep this hidden. Only those you trust and love are allowed to know of its existence. You will be changing the world and there will be others – human and full-bloods - who do not want that to happen.' He looked her straight in the eyes. 'You have a huge responsibility that comes with a heavy burden. *Never* let your guard down.' He ushered her out of the room and into the church. 'Now go!' he hissed. 'Go and hide it well. Learn from it, and from those like your mother and Nathan. May light be with you.'

Crystal shoved the book into her bag and, head down, walked away from the church.

19

Crystal heard the front door open at just after 11pm. She heard her mum switch first the kitchen light on, then the kettle. Five minutes later, she listened to Nathan return. She stayed sat on her bed, the old, brown leather covered book on the duvet in front of her. Torn between going downstairs and staying safely cocooned in her bedroom, she sat a few minutes longer staring at its cover, the sound of her beating heart echoing in her ears.

She wanted to open it and look within its pages, to satisfy her curiosity, however she was also frightened. Her trembling hand rested temporarily on the cover, before she swiped it away again and folded her arms. Finally, she swung her legs off the bed, wrapped her cardigan around both herself and the book and headed downstairs.

'Mum, Nathan, did you both have a nice evening?' Crystal stood in the kitchen doorway, unsure on how to broach the subject of the book.

'Yes, thanks hun. Did you?' Izzy looked enquiringly at her daughter; Nathan just nodded his response and continued drinking from his glass.

'Kinda.' Crystal walked hesitantly forward. 'Until I bumped into Father Javier.' Nathan shot his head round to look at her, and Izzy gasped as her daughter opened her cardigan and placed The Account on the table.

'Oh my God! Is that what I think it is?' Izzy's held a trembling hand to her mouth.

'Yep.' Crystal walked round the table and settled in the chair next to her mother. Her eyes never once left The Account, as if she was waiting for it to spring into life. 'He gave it to me, along with a speech about my destiny and a warning not to go back to see him.' She leant her chin on her hands.

'I knew you were meant to have it!' Nathan clapped his hands together in delight.

'Are you nuts?' Izzy flung her chair back and stood in front of him. 'This isn't a game. This is my daughter's life!' Grabbing her chair, she sat quickly back down again. Running a hand agitatedly through her hair she continued, rather more quietly 'This is our life.'

Crystal reassuringly patted her mother's arm. 'It's fine Mum. It'll be okay.'

Izzy looked at Crystal through tear-filled eyes. 'I didn't want this for you. We didn't want any of this.' She gestured to the book sat on the table.

'Izzy, we need to focus on helping Crystal now,' Nathan chipped in.

'Don't you dare!' She spun round to face him. 'I've done nothing but help my daughter. I've protected her from the moment she was placed in my arms!' She glared at him through narrowed eyes. 'I blame you for this! You didn't need to drag my daughter into your plans. You could've easily started a rebellion without her. Destiny could easily be changed!'

'You knew, as well as I, the risks in having a half-blood child. I warned you and Samuel, but you didn't listen.' He got to his feet and glared at her across the table.

'What was I supposed to do, not have her?' Izzy bit back, her voice rising.

'If you wanted a quiet life, then yes!' he yelled back at her.

Izzy shot to her feet. 'I was not going to get rid of a baby that both Samuel and I yearned for!'

'We all knew the prophecy.' He waved his index finger in her face. 'We all knew if a flyah and a healah had a child, it would be an angel.'

'I didn't know Samuel would have to suffer as a result!'

'He wasn't the only one who suffered.' He stabbed his finger against his chest to emphasis each word. 'I did too! I was, after all, his mentor.'

'Stop it, both of you!' Crystal banged the table hard with both hands. She lowered her voice slightly, 'Sit down.'

Izzy and Nathan glared at each other before slowly taking their seats back at the table.

'*I'm* the one this affects the most. *I'm* the one who decided to take the book when it was handed to me. *I'm* the one that could've said 'No' and that would've been the end of it.' Crystal looked at each of them in turn. 'Arguing isn't going to help anybody.' She turned to her mother. 'I appreciate what you have done for me, and what you have had to give up as a result. And you,' she turned to Nathan. 'You, I've only known five minutes and you're already doing my head in! I've not signed up to any war or rebellion. I'm not agreeing to do *anything* until I've had a chance to read some of this and get my head around it.' She took in a very deep breath to calm herself down.

'You're right, I'm sorry. I just can't help but worry about

you.' Izzy managed a weak smile. 'You're my daughter and it's my job.'

'I know Mum, but I'm an adult now and, now I have all the facts, I can make my own mind up.'

Izzy held up her hands in resignation. 'I guess you are.'

Nathan stood up and stretched. 'Well, I'm gonna say nothing apart from 'Good night'.' He walked from the room with his head held high.

They both watched him go, before Izzy stood up and, walking over to her daughter, gave her a big hug. 'I love you. I don't say it enough but I'm proud of how you've turned out. Your dad would be too.'

Crystal sighed. 'I just wish he could be here.'

'Me too hun, me too.' Izzy straightened herself up and picked The Account up off the table. She handed it to Crystal. 'You'd better put this somewhere safe. I'm behind you one hundred percent, whatever you decide to do.'

'Thanks Mum.' Crystal took the book and wrapped her arms around it. 'I appreciate that.' Walking out of the kitchen, she stopped in the doorway and turned around slightly. 'Night Mum. I love you.'

'Night hun, try to get some sleep.'

'I'll try – although I've got some Hebrew to learn!' She turned and walked towards the stairs.

20

E ven with the curtains closed, the moonlight lit up the bedroom better than a 60-watt light bulb. Crystal groaned and rolled over to look at the clock.

God, is it only five past one? She grumbled to herself. Fluffing up her pillow for the umpteenth time, she tried to settle. It was useless. She glared at the leather-bound book laid on her bedside cabinet. The moonlight beamed straight onto The Account, illuminating the very thing she was trying not to think about.

Rolling her eyes, Crystal finally gave in. Throwing back the covers she switched on her lamp, swung her legs over the edge of her bed and grabbed the book from the cabinet and flung it onto her bed, where it came to a rest on the duvet. She stood looking at it, lying there, taunting her. She sat back on the bed, crossed her legs and stared at the cover.

It wasn't very special looking. The brown leather cover was quite plain, no writing or intricate designs to show it as anything special or significant. It was held closed by a leather string, wrapped around the book three times and tied loosely in a bow. She untied this string and grudgingly flicked through the vellum pages. The writing varied throughout – the only thing they all had in common was the fact that she couldn't read any of it, as it wasn't in a language she knew, or had any real interest in learning.

As Crystal flicked through the pages, she became more certain that this wasn't meant for her. It felt wrong, as if she was reading someone else's journal. She closed the cover and retied the string, before putting the book back on her bedside cabinet. Getting back under her bed covers, Crystal resolved to visit Father Javier in the morning to let him know he'd made a mistake. She leant over and set her alarm a half hour earlier, so she could go before work. Feeling slightly more relaxed, she managed to go back to sleep.

~

The ringing of her alarm woke Crystal from her sleep at 6.15am. She wearily stretched out and shut off the noise.

Is it really time to get up already? she groaned to herself. She pulled herself to a seated position and rubbed the sleep from her eyes. Well that's an improvement, she thought. I actually woke up whilst still under the covers for a change. She swung her legs out of bed and pulled on a pair of black leggings, followed by a vest top and mustard coloured jumper. After dragging a brush through her hair, she pulled on her coat, shoved The Account into her shoulder bag and gently opened her bedroom door.

Knowing that it was far too early for Nathan to be awake, she tiptoed past his bedroom door, carrying her boots to avoid making any noise. As she passed her mother's room, she heard the shower running, so knew she could make it downstairs and out the back door without being detected.

Grabbing a muesli bar from the cupboard on her way through the kitchen, Crystal quietly opened the back door and stepped out into the still dark early morning chill. Closing the kitchen door behind her, Crystal paused only to sit on the back doorstep to tie her boot laces, before heading out the garden and down the road.

The floodlights lit up the church, making it an eerie, intimidating structure looming, larger than life, surrounded with brightness and light. In stark contrast, the headstones around the church yard loomed ominously in the darkness; a darkness to not only counteract the building, but also to make you want to be inside the church; to be inside the light and safety it represented. The gravel path crunched loudly beneath her feet, as she walked up the path to the church entrance. Each step she took seemed louder than the last. Crystal pushed open the heavy wooden door and stepped into the candle-lit serenity of the nave.

Walking past the dark oak pews, Crystal made her way to the vigil candles that stood by the pulpit at the rear of the church. She paused for a moment, looking slowly at the scene around her. The stained-glass windows were lit up by the spotlights outside. The deep reds, bright orange and blues shone brightly; the pale face of Mary, holding baby Jesus, looked down on Crystal with a look of pity. One of the other windows had a flowing haired Christ nailed to a cross. A look of love, mixed with compassion, was etched across his face. Crystal looked at the votive vigil candles in the black metal stand, burning brightly for loved ones that needed remembering or forgiving. Crystal felt an uncomfortable feeling deep inside her, as she cast her eyes over those candles, dripping wax slowly down their sides. The hopes and wishes of the people who lit them were almost tangible.

What if it's all a lie? She closed her eyes, as that uncomfortable feeling turned to a sense of sadness – a sadness that could only come from the certainty of knowing your gut feeling was actually right.

She opened her eyes as the sacristy door opened and Father Javier, dressed in jeans and a vest top, marched into the room. He looked up and momentarily stopped in his tracks, as he registered who was stood in front of him.

'I told you not to come back!' he whispered angrily.

'But I think you made a mistake.' Crystal bent her head down and rummaged briefly in her bag, before starting to pull the book from inside. 'I don't think this is meant...'

'For crying out loud, put it away before anyone sees!' Father Javier cast his eyes anxiously around the empty room.

'There's no one else here. It's far too early, isn't it? You did say I should contact you if I had any questions.' Suddenly she wasn't so sure of that fact any more.

'I told you to *text* me. I specifically said not to come back! Quickly, follow me – we'll go in the tower room, at least it'll lessen the risk of being seen.'

Crystal followed him and stayed silent until they'd gone up the stone steps to the tower room and Father Javier had closed the door behind them.

'I wanted to give this back to you. I think you've got the wrong person.' She tried to hand him back The Account, but he stepped back from her, holding up his hands.

'I'm not mistaken. I have the right person.'

'I'm not big enough for this!' She put the book on top of the bookcase. 'I'm sure your faith would be better placed with someone who is older, more experienced in all of *this*. I'm too young and too naive to be the angel you're after.'

'It is your destiny – and yours alone. You will bring enlightenment to the world.' He smiled gently at her.

'I can't even bring enlightenment to myself – let alone anyone else. There must be someone else.' She pleaded with him, her eyes silently begging him to admit his mistake.

'There is no one else. You cannot hide from your destiny, no matter how hard the road ahead may appear.'

'What do you know of destiny and hardship?' She sat down on a stool and lowered her head to her hands.

Taking the seat next to her, Father Javier placed a hand gently on her shoulders.

'I've been a Guardian since I was twelve. My father bought me up with stories of martyrs, knights and princes who endured every type of hardship in the quest to fulfil whatever they set out to do. No obstacle was too big. He told me he was a Guardian to a special book that must be kept hidden and protected – no matter what – and that my destiny was to be a Guardian one day too.' He reached up to the cross around his neck.

'I took this from my father, as he lay dying.' He looked up and met her horrified stare.

'You watched your father die?'

Father Javier nodded. 'We got word that they had found him – The Others – five minutes before they turned up at our door. My father sent me away to a friend's house, but I sneaked back. I saw them trash our house, and instinctively knew they were after that special book. I saw how brave he was – stood defiantly in front of them.'

'What happened?' Crystal whispered.

'They killed him when he refused to give them the location.' He continued to fiddle with the cross around his neck. 'I knew where it was hidden, and that my father kept the key inside his cross – this cross.' His hand fell back down to his side and he looked at Crystal. 'I was twelve and knew that I had just become a Guardian. A role that got my father killed, but also a role that he would rather die than betray.'

'I'm sorry about your dad.'

'I'm proud of him. He showed me what strength and dedication was. He taught me so much in those twelve years, things I didn't realise until I was old enough to understand their significance.' He turned to face Crystal. 'I *know* you are the only angel left – that makes you the right person, by default. You may not want the responsibility – I didn't want the responsibility at twelve years of age – but it has been handed to you, and you must deal with it.'

'But I don't know what to do, or how to do it.' Her voice sounded pathetically child-like, even to her ears.

He stood up and took The Account, handing it back to Crystal. 'Everything you need to know is in here. What you do with that information will be dictated by your instincts and feelings – so trust your gut feelings, they're your guidance system – and believe in yourself. '

Crystal took the book back and put it in her bag. 'I'm sorry if I've caused problems by coming back here.'

'Don't worry, if anything comes of it, I'll deal with it. Just make sure you keep to contacting me by text, instead of turning up in person, in future.' He smiled at Crystal and stood up to lead her from the room and towards the church entrance. 'Now go and put that book somewhere safe – for all our sakes.'

'Thanks Father, I will.' Crystal started to pull open the church door, before pausing to turn back to him. 'And I am sorry about your father.'

Father Javier nodded his acceptance before turning and walking back into the candlelit room. Crystal pulled the door shut behind her and crunched her way back along the pathway through the graveyard.

As Crystal reached the end of the gravel path, she paused to check her watch and, deciding she had time to go home before work, she headed back along Church View. The postman was already delivering mail to the residents of those houses next to the church. He nodded at Crystal as she walked past him, and she could sense him continuing to stare at her until she disappeared from his view.

21

Her mother was already in the flower shop when Crystal returned home. She'd sneaked back past Nathan's door before letting herself into her bedroom and grabbing a quick shower. She was towel drying her hair when she realised that The Account was still sat on her bedside cabinet. 'Shit!' She looked frantically around for somewhere safe to hide it. She looked around her room to weigh up her options. There was a large bay window with a window seat underneath, a sealed up fireplace with a white painted wooden surround, her metal bedstead, white wooden bedside cabinet and a wardrobe in the main part of her room.

She walked past her desk and through to the en-suite, and looked, firstly at the shower base then the toilet cistern. No, that's far too obvious, she thought. Walking back into the bedroom, her gaze stopped at the bay window. The seat might be too obvious, but she remembered that the left-hand side of the window sill was a bit loose. She grabbed the paper knife off her desk and dislodged the sill. 'Perfect!' There was a gap just big enough to slide the book inside.

She replaced the sill and stood the potted prayer plant on top.

~

A my waved at Crystal as she made her way to her desk. She waited for Crystal to take off her coat, impatiently tapping her purple stiletto-clad foot until Crystal had sat down on the seat behind, before spinning her chair around.

'Morning! You'll never guess whose house I ended up round last night?' She didn't wait for Crystal to respond. 'Only Matthew Freidman. You know, the new lad from HR.'

Crystal flicked the 'on' switch of her PC base unit and it flickered to life. 'I'm so glad IT managed to fix my PC last night!' She let up a silent 'thank you'. 'So, when you say you ended up at his house last night – do you actually mean all night?'

'Yep. It was amazing. Hell, I was amazing!' Amy flicked a bouncy strand of black hair behind her ear. 'Did you get up to anything last night?' She gave Crystal a puppy-dog look before continuing. 'Of course, you had your girly night in with Emily, didn't you. So that would be a 'no' then. I'm off to get a mug of coffee. I need the caffeine to replace my lost energy.' She swung off her chair and wiggled her way to the coffee machine.

That's okay, I didn't want one, Crystal thought as she watched Amy teeter her way across the office in her favourite four-inch-high purple stilettos. She opened her drawer and took out a can of cola, swigging from it as she waited for the software on her PC to load and for Amy to return.

'So, do I take it you've finished with the lads from IT now?' She spun her chair round and smiled sweetly at Amy.

'You're making it sound like I've slept with them all! I've only been out with two of them. I don't know what their problem was.' Amy pulled a face. 'I think neither of them knew how to handle someone like me.'

'Yeah, I guess that's why they're not talking to you anymore.' Crystal spun her chair back to her desk. 'That'll be why they send the older ugly guy up to fix my PC every time it goes wrong.'

'Well, he does seem to be up here a lot, looking at your PC.' Amy's purple varnished nails clicked on her keyboard. 'Who knows, maybe he's more your type.'

Crystal ignored her and started sorting through all the papers in her 'in' tray.

~

Amy threw the scraps of paper into her desk drawer and slammed it shut. 'Thank God it's time to go home!' She stood up 'I can't believe I chipped my varnish. I'll have to redo it now.' She pouted at the offending fingernail.

Crystal cleared the papers off her desk and put them in her filing tray. 'Are you walking home, or have you got a lift?' She glanced in Amy's direction.

'I'm walking. Why, did you want to walk with me?'

Crystal didn't fancy walking the twenty-minute walk on her own, especially as the autumn evenings were drawing in. 'Okay.' She nodded and grabbed her coat from the back of her chair. They walked across the office and down the stairs to the foyer. Amy spotted Matthew Fieldman coming out of the HR department and waved at him. Crystal watched her face drop as his colleague nudged him and they both quickly looked the other way, laughing.

'Don't worry, he probably didn't see you.' Crystal offered helpfully.

Amy stuck her nose in the air. 'I don't care. I didn't really like him that much. I just wanted a shag.'

Crystal shook her head slightly. 'Are you and Chris still having that stupid competition?'

'It's not stupid, it's fun. I'm not losing £50 to him. The bet still stands – whoever shags the most people by the end of the year gets £50.'

Crystal wrapped her cream scarf around her neck and buttoned up her coat. 'It's a stupid bet.' She softened her voice slightly. 'I'm only worried you'll get hurt.'

Amy, head down, busied herself with her coat buttons. 'I won't get hurt. Men are only good for one thing.' She looked up. 'And, in my experience, they're not even very good at that.' She held the door open for Crystal then followed her outside, before shoving her hands into her coat pockets. 'Let's face it Crystal, you have to hurt them before they hurt you.'

'Not all of them are bad!' Crystal laughed. 'Look at Chris... okay, maybe he's not a good example...' She paused, realising he was treating the girls he slept with as badly as Amy was treating the boys. 'Well Mark is nice. He's invited Emily over for dinner at their house on Friday.' Even in the failing light, she could see Amy wrinkle up her nose in disdain.

'Yeah, but Emily is such a drip, she'd be happy with *any* lad who paid her attention.'

'Don't be so mean to her.'

'Well, she may be my cousin, but I don't have to actually *like* her that much.'

'What is your problem with her? She's really sweet – she wouldn't hurt *anybody*.'

'Exactly! She's so... *girly*. All sweetness and light – *everybody* loves Emily.' The jealousy dripped off her tongue. Flicking her hair, she continued. 'She has all those cutesy bows and hair bands; all those *shiny* little fake brooches. Ugh!' She brushed an imaginary piece of fluff from her coat. 'She's like a little doll stuck in a bad 1950's movie.'

'Don't be so nasty.' Crystal turned to Amy. 'It wouldn't hurt you to be a tad nicer to her. She just wants to be friends with you.' She sighed and continued, 'For crying out loud, you're family. You should stick together!'

Amy laughed bitterly. 'We both know family is overrated. If family was really that important, we'd both have dads at home, wouldn't we?'

Crystal didn't respond, she just kept her head down and walked on. At Bellamy Place she bade Amy goodbye and continued walking on her own. Five minutes away from home, she became aware of another set of footsteps, echoing in time with hers.

She shook her head. Don't be so paranoid, she told herself. Keeping her head down, she sped up her pace slightly. Her heart skipped a beat as the echoing footsteps increased their speed too. She didn't want to look round, worried about what she'd see. Come on, get a grip, she thought, as she clenched her fists and crossed the road. The echoing footsteps followed. Her heart was pounding in her ears and thousands of tiny needles seemed to be prickling her skin. She turned right at the end of the road, chancing a quick glance behind her as she rounded the corner. She spied a slim figure dressed in dark clothing and wearing a hoodie. Not too suspect looking then, she thought sarcastically, picking up her pace again.

She couldn't hear the footsteps anymore. She turned and saw the figure receding down the road in the opposite direction. Silly cow, she thought as she placed a hand over her heart and took a couple of deep, steadying breaths. She leant back against the brick wall, let her bag slide off her shoulder and swing gently from her hand. Closing her eyes momentarily, she let out a huge sigh. It was in that split second that she felt her bag strap get wrenched from her hand.

'Hey!' Her eyes flew open and she attempted to chase after the man running rapidly down the road. 'Damn!' It was no use, running in heels disadvantaged her too much and the man was surprisingly fast for such a stocky build. Her eyes filled with tears. She continued walking home, disappointed and defeated – wishing she'd keep her boots on all day instead of going home and changing earlier.

Luckily someone was home as the back door was unlocked. She let herself into the house and into the sitting room.

Izzy and Nathan were both sat watching TV. 'Hi hun, have a good day?' Izzy enquired, her eyes still fixed on the TV.

'Not really.' Crystal collapsed onto the sofa, next to Nathan. 'I've just had my bag swiped.' She suddenly had their full attention.

'What happened? When?' They cried in unison. Izzy started to get up.

'Don't get up Mum; I'll cry if you cuddle me.' She smiled weakly at her mother. 'I was only a couple of minutes away from home.' She let her head fall back against the sofa and closed her eyes. 'My iPod, phone *and* purse were in that bag!' She rubbed her palms over her brow.

'I'm guessing your house keys were in your bag too?' Nathan stood and started to walk out of the room.

'Where are you going?' Izzy called after him.

'Going to buy new door locks. Can I borrow your car?' he called back from the direction of the kitchen.

'Yes. The keys are on the hook.' She turned to face Crystal. 'He's made a good point.' She nodded her head slightly and sighed. 'Stay there. I'll make you a cup of tea.' She patted Crystal on the shoulder and walked into the kitchen. 'It was probably just a random chancer,' Izzy shouted from the kitchen. Crystal could just detect the slight waver in her mother's voice.

'Yeah, probably.' She sounded about as convincing as her mother had.

Izzy handed her a mug of tea and they both sat in worried silence.

Twenty minutes later Nathan returned with the locks and, after finding Samuel's old tools in the shed, he got to work replacing the door locks whilst Crystal and Izzy cooked something to eat.

They were halfway through eating, when Izzy's mobile rang. She glanced at the screen before looking puzzled. 'Apparently, you're calling me.' She showed them the screen before answering.

'Hello?' Izzy's hand hovered over her throat, fiddling with her silver heart locket, whilst she listened. 'That would be great, thank you.' The relief was evident in her voice. She finished the call and laid her mobile on the table, before letting out a huge sigh of relief. 'That was Amy. She found your bag at the end of her street.'

'That's great!' The smile spread across Crystal's face. 'They obviously didn't take my phone then.'

'No they didn't.' Izzy picked up her knife and fork and

continued eating. 'Your purse and iPod were still there.' She glanced worriedly across at Nathan. 'And your house keys were there too.'

Nathan's quizzical eyes met Izzy's as she continued. 'So, you didn't have to change the door locks after all, but thanks for acting so quickly anyway.'

'That's all right. Better to be safe than sorry.' He continued to stare at Izzy. She finally flung her cutlery down. 'Okay, I agree! It's a bit strange that this should happen straight after Crystal is given The Account, but we shouldn't jump to conclusions – and anyway, we can't do anything until we get the bag back.'

'Do you think they might be connected then?' Bemused, Crystal glanced from one to the other.

'Well, I for one don't think it was random,' Nathan said quietly. 'Your mother doesn't either.' He glanced up at Izzy and she nodded in agreement. He turned to Crystal. 'Do you have The Account well hidden?'

'Yes, I put it...'

He held his hands up to stop her talking. 'Don't tell us where you've put it. It's probably safer that way.'

'Is that why you think they stole my bag, to get to The Account?' She shook her head. 'No one knows I have it, apart from us three.'

'And Father Javier.' Nathan chipped in.

'He wouldn't tell anyone, he's the Guardian, it's his job to protect it. He told me so.' Crystal frowned at him.

The doorbell sounded and Nathan went to answer it. He returned with Crystal's bag. 'A pretty redhead gave me this.' He handed the bag to Crystal. 'I'm guessing it was her mother in the car that was cutting me the evils.'

Crystal rummaged through her bag to check the

contents. 'Don't worry about Mandy; she's like that with everyone.'

'Oh great!' Izzy groaned. 'So Mandy knows you're here now. It'll be halfway round town by the morning.' She ran her hand through her hair. 'I can see her and Frank making up theories as to who you are and what we're doing.'

'Well, everything seems to be here.' Crystal went to put the bag on the floor.

'Wait a minute. Did you check that the lining hadn't been tampered with?' Nathan asked.

'You're being ridiculous.' Crystal picked up the bag anyway and examined the stitching and seams around it.

Nathan shrugged. 'Well, if nothing was taken, maybe something was put in?'

'Nope. It's all fine.' Crystal went to put the bag down again, but stopped and started rummaging through it again. 'Wait a minute... there is something missing, but it's probably nothing to worry about.' She glanced up at him.

'What's missing then?' Izzy asked.

'Father Javier gave me his business card. That's what's missing.' Nathan opened his mouth to speak, but Crystal stopped him. 'It's okay though. It only had his mobile number on it, nothing else. Not even his name.'

'Have you called him on that number at all?'

'No.' Crystal shook her head.

'That's good then, so if they checked your phone, they'd not see his number on your call log. And you're sure no one saw you meet with him yesterday?'

'I'm sure no one saw me yesterday.' A recollection from this morning entered her mind. Izzy heard the doubt in Crystal's voice.

'Hun, what is it? You don't sound sure.'

Crystal looked guiltily at her mother. 'I did bump into a postman this morning.'

'You went out this morning? I didn't hear you.' Izzy looked puzzled.

The penny suddenly dropped for Nathan. 'Please tell me you didn't go to see Father Javier.'

'I thought he might've given the book to me by mistake,' Crystal began apologetically. 'I had to be sure it was meant for me. You'd have done the same in my position.'

Nathan rolled his eyes and stood up. 'Do you realise what you've done?' He tried to keep his voice calm. 'He told you not to contact him for a reason! Now I'll have to go and warn him.' He pulled his coat from the back of the chair. 'A business card with just a number on it *is* unusual-looking. They will probably run a trace on it. And it will lead them to the Guardian.' He pulled the collar of his coat up. 'And the Guardian could lead them to you – especially if the postman who saw you tells anyone that you were there.'

Izzy stood and started clearing the dishes from the table. There wasn't anything else that she could really do.

'I'm sorry. I didn't realise.' Crystal got up and started stacking plates in the dishwasher. Nathan didn't reply – he just marched out of the back door and into the night.

Nathan didn't return that evening. Neither Crystal nor Izzy managed to get much sleep that night.

22

Nathan crept across the graveyard. The floodlights were lighting up the church, the black van parked out the front cast a huge ominous black shadow across the gravel walkway. Using the gravestones as cover, he inched forward. He could see the driver inside the van, sitting bolt upright, staring down the gravel walkway. Nathan scanned the area around the church. Satisfied there was only one person in the van, he crept round the graveyard and towards the door at the rear of the building. He quietly opened it and let himself into the sacristy, then on into the cool, dim confines of the church interior.

It had been years since he had sneaked around the church at night. The last time he had been twelve and he, along with the other choir boys, had often snuck into the church to tell each other ghost stories and play dare, to see how far they could go before God would punish them. He remembered one of them had dared him to piss in the font...

'Focus, god dammit!' he sternly reminded himself, in a hushed voice.

The people, who were in the tower room at the other

end of the church, had no such qualms about being quiet. Amid the shouting he could hear the sound of metal hitting the stone floor, as well as the dull thud and crash of wooden bookcases being knocked over. The candlelight from the vigil candles and candelabras at the altar didn't reach the walkways between the rows of pews and the church wall, so he used the shadows to his advantage and silently strode towards the ruckus at the rear of the church. As he made his way up the stone steps in the tower, the hairs on his arms and back of neck were tingling, as if a tiny electrical pulse was being sent around his body. The adrenaline was causing his heartbeat to echo in his ears.

The door was only slightly ajar and, at first all he could see was a thin slither of mixed light and shadows. He inched forward and gave the door a slight push. There were four men in total. All dressed in black, with hoods obscuring their faces. Two of them were holding Father Javier by his arms, whilst the third, slimmer built man systematically punched him in the face and stomach. The fourth was ransacking the tower room. Nathan briefly shut his eyes at the sight. God, he looks a state, he thought to himself. He tried to see their faces but their hoods were casting a shadow over most of their features and the third man had his back to the door. He looked at Father Javier. They'd obviously been here for a while, as Father Javier's face was a bloody mess. Blood was running from a gash in his temple, his mouth and jaw line were swollen and his lips were split open.

'Tell me where The Account is.' The third man aimed a blow at Father Javier's kidneys. Father Javier groaned at the impact, but didn't reply.

'It's not here I'm telling you. I've pulled this room apart.' The fourth man threw his arms out in defeat, before wiping his hand across his face. When he put his hand back down it was glistening with fresh blood. Good for Father Javier, Nathan thought. He obviously managed to cause a bit of damage himself. Nathan smiled slightly. The fourth man continued. 'I'm guessing that it was hidden in this panel though.' Nathan could see him point to one of the up-ended bookcases. The books had been unceremoniously dumped onto the floor and the false back panel had been ripped off.

The third man momentarily cocked his head to one side, as if listening for something. He turned his head slightly towards the door. Nathan got a glimpse of his side profile and could just make out the slight twitch of his lips, as if about to smile. He clenched and unclenched his fist for a couple of seconds, before turning his attention back to Father Javier.

'Who has it? Did you give it to the girl?' The third guy's fist made contact with Father Javier's nose, with a sickening crunch. His body hung limply between the two men restraining him.

The third man went to take another punch, but the fourth man grabbed his arm, preventing him from making contact. 'He's not going to tell us anything. We're under instructions to bring him back alive.'

The third man angrily shook him off before nodding to the other two to let Father Javier go. He groaned as he fell to the floor, before summoning up the energy to lift his arm and beckon the third man to come closer. The third man crouched down to listen.

'May light be with you.' Father Javier managed to say.

The third guy stood up in disgust and shoved Father Javier over with his foot. He then examined his knuckles and wiggled his fingers, to try and ease the aching. 'Pick him up and put him in the van.'

Nathan edged his way from the door and ran swiftly back down the stone steps. Hiding in the shadows by the church notice board, he watched as they dragged Father Javier out of the tower doorway and towards the entrance door. One of the men was limping and the other man was still wiping his bloody nose. Nathan considered his options. He could try to rescue him, but Father Javier wasn't in any fit state to help take out the four guys – five, if you counted the driver. His only other option was to find out where they were taking him. He watched them bundle Father Javier into the back of the van before he crept back up the steps to the tower room.

The third man paused, his head cocked slightly to the side again. He slowly pulled his hood off and, with hands on his hips, casting his icy blue eyes around the mess that surrounded him. Nathan had a clear view of his face this time. His black, chin length, slightly wavy hair was damp with sweat and the dimple on his chin was all the more pronounced by the clenching and unclenching of the muscles in his jawline. As he bent down to check through the books one last time, his sleeve rode slightly up his arm, revealing a small circular tattoo on the outside of his left wrist. He looked up at the open doorway, his piercing icy-blue eyes peering into the darkened room beyond, before standing up straight and kicking the books, scattering their precious contents across the room. Nathan disappeared back down the steps, managing to get back into the shadows just as the man appeared through the tower doorway. He paused to pull his hood back on and stormed out of the doorway, heading back to the van.

Nathan heard the van start up and the wheels scrunching across the gravel as they made their way out of the graveyard. He hurriedly left the church the way he had entered, to ensure no one in the van would see him.

Unfortunately, neither Nathan nor the four other men had seen Frank sitting, quiet as a church mouse, on a pew in the darkest shadows at the rear left of the church.

Nathan stood outside the church watching the van drive away. He hadn't flown for a while. He didn't even know if he was still capable, after being tanked on so much alcohol for all these months. But he had been drinking nothing but coffee all day and he knew it was the only way he would be able to follow them, to see where Father Javier was being taken. And a chance to see who had sent them.

He closed his eyes and focused his attention. Holding out his arms slightly, he placed his hands, palms downwards, as if pushing the air between them and the ground. He felt the all too familiar buzzing through his body; all his nerve endings sending tiny electrical pulses in unison; the tensing and relaxing of his shoulder blades, as if they were supporting and flapping a huge pair of wings. His feet left the ground and he opened his eyes.

It was harder than he remembered, even for a full-blood like him. The problem was clearing your mind of everything except the intent. His intent had been to stay hidden for so long that his brain automatically wanted to ping useless information around inside, in an effort to prevent him thinking of flying.

He followed the black van, using the both the weather and the natural layout of the land as camouflage. Nathan was glad it was a cloudy night; the stars were hidden and the moonlight barely made it through the clouds. He kept low, as near to the tree lines as he could without being so low that they'd cause him problems. He followed the van from when it left the church until it turned off the main road and down a gravel track, before stopping outside a large three storey house roughly half an hour away from Thatcham. The concentration it had taken to stay focused had wiped out his energy. He was grateful the van eventually stopped as it meant he could land and recover. He looked around for a suitable place to land.

He noticed a small copse just a short way from the building where the van had pulled up. It would make an ideal landing place. He headed for the trees and, struggling to keep up the concentration, he rapidly fell the last six feet to the ground. Nathan lay in a heap on the ground, gasping to get air back into his lungs and give his limbs a precious few seconds to recover. After a couple of minutes Nathan finally hauled himself to his feet and jogged towards the building.

Nathan made his way over to the van – it was empty. All five men must've gone inside. The garden and surrounding areas were in darkness – as was most of the building. Nathan walked around the imposing structure, using the moonlight to check it out. It was Victorian he guessed, noting the huge windows and impressive columns, and built during the Gothic revival, judging by the variety of gargoyles staring down at him. They included chimeras and grotesque looking human-beast distortions. Although the windows were in darkness at the front of the building, he still ducked as he made his way around the building just to be sure he wasn't seen.

Around the back he found a double patio door that opened into a room that looked like a study. He carefully tried the door – it was locked. He worked his way along the rear of the building towards a set of steps, roughly halfway along the rear of the property. They led downwards, to a plain, heavy wooden door. He glanced up, noticing that a couple of the third floor windows were lit, but the curtains were pulled closed and the light from them wasn't strong enough to reach down to where he was stood, so wouldn't cause him any issues with going down the stairs. *I must be bloody mad!* he thought, as he silently ran down the stairs and turned the door handle before he changed his mind. It opened silently and smoothly.

Immediately in front of him was a brick wall, covered in crumbling greying plaster. To the right, there was a narrow unlit corridor with several doors along its length and a left turn at its end. He closed the door behind him and crept towards the turning, ducking as he passed each darkened room to avoid the chances of being seen in the single small glass panel inlaid roughly five and a half foot high housed in each door.

Nathan turned the corner. Light was being emitted from two rooms at the far end of the corridor. The first doorway housed Father Javier and two of the stocky men. Nathan could sense the heaviness around their auras, as if they both had their own personal thunderclouds with them. His nostrils were assaulted with a damp earthy smell. Nathan screwed his face up in disgust. Bloody digahs. Scum of the earth! He quickly chanced a peek in through the glass window again. Both men had also removed their hoods.

Nathan shook his head. Things didn't bode well for Father Javier, he thought to himself. They're obviously not worried about being identified anymore. He agitatedly ruffled his hair, whilst thinking about how best to help Father Javier. Military training kicked in. 'Number one, assess the enemy.' He nodded in agreement with his thoughts and, decision made, went back along the corridor to check there was no one in the other rooms. That just left the second doorway at the far end of the corridor. He quickly checked on Father Javier. The two men were just guarding him. Immediate danger is over, Nathan thought to himself and he crept towards the second doorway.

A faint glow was emitting from this room and, as he got closer to the door he felt the familiar tiny electrical charge, bringing the hairs on his arms and back of neck to stand to attention. His breaths deepened; the echoing beat of his heart grew to a crescendo in his ears. He leant back against the wall to catch his breath. Only a dark flyah – or dark angel – could cause that kind of response. He shakily took a swig from his hip flask, in a vain attempt to block the energy emitted from his own ability and to calm his nerves.

In that second, Nathan knew trying to save Father Javier was pointless.

Standing right outside the door Nathan chanced a glance through the glass window. The light was coming from a woman's hands, as she knelt; face downwards, in front of a man. He was stood with his arms towards her, fingers outstretched and palms facing downwards. She placed her hands on top of his, covering both sets of badly bruised knuckles, and the light turned orange as the healing power began in earnest. The same dark, curly haired man Nathan had seen beating Father Javier earlier, was stood proudly soaking up the healing light, his head cocked to one side, and turned slightly towards the door, as an owl listens for prey.

Nathan knew if he didn't leave now, whilst the euphoria of the healing energy was captivating the man, he wouldn't be leaving at all.

23

Frank sat in the front pew, as usual. Mandy arrived five minutes after Frank had. She sat on the pew, next to him and they both bowed their heads in silent prayer. Presently, Frank lifted his head and smiled at Mandy.

'I'm glad you could come this evening, at such short notice.'

'That's all right, Frank. It's a pleasure, as always.' She smoothed invisible creases from her long skirt. 'So, he's gone then?'

'Yes. When I arrived I heard lots of shouting coming from the tower.'

'Did you hear what they were saying?'

'It's not our place to gossip.' He frowned at her.

Mandy bowed her head. 'Of course not. I'm sorry Frank.'

'I tried to help him of course.' Frank puffed out his chest like a cockerel fluffs up his plumage. 'But there were too many of them.'

'I'm sure you did. You're so brave, Frank.' She dared to reach across and gently pat his hand.

He lowered his voice to a whisper. 'I did hear the odd

word. Of course, it would be inevitable that I would hear something, as I went to help.' He remembered nervously edging up the steps and towards the room at the top. He remembered seeing the two men wrestling Father Javier to the floor. He'd wanted to help, but his flight or fight mode kicked in – and he fled back down the stairs, before hiding in a pew at the front of the church. He leant towards her. 'They kept asking for the account.'

She flushed as she realised they were almost head to head. She held her hand to her chest to steady her racing heart. 'I wouldn't mind betting they wanted him to account for his actions. A couple of us wrote to the diocesan bishop in Portsmouth to insist on his removal, as he was a having an adverse influence on the young girls. You can't have a priest walking around in vest tops showing off his muscular physique.' She tutted and shook her head.

Frank sat back upright and placed his hands on his lap. 'We will have to wait and see who they replace him with. I hope it's someone with a bit more experience. This town's younger generation needs stronger guidance. In the meantime, they'll have to close the hostel, of course. They can't run it without a man of the cloth to oversee it, as it's part of their duty to the community.'

Mandy nodded. 'It's not just the younger generation that needs the guidance.' She lowered her voice. 'I drove Amy over to Izzy's house to return Crystal's lost bag. You'll never guess who *she* had in her house.'

'Who Crystal?'

'No, Izzy. She was only entertaining that scruffy unkempt looking blond man. You know the one that I bumped into in the graveyard. The one who you said was arguing with Father Javier the other day.'

Frank rubbed his chin.' Hmmm. That *is* interesting.' He replied. 'It may be worth finding out more about who he is.'

'I'll help you with that Frank,.' Mandy offered, helpful as ever.

24

The sunlight was streaming through Crystal's window when she opened her eyes and fell back onto her bed. This is getting ridiculous! She sighed and rolled her eyes, giving herself a second to recover from the fall and to summon up some energy, before sitting bolt upright as she remembered that Nathan hadn't come home last night. She glanced at the clock before swinging her legs out of bed, grabbing her dressing gown and heading downstairs.

A tired-looking Nathan was sat drinking coffee at the kitchen table. 'Your mum's in the shop, sprucing up the flowers.'

'Were you out all night? You look shattered. Well, even more shattered than you usually look,..' Crystal muttered.

'Thanks, and yes, I was out all night.' He agitatedly ran a hand through his hair.

'Was Father Javier okay?' She reached for the cornflakes and grabbed milk and a can of cola from the fridge.

'No, not really. I got there as he was being taken away.'

Crystal held a hand to her mouth. 'Did you see who took him?'

Nathan shook his head. 'They were wearing hoodies and they bundled him into the back of a black van.'

'Did they hurt him?' she asked quietly.

Nathan averted his gaze to the paper laid out on the table. She was only a kid after all and he'd promised Izzy he would shield her as much as possible. 'Is there any more missing people in here?' He started flicking through the pages.

'Did they? Nathan, did they hurt him?' She was more insistent this time.

He put the paper down and sighed. 'What do you want me to say? They got to him before I could and they beat the shit out of him before carting him away in a van to certain death. Satisfied now?'

'You don't have to be nasty. I just wanted to know if he'd been hurt or not.'

'Grow up, Crystal. Of course they were going to hurt him! They hate people like him and you, even more than they hate not being in control.'

'Well, you don't have to shout you know.' She sprang to her feet, glaring at him.

'Don't be such a stupid bitch then.' He rubbed his forehead and closed his eyes.

'I'm not stupid.' She stood in front of him, hands on hips, eyes full of blazing defiance.

'You are if you don't know how serious this all is. I'm tired; I've been up all night. I don't have time to play nice. If you'd read The Account, I wouldn't need to remind you what we're dealing with.'

'I *am* reading it.' The flicker in her eyes gave the lie away.

'No you aren't. If I told you Father Javier was taken by Digahs,' Nathan couldn't hide the contempt in his voice at the word 'Digahs', 'you wouldn't have a clue what I was talking about, would you?' His narrowed eyes and sarcastic tone caused her lie to explode in a red flush across her face and neck. 'I bet you're not even practising using your abilities!'

She threw her hands in the air. 'Okay! I'll start reading it.' She sat back down, elbows on table and hand playing with the spoon in her cereal bowl. 'I just think sometimes it's better not to know things. You know, ignorance is bliss, and all that...'

'Oh for God's sake!' He took a steadying breath. Screw shielding her, he'd risk Izzy's wrath over stupidity any day. He leant across the table and purposely quietened his voice. 'News flash, girlie. You're either gonna have to wise up and get up to speed fast or bury your stupid little head in the sand and die in blissful ignorance. Because The Others are coming, whether you're ready or not.' He pushed his chair back and stood, resting his fists on the table, leaning slightly towards her. 'They're coming for us all, but especially *you*. And you've got more than Digahs to worry about.'

'What's that supposed to mean? What else is coming? What should I be worrying about?' she yelled after him as he walked down the hallway towards the stairs.

Nathan ignored her and climbed the stairs to his room. He kicked his boots off and collapsed onto the bed. His shoulder and arm muscles cried out in pain – they hadn't had such a workout in a very long time. He laid there, eyes closed and body shaking – partly down to adrenaline but mostly down to the lack of alcohol in his system. As he drifted off to sleep one thought kept running though his mind: Do we really all have to put humanity's future in *her* hands?

Crystal sat at the table eating the rest of her cornflakes. He's such a jerk. She was annoyed, partly at the way he spoke to her – but mostly because he'd made her feel bad. She knew she should be reading The Account and practising her flying, but a childish part of her hoped that it would all just go away if she ignored it for long enough.

Her spoon rattled in the empty bowl, the cornflakes sitting heavy in her stomach – along with the sick feeling of cold hard reality. Leaning back against her chair, Crystal closed her eyes, waiting for the sickness to recede. 'Why *do* I have to get involved in all of this? How do they know I'm the *only* angel left?' She opened her eyes as the answer hit her 'They don't really – they *can't* really know I'm the only one. There are probably more of us out there, somewhere.' She felt the heavy sick feeling subside slightly, lightening both her mood and the feeling or responsibility hanging around her.

What the hell, there's no time like the present, she thought, grinning to herself and, after putting her bowl in the dishwasher, stood in the middle of the kitchen and closed her eyes. Remembering how Nathan had stood, she copied his stance – hands parallel with the ground, arms held slightly away from her sides. Clearing her mind of everything was a lot easier now she'd lost the heaviness of her supposed responsibility.

After a minute or two, she felt a buzzing tingle working around her body as, at the same time; a slight cold breeze blew between her hands and the floor. Her back felt as if she was wearing a backpack on it, resting over her shoulder blades and her back and shoulder muscles systematically tensed and relaxed in response. Her heart racing, she forced her attention back to focus on nothing but flying. Her feet and ankle muscles relaxed as they left the floor causing Crystal to grin in response to her achievement. She opened her eyes and giggled in delight. What a rush! The adrenaline pumped rapidly around her body, her heart beating loud and fast in her chest.

Standing with her head inches from the ceiling wasn't how she envisaged flying so, slowly leaning forward, Crystal tilted her body so it was parallel with the floor. The backpack feeling of weight on her back and shoulders increased slightly and she felt the cold breeze shift from her hands to her stomach and chest. She worked her way from the middle of the kitchen to the end wall, just above the back door. Realising she didn't know how to stop, the panic spread through her body like a fire spreading through a tinder dry forest. As her head made contact with the wall, she stifled a scream and fell in a heap on the floor.

Glad no-one was there to witness the fiasco, Crystal sat there rubbing the top of her head and frowning to herself. 'Maybe that's enough to start with.' She stood up and rolled her head slowly left to right, easing the aching in her neck and shoulders. Feeling slightly shaky, she reached for a can of Red Bull from the fridge. Sitting back on a kitchen chair, she pondered over what had just happened. No wonder I need to practise, she thought, if a session that quick can leave me feeling so shaky and tired.

Feeling the caffeine working its magic through her system, Crystal got to her feet and made her way up the stairs to her bedroom. I'll start slow with the flying, she decided, in the meantime, I'll make a start on reading The Account – it's a lot less effort. She closed her bedroom door behind her and pulled down the blind in the bay window, before removing the part of the window sill protecting The

Account's hiding place. Carrying it over to her bed, she sat cross-legged with the book in front of her.

The cover was very plain looking; brown with black ornate lettering. She ran a finger over the indented letters, delaying for a moment the inevitable opening of its cover and revelations of the pages inside. Taking a deep breath, Crystal untied the brown leather cord tied around it and opened the cover. The first page was blank – but the second page was full of muddy-brown lines of handwritten text. At first, the wording was unrecognisable but, as Crystal stared at the page, it was as if the letters suddenly straightened out to reveal themselves in English. She turned to the next page. Again, the unrecognisable words become recognisable the longer she stared at the page. She couldn't decide if the actual words were changing to English text or if her subconscious brain was processing the foreign language and translating it before her conscious mind kicked in. She flicked through the pages, noting that the shape and size of the handwriting changed throughout the book, indicating it was, in fact, written by several different people.

Flicking back to the first page of text, Crystal settled back to read.

This Account has been written by specially designated persons throughout the decades. They pass this honour onto future generations, rarely passing it outside their immediate family, to ensure the secret location is not endangered. (It was decided in 1455 that the older works, originally written on scrolls made from papyrus, be rewritten onto vellum and placed at the beginning of this journal – for easy reference and also to ensure the works were preserved and easily hidden. Papyrus was notoriously fragile – and in hindsight it was a brilliant idea, as only a couple of fragments from the original scrolls remain, due to the drying and cracking nature of papyrus. These fragments are now referred to as both 'The Book of Shadows' and 'The Secret of The Way Things Are' by the Israeli museum, where they and the other Dead Sea Scrolls are now housed.) These scribes also protect the words in The Account from being destroyed – they are therefore guardians of the word – protecting the only source of knowledge detailing the true origins of human life and the planet we inhabit.

So that explains why Father Javier had the guardian job, Crystal thought. She flicked to the next page, giving her eyes time to adjust to the change in writing and her brain time to make sense of the words.

In the beginning was 'The Others'. A source of energy, desperate to experience the feeling of separateness, they wanted to create something tangible to experience this feeling through. They created planets out of pieces of their own energy source to amuse themselves – one of which they called 'Earth'. Earth was formed, but void of life and feeling, as were their other attempts. Darkness covered it so The Others set about creating other planets from pure energy. Some sparkled brightly, whilst others – those with more concentrated energy – continually pulsed the captured energy, causing them to burn so brightly they had to place them away from Earth and the other planets to avoid turning them to ash.

The Others were pleased with the results of their efforts and, after creating smaller energy balls, decided to house them inside different shapes that could walk around the Earth planet and live separate from the source. They called some of these smaller balls of energy animals, whilst others were called 'humans'.

Crystal leant back against her pillow and took a swig from the can she'd brought up with her. She realised the enormity of what she was reading – it was The Bible, but not in the conventional sense. She hesitated, wondering whether to read on or not. She stood up and stretched before pulling her window blind up and opening her window, just a crack, to let in some fresh air. She glanced across at the book on her bed – its pull was just too strong. She sat back down and skimmed her eyes across the page.

As humans were made from 'The Others' source energy, they could do everything The Others could do, so they decided to partition off the memory of these abilities in humans, so they could have control over them and use them as they saw fit. They realised that these humans still felt part of the source, so blocked off their memory of how they were created. The Others could experience feeling through these humans, but the heavy feeling of loneliness filled their minds, so they gave them the right to interact. They lifted the partition blocking some of their abilities, different for each group of humans, and gave each group a different name and job. Digahs would plough the soil and partake in any manual labour job – such as heavy lifting, healahs would use energy to create plants, as well as healing others that were injured and flyahs would supervise them all to ensure everything was as it should be.

Talk about mind control, Crystal thought indignantly. She skimmed the rest of that page and turned to the next. Scanning its contents, she was looking for what would make Nathan have so much contempt for Digahs. She finally found descriptions of the three groups of humans, written by a different person, judging by the change in handwriting.

Digahs are made from the least amount of energy, but are housed in the larger shaped bodies. This makes them easily controlled, however they quickly manage to fester the heavier energy-based emotions such as anger, hate and jealousy. They therefore, cannot experience lighter based emotions such as love, peace, happiness etc. This makes them totally resentful and bitter of their position, nasty to others.

Digahs are baddies then. She sighed and continued reading.

Healahs have lots of energy. They are only capable of feeling the lighter based emotions such as love and unity etc. They may get occasionally feel a heavier emotion however; as love is at their core, they are incapable of holding onto a heavier-based emotion...

Crystal smiled. That's my mum to a tee – not a bad bone in her body, she thought.

Flyahs are middle ground energy. They can feel both heavy and light emotions but seldom can be bothered enough to experience any, either way. They have a job to do and just get on with doing it...

Crystal thought about how Nathan had spoken to her earlier. He definitely had been swayed to focus on getting a war started with The Others.

She closed the book – she'd made a start and needed a change of scenery. Placing it carefully back in its hiding place under the window sill, she went to see how her mum was getting on in the shop.

Izzy stopped healing the plant in her hands when she

heard the door open. She turned to see who had entered, smiling at her daughter's unexpected visit.

'Hello hun. You okay?' She cupped her hands back around the plant pot, her hands emitting a slight orange glow.

'I'm fine Mum.' Crystal shifted from one foot to another.

'You sure?' Izzy didn't need to shift her gaze from the plant. She could sense Crystal wanted to talk.

'Yeah... It's just that I've started reading The Account...'

'How do you feel about that?'

'A bit weird to be honest.' Crystal leant against a stand housing several containers of cut flowers in water. 'These flowers look good. Have you been healing them?' She fiddled with the leaves of a gladioli stem.

'Yes, I have.' Izzy put the plant pot back in its place on the shelf and turned to face her daughter. 'Weird, how?'

'Maybe weird is the wrong word.' She kicked her toe against the leg of the flower stand. Izzy stayed silent, giving her time to collect her thoughts. 'I suppose I feel a combination of feelings. I feel uneasy, nervous, scared. Is it really the only copy – the one I have?'

Izzy nodded. 'It is. And it's okay to feel all of those feelings. In fact, it's understandable. You have a big responsibility on your shoulders.' She walked over to Crystal and pulled her close, wrapping her arms around her in a bear hug. 'You'll cope though. I have every faith in you.' She kissed her head and gave her a quick squeeze, before taking a step backwards. 'You're twenty-one and have had an easy life up until now. Don't make the mistake of constantly staring at the overall mass – whether that's the responsibility, destiny, and plan – whatever you want to call it. Focus on the individual steps. You may feel as if you have this huge responsibility on your shoulders, but that doesn't mean you have to do it all today. Do you understand?'

'I guess so. Do you honestly think it's *my* destiny? I mean, how do you know there aren't any other angels on Earth?' Crystal tried to keep the hope in her voice to a minimum.

Izzy smiled at her daughter. 'Hun, there are no other angels. You are the only one.' She sat down on a chair in the corner of the shop and gestured for Crystal to sit on the adjacent one. 'I know it would be a lot easier for you if you didn't have this burden, but I'm not going to lie to you – however uncomfortable it makes you feel.' Izzy reached over and held Crystal's hand.

'But how do you know I'm the only one?' There was less certainty in her voice this time.

Izzy gave Crystal's hand a gentle squeeze. 'When I fell pregnant with you, both me and your dad couldn't have been happier. You made our life complete. But we'd heard stories about the angel prophecy – and we knew that The Others wouldn't let you live as inter-breeding was forbidden. We knew we'd have to pay a high price for keeping you safe until you were of age. We'd have to stay hidden from The Others and to do this meant we could only stay together for a short while.' She patted Crystal's hand reassuringly. 'But we were both happy to pay that high price – because not having you, would have been so much worse than anything The Others could've put us through.'

Crystal smiled weakly at her mother. 'But...'

'Crystal, we know you are the only one because, after we escaped, The Others ordered those that helped us, as well as any other angels to be hunted down. They herded each group up and somehow got inside their heads and did something, because no one inter-breeds anymore.'

'So, did they get everyone who helped you? Because, obviously they didn't get Nathan.'

'No. There are others on Earth who, like us, worked out how to keep from being detected. They keep intense ability usage to a minimum to avoid coming onto The Others' radar. Nathan's part in our escape was never discovered. He stayed after we left – only coming back to Earth after your dad went back. As you neared your twenty-first birthday your dad sent him to watch over us – like our own guardian angel.'

'Why did dad have to go away at all?'

Izzy looked at Crystal and saw the heartbroken eyes of a little girl staring back at her. 'He knew they wouldn't rest until they had us back. He had no choice – even though he loves us so very much. In their eyes, at that moment in time, your dad was the bigger traitor as he was a Flyah – he held one of the highest ranks allowed for a human. Does it mention about the different ranks in The Account?'

'Yes, I've just been reading about them. Flyahs are like supervisors, right?'

'They are. The Others bestow a certain amount of trust in them doing that job. They are not supposed to go against the wishes of The Others – they are supposed to be impartial and unemotional. So when your dad did exactly the opposite, they're naturally going to want to know why. Dad knew that by going back, they would concentrate their efforts on him, as they did after all know that you'd only be a threat once you turned twenty-one. He gave us the gift of time and a relative amount of safety by going back. He believed love would conquer all they could throw at him.'

Crystal looked at the floor whilst kicking the heel of her right boot with her left one. 'So, how do you know he's not dead?'

'Oh hun, he's not. He will come back some day. Come here.' She put her arm around Crystal and pulled her close. 'That love we have for each other does sometimes make us feel so utterly heartbroken. But it's also what unites us and keeps us strong. *Never* doubt how much we love you – or how much we love each other.'

'So the quicker I face up to my destiny, the quicker he'll be able to come back?' Crystal mumbled from the confines of her mother's embrace.

'He'll come back when it's time for him to come back.' Izzy let go of her daughter and stood up. 'Your focus, at the moment, is to read The Account and find out exactly what your destiny is – regardless of what Nathan or I think.'

Crystal stared up at Izzy. 'Nathan said Father Javier was taken by Digahs and that they would probably have killed him. He also said I had bigger things than Digahs to worry about. Do you know what he meant?'

'No I don't. I've heard rumours; however, rumours are rife amongst our types. But if you want facts, you'll have to read The Account.'

'Can you point me in the right direction? The Account's a rather long book.' She smiled up at her mother.

Izzy shook her head. 'The guardians and the selected ones are the only people that can actually read what's written within its pages. No one else can decipher it.' She looked up at the clock. 'I really need to get some work done. Your best bet is to study The Account at every opportunity you have. Because, quite frankly I don't want to worry you, but I really don't know how long we actually have.'

'No pressure then.' Crystal got to her feet. 'Don't worry Mum. After everything you and Dad have had to sacrifice, I'm not going to let you down.' She hugged her mum and started to walk to the door, before turning to look back at her. 'Besides, the quicker I do whatever I'm destined to do, the quicker Dad can come home.'

Izzy smiled back at her daughter. She didn't want to burden her down with the knowledge of how long exactly that might take.

25

The house was in darkness. Crystal glanced over at the clock. It was 1.35 am. Her alarm had gone off five minutes ago. She'd heard her mum and Nathan go to their separate rooms a couple of hours ago, so knew they'd both be asleep by now.

She swung her legs out of bed and sat up. She pulled on her black leggings and jumper and ran a brush through her hair. She sat for a couple of minutes more, settling her nerves. She'd been quietly practising for days; so knew she was ready. Checking that she had a can of cola in her drawer and a bar of chocolate in her pocket, she picked up her boots and tiptoed downstairs and out the front door, ensuring that it clicked quietly shut behind her.

She sat on the doorstep and pulled on her boots. Her hands were shaking slightly as she did up her laces – shaking from a mixture of nerves and anticipation. Standing up she walked quietly down the road and into the night.

It was only a ten-minute walk to the house. She flicked open her phone and checked the message Emily had sent her. Yep, I have the right address. She glanced up at the two up, two down, house. Now to work out which room is actually the main bedroom. Crystal walked round to the back garden and back again. She didn't really want to use her flying ability until she really had to, but she wanted to make sure she had the right room. She glanced up and down the street before focusing her attention.

She closed her eyes and focused on her breathing first; the rise and fall of each breath. Then on the feeling of weightlessness; the feeling of cool air around her legs, of each muscle relaxing. She held her arms slightly away from her sides and slowly raised them, palms downwards, as if pushing herself away from the ground. When she opened her eyes they were level with the upstairs window ledge.

She peered inside. Luckily the curtains were open, so she could make out the figure of the elderly lady quite easily. She took a closer look at the window, it was on the latch. She could just get her fingers inside and push the latch open. The window squeaked slightly as she pulled it open; she held her breath and flicked her eyes to the woman asleep under the covers, to see if it had disturbed her at all. Satisfied that it hadn't, she floated in through the window and across to the bed.

She settled to the floor and stood there for a couple of minutes, watching the woman sleep. She looked so peaceful. But holding her hand above the woman, she could feel the darkness of her illness. Her hand glowed white in the darkness, darkening to orange as she worked on healing her. When it finally went white again, she knew it had worked. She hovered her hand from top to toe, checking for any heaviness. Satisfied she had finished, she rose from the floor and floated back out of the window. Landing quietly back on the pavement, she looked around to make sure no one had seen her, before walking quietly away.

She walked home feeling tired yet exhilarated. I've healed my first person! She could barely contain her glee. She pulled the chocolate bar from her pocket and quickly ate the contents to replace the energy she'd lost. She then took her phone from her pocket and typed a text message to Emily, thanking her for giving her the lady's details and address. It obviously woke Emily up, because Crystal's phone sprang into life with an incoming call.

'Hi,' she whispered.

'Did it go all right?' Emily asked, in a rather sleepy voice.

'It was great!' Crystal realised she was raising her voice in elation, so promptly lowered it to an exaggerated whisper. 'This was a brilliant idea – you should've seen it! My hands glowed white then orange. I flew Emily!' A huge smile spread across her face. 'I really did it!'

'That's great. Did anyone see you?'

'I checked, before and afterwards. No curtain twitchers and no-one about outside.'

'What about Mrs Clements? Did she wake up when you were healing her?'

'Nope,' Crystal grinned. 'And it wouldn't have mattered if she had. Being as you got her information from your dad's prayer list, she'll just think God sent an angel to heal her!'

'I guess. Glad it went well. I'm going back to sleep now.' She yawned.

'Night Emily – and thanks.'

Crystal put the phone back in her pocket and walked back home.

When she got to her front door, she sat back on the step and took off her boots before carefully placing her key in the door lock. Once inside, she crept past the spare room where Nathan was sleeping and slid round her door and into her room. There weren't any tell-tale signs that anyone was awake or moving around, so she slipped out of her clothes and into her pyjamas before climbing into bed.

Nathan rolled over in his bed and closed his eyes. He slept so lightly, all those years of hiding had taught him to keep his senses alert – even when he was asleep. He'd woken when Crystal crept past his door and had heard her leave. He'd also heard the front door open and had seen the shadow of someone walking past his bedroom door – as that someone had been emitting a slight glow. Crystal would really have to be more careful, he thought, before huddling back under the duvet.

26

S unday mornings were usually quiet relaxing days in the Meadows' household. A day to laze around in jogging pants and baggy jumpers. Izzy loved having Sundays off as she could sit and read the paper at the kitchen table – a mug of tea in one hand and a piece of toast in the other. This morning the early morning sunlight poured in through the patio door, surrounding her with its warming, healing energy. She glanced up at the clock and, deciding that 8.20am wasn't too early, she picked up her mobile phone.

'Morning Mel, it's me. Can you make your excuses to Frank? I'm think it's about time we caught up.' She paused to listen to Mel, before continuing. 'No, Nathan won't be here but Crystal may be around. Great, so shall we make it a date for 10 am? Cool, I'll give Kitty a call and let her know.'

She rang Kitty and, as her phone went to voicemail, she left a message and, upon hearing the creaking of the upstairs floorboards, flicked the switch to turn the kettle on. Nathan came into the kitchen. He was already dressed and wearing his boots.

'Morning, did you sleep well?' Izzy placed a mug of coffee in front of him. He pushed it out of the way and took a flask out of his pocket.

'Don't you think you should be cutting back a bit on that?' She pushed the coffee mug closer to him.

'If I wanted a mother, I'd have gotten myself adopted.' He took a gulp from the flask, eyes never leaving Izzy's face.

Izzy sat down in the chair opposite him and leant across the table. 'Samuel sent you to protect us.' She stopped and momentarily gathered her thoughts before starting again. 'You expect me to trust you, Nathan. No, actually you want me to place mine and my daughters' lives in your care? You're no good to anyone if you're never sober.'

He groaned and ran a hand through his already messy hair. 'I told you, I need it to stay hidden. Especially after what happened to Father Javier the other day.' He glanced up at her. 'If you've got any sense, you'll stay hidden too.'

'You never did tell me about that. I heard from Crystal that you said Digahs were involved. What else did you see?' Izzy tried to hold his gaze, but his eyes darted quickly away from her gaze.

'Nothing.' He grudgingly picked up the coffee and took a sip, before pushing it away and taking another swig from his flask.

'Well it's obviously something, as you're even more hell-bent than usual about us all staying hidden.'

'I've been saying for years about the war coming. You knew what you were getting into when you and Samuel had her.' He jerked his head in the direction of the ceiling.

Izzy decided to change tactics – going for a more direct approach. 'You keep going on about a war or rebellion that's coming. A war that is inevitable, so you say, now that Crystal has The Account. But how can you fight when you are so desperate to stay hidden all of the time?' She slammed the mug of coffee back in front of him. 'You want us to trust you, well drink this then!'

He tried to stare her out, but determination was written all over her face. Her jaw was clenched tight and her eyes were burning back at his. It was a battle of wills and, Nathan in his slightly hung over state, was no match for Izzy. He picked up the mug and downed its contents.

'Thank you.' Izzy let the air escape from her lungs and relaxed her shoulders. 'I don't want any part in this war, *if* it's even coming, which I *don't* believe it is.' She held up her hands to stop him interrupting. 'I'm always willing to see the best in people – it's just part of my healah DNA. But I *do* believe that as flyahs, you and Samuel will be the first to know about it – if it does happen. And Samuel wouldn't have sent you to us if he didn't believe we needed protecting.' She looked him in the eyes. 'And I don't believe he'd have sent you if he didn't believe you were strong enough to handle whatever may, or may not, be coming.' She rested her hand momentarily on his arm before standing up to re-boil the kettle, as she'd heard Crystal moving around upstairs. Turning to face him again, her face full of concern and her voice slightly lowered, she uttered, 'I've said it before, and I'll say it again. All I ask is that we shield Crystal from as much as we can, for as long as we can, okay?'

Nathan nodded his agreement, picked up his mug and placed it by the sink. 'Thanks for the coffee. I'll see you later.' He pulled on his coat. 'I've got people to see.'

He went out of the back door as Crystal came in the kitchen door.

'Morning Mum. Was it something I said?' Crystal pointed in the direction of the back door.

'Oh, don't worry about him, he's fine. Here, I made you a mug of tea.' She handed the mug to her daughter.

'Thanks Mum.' Crystal gratefully took the mug from her mother and sat down on a kitchen chair.

'I've got Mel and Kitty coming over at ten, have you got anything planned?' Izzy gathered the newspaper pages together and folded it neatly up.

'I'm not planning on going anywhere today.' She sipped from her mug. 'I'll probably do some more work on reading The Account.'

'Oh, okay.' Izzy busied herself with brushing imaginary breadcrumbs off the kitchen counter. 'Well, yell if you need any help with anything, Kitty and Mel won't mind being interrupted – or helping for that matter.'

'Do you think we should tell them about The Account then?' Crystal got up and put some bread in the toaster. 'How much do they actually already know?'

'Not much.' Izzy averted her eyes. 'I'll leave it up to you. After all, it's your decision to make.'

'Father Javier told me not to tell anyone. I feel I should honour that for the moment. I'd better make a start with today's reading session. I'll take my breakfast upstairs with me.'

'Okay.' Izzy turned and managed a brief, tight smile at her daughter. She watched Crystal walk out of the room before letting the smile drop from her face. You may have promised Father Javier, but I haven't promised anyone anything.

~

Mel arrived first, at precisely 10 am. She'd just sat at the kitchen table with Izzy when Kitty rushed in the back door.

'Hi. Sorry I'm a bit late.' She collapsed onto one of the kitchen chairs. 'It's been a bit of a hectic morning.' She took a couple of minutes to catch her breath and to let her flushed cheeks cool down. Izzy handed her a cup of coffee.

'No worries. Everything okay?' She hid her grin behind her mug; her eyes caught Mel's glance – before they both started sniggering.

Kitty ran her hand over the back of her head, calming down her slightly stuck up hair. 'What're you both sniggering about?' She took a sip of her coffee.

'Hectic morning eh?' Mel glanced down at Kitty's blouse. 'Looks like you got dressed in a hurry.' She laughed as Kitty flushed red again, realising her buttons were all done up in the wrong holes. 'Were you and Peter taking advantage of an empty house?'

Izzy laughed. 'Don't wind her up. At least one of us is enjoying a fulfilling marriage!' She caught Kitty's attention; eyes full of embarrassment and humour in equal quantity. 'Are you aiming for another child to add to your brood?'

'I'm ignoring you both now. You can be so childish!' Kitty stifled the humour in her voice and tried to hold her head aloof. 'Neither of you have changed since primary school. Haven't you got anything else to talk about? I'm sure you didn't call an impromptu coffee morning to take the mick out of my sex life.'

Izzy put her mug down and glanced towards the hallway, ensuring they were alone. 'I have to be a bit quiet, as Crystal's upstairs.'

Both Kitty and Mel leant forward across the table. 'What's going on?' Mel asked, keeping her voice low.

'Crystal had her bag swiped the other evening.' Both women stared at Izzy, faces shocked. Izzy held her hand up to stop them. 'She's fine. Amy found her bag down her road. Mandy drove her over to give it back.'

'Did my lovely sister-in-law come in?' Mel enquired.

'Don't be silly – she's kept her distance since Kevin disappeared! But the point is, shortly after, Father Javier was attacked and taken away. The Others got to him.'

'Frank said Father Javier was taken away because he was immoral. Something about inappropriate behaviour with the young girls in the congregation. He also said he was a bad role model. Said the church took him away, after Mandy and the other women wrote a letter of complaint to the Diocese Bishop,' Mel replied.

'Might've guessed Mandy was involved somewhere. I don't see how the two are linked though. How'd you know he was taken by The Others?' Kitty was frowning at them both. 'Am I missing something?'

Izzy lowered her voice again. 'Father Javier was the Guardian of The Account. He gave it to Crystal, along with his business card, the day before he was taken away.'

'But how do you know they're related? I still don't get it.' Kitty sipped her coffee, still looking puzzled.

'Don't tell me Crystal had the book in her bag?' Mel covered her mouth with her hand.

'No, she didn't – she's more intelligent than that! But she did have the business card in her bag and it was the only thing missing when she got her bag back.' She looked to Kitty. 'And *that's* what links her to Father Javier. Crystal said Father Javier warned her that she was being watched too. As soon as we realised the business card was missing and realised he might be in danger, Nathan went to the church to warn him.' She put her head down slightly. 'But he was too late, they were already there.

'What can we do to help?' Kitty asked, putting her hand over Izzy's and giving it a slight squeeze.

Izzy gave her hand a replying squeeze. 'How's things going with Emily and Mark? Did dinner go well the other day?'

'Yes, they're getting on like a house on fire.' Kitty smiled at Mel. 'She's an absolute treasure, your daughter. She helped me with the washing up. *That's* something my boys have never done!' She put her mug down. 'All joking aside though, it's nice having female company in a house full of men. And, she settles in really well with them all.'

'That's good,' Mel chipped in. 'That should make her nice and relaxed enough to really start noticing her intuition. It's just a shame that she can't do that in her own home.' She looked somewhat disappointed at that statement as she uttered it out loud.

Izzy touched Mel's hand. 'Talking of that – how are you getting on? Any progress on your intuition yet?'

'It's just so difficult with Frank around. I know he doesn't have a job to go to, and he's at church so often, but I never know when he's going to walk in the door.'

'Don't worry, just practise when you can. We're going to need your input soon.' Izzy laughed. 'It's a shame we can't get Frank a job at the church – he enjoys going there so much!'

'Oh, that reminds me.' Mel widened her eyes. 'I can't believe I forgot to tell you this part! Frank was *there* when Father Javier was taken.'

Izzy swung her head back round to face Mel. 'He was there! Nathan never said.'

'He saw Nathan though – well, I'm guessing that's who he saw, as he mentioned a scruffy blond haired man in a dark oilskin overcoat.'

'Sounds like Nathan.' Izzy replied. 'But he said he was alone in that church. Does Frank know who he is?'

'No.' Mel shook her head 'but he does know he's staying with you, so that raised his suspicions.'

'I bet it did! I didn't think it would take Mandy long to spread the gossip.' Izzy frowned. 'I can't believe she still blames us for her bad choices in life.'

'Well, we all know she thinks we pushed her towards the wrong brother. Anyway, Frank was probably hiding somewhere in the shadows, which is why Nathan didn't see him. You know what Frank's like. He knows that church like the back of his hand.' Mel smiled but there was a sad air about it. 'He likes to know what's going on, but doesn't want to get involved or be seen as being nosy, so he probably had an excellent vantage point.'

'I still can't believe you chose to marry him,' Kitty mumbled into her coffee mug.

'Well I am married to him now. So for better or worse, I'll make do with the situation.'

Izzy could sense the atmosphere go slightly cold, as Mel hated Kitty criticising her marriage – especially as Kitty had such a great relationship with her husband. 'So anyway, back to the point at hand. Crystal now has The Account and has started reading it.'

'How's she coping with it all?' Mel was grateful for the change in topic.

'She's doing okay.' Izzy nodded, before standing up and walking over the rather wilted orchid in the kitchen window. Placing her hands around the plant's pot, her hands glowed slightly orange as the healing commenced and she continued with the conversation. 'Obviously, we don't know how long we have before everything kicks off. That's why we need to make sure everything is in place and that we're all ready.'

All three of them watched the orchid straighten and the colour increase on its petals.

'I wish you could do that to my garden.' Kitty sighed. 'It's so beautiful to watch and you can almost feel the love radiating from it.'

'There'd be no point,' Mel butted in. 'Your garden doesn't stand a chance with your hyperactive dog and those whopping great lads of yours!'

'I know.' Kitty replied, head resting on her hands. 'But it would be nice.'

27

Crystal pulled down the bedroom blind and pulled out The Account from its hiding position under the window sill. Sitting cross-legged on the bed, she took a swig from her Red Bull can and took a deep, relaxing breath in. Closing her eyes momentarily, she calmed herself before opening the book at a random page and starting to read its contents.

The Others leave us to lead whatever life we choose on Earth. When they have a need for us and our skills, we are taken (usually temporarily) to whatever planet they are currently building. Frequently this experience is then removed, or blocked somehow, from our memories. The enlightened few are able to retrieve these memories for us, which enables us to write up the details of 'the account' in this book. The Others however, are learning that these enlightened ones exist – their safety is paramount to us remembering our true origins, so they are learning to hide amongst us.

Flicking through a few more pages, Crystal realised

there were no dates assigned to these entries, although it did resemble an ongoing journal of facts and events. She wasn't really sure whether she should be reading it in order or not, so she chose another page at random.

The purge was ordered on all angels and half-bloods. I managed to keep my son hidden for two long years after the purge commenced, but eventually, those sent by The Others found us. Although he wasn't an angel, he was still taken by the flyah sent to find him. As mentioned in a previous entry, my son was born a half-blood, comprising of a healah and digah mix. He's just turned twenty-three and is a strong, somewhat simple lad, with a love of nature and animals. He wasn't killed, so I believe he may be returned at some point – however, I am fearful and unsure of what his personality will be like upon his return.

The dark side of him is kept at bay by our simple lifestyle – we live in a small wooden cottage in the woods, surrounded by nature. Our interaction with others is limited and on a 'needs must' basis. Those raising a healah-digah child must remember the healah gene is prominent from birth – but the digah dark side rears its head once the child turns twenty-one. To keep it at bay the child must have a calm, almost reclusive lifestyle. Saul spends most of his time in the woods, healing trees and plants, butterflies and any injured animal he comes across. I home schooled him to ensure he isn't around those that may take advantage of his simple nature.

After he hit his 'coming of age', we only had a couple of incidents involving his darker side and, even though I know he has dark at his centre, the light and love he receives from healing things is enough to keep that darkness at bay. Now I fear that the light and love that has surrounded my son all his life, has now been driven out by that darkness – as even my light has dimmed as a result and, although my heart feels like it has been shattered in a million pieces, I keep healing myself and believing that some good will come out of this life. If it's too late for my son and I, then I hope that my words will be of hope and light to others.

Poor Saul, Crystal thought, his mother's heartbreak was clearly evident, yet she still believed it was important to write about it in The Account. She felt her heart skip a beat as she momentarily put herself in the mother's position. How would my mother react if I was taken? Crystal didn't want to think about it, but the more she sat and thought about this woman and her son, the angrier she became. How dare they put people through this kind of pain! More to the point, why do they put others through this pain?

The mobile phone on the bedside cabinet sprang into life, vibrating its way across the wooden surface. Crystal glanced at the caller ID before picking it up and speaking.

'Hi Emily, everything okay?'

'Yeah, are you busy?'

Crystal glanced at The Account before closing the cover. It could wait a bit longer – friends came first. 'Not really, do you want to come over?'

'Yes please. I've just had a run in with my dad, so could do with a change of scenery and a breather.'

'I'll meet you halfway. See you in five minutes.' Crystal closed the mobile and picked up the book, storing it carefully back in its hiding place. She ran a brush through her hair and pulled on her trainers, before running down the stairs and into the kitchen.

All three women in the kitchen turned in unison and

stared inquisitively at Crystal. Izzy raised an eyebrow at her daughter. 'Everything okay hun?'

'Emily's coming over, if that's all right?' Crystal glanced firstly at her mother, then at Mel.

'Of course it's fine.' Izzy smiled at her daughter and turned back to Mel and Kitty.

'Great. I'm just going to meet her now.' Crystal pulled on her coat and swung the back door gently shut behind her.

Mel glanced round at the clock behind her, before turning back and facing both of her friends.

Kitty and Izzy were both staring at her. Kitty spoke first. 'How are things between Emily and Frank?'

Mel sighed loudly before rubbing her fingertips in a circular pattern around her temples. 'Let's just say he's not too happy about her having a boyfriend.'

Izzy checked the kettle had enough water in it, before flicking it back on to heat up. 'He's not going to be a problem, is he?'

'I can deal with him, it's fine. Honestly.' Mel handed her mug to Izzy for a refill.

'Are you sure?'

'I said it's fine, Izzy!' Mel snapped back at her, before rolling her eyes and sighing again. 'I'm sorry; I didn't mean to bite your head off.' She rubbed her temples and glanced guiltily at Izzy. 'I'm so used to being stressed and on the defensive I sometimes forget I don't need to be that way with you both.' She smiled weakly. 'I'm fine – it's all fine, honestly.'

Izzy placed a fresh mug of coffee into Mel's hands. 'Don't worry about it. I understand.' She placed her hands around Mel's, as she'd done earlier with the plant pot.

'You shouldn't...' Mel started to protest, the panic spreading across her face.

'Shush. It's fine, I'm only doing it slightly.' Izzy closed her eyes and let the glow from her hands burn a slight orange shade. Mel closed her eyes too and, after a few minutes, both her shoulders and the taut muscles in her face relaxed.

Izzy opened her eyes and the orange glow faded through yellow and white, before it disappeared. When Mel opened her eyes she was visibly calmer and serene. She didn't say anything, but slowly picked up her mug and took a sip, only closing her eyes momentarily whilst she appreciatively inhaled the coffee-aroma and steam emanating from its contents.

Finally, Mel spoke. 'It's been difficult. Frank isn't happy about Emily seeing Mark, or about her seeing anyone for that matter.'

Kitty's eyes were full of pity for her friend – her voice quiet. 'It must be hard for you.' She reached across and grabbed her hand, squeezing it gently. 'I can only imagine what you are going through.' She glanced across at Izzy. 'What you are both going through, for that matter. I don't have any special ability, but I worry for you both and am here for you both – no matter what. It must be so difficult keeping your gifts hidden – I know I feel bad enough hiding the things I know about you both from Peter. But I will do whatever you need me to do, to make this easier for both of you and your daughters.'

They were all sat around the table holding hands, when the back door opened and Crystal walked in, followed by Emily.

'You three look like you should be wearing witches' hats and chanting!' Emily laughed. 'Hi Mum.' She glanced sheepishly up at her mother before grabbing a couple of cans of cola from the fridge and heading out of the kitchen.

'I'm assuming we're going up to your room?' She glanced back at Crystal.

'We can, if you want to.' Crystal shrugged her shoulders apologetically at the women, before following Emily out of the room.

'I'll give you a shout when I'm leaving then!' Mel shouted after her daughter, before shaking her head slightly. 'She'll talk to me when she's ready,' she continued for the benefit of Kitty and Izzy.

'They usually do, eventually – talk to their mums, if my boys are anything to go by.' Kitty replied.

Both Mel and Izzy absentmindedly nodded their heads – both preoccupied with thoughts of their respective daughters – and the burdens and trials they had yet to face.

28

The train pulled away from Thatcham Station at 7.58 pm. Crystal was quite anxious over meeting the other full-bloods. Nathan was rather more relaxed, slumping against the window next to his seat in the railway carriage. He'd only announced Monday evening that he was taking her somewhere special the following evening, so Crystal had worked herself into a nervous wreck, as she hated surprises. She gnawed absentmindedly at the nails on her right hand whilst her eyes scanned the other occupants of the carriage.

'I've checked everyone already.' Nathan's voice broke into her thoughts.

'I know, but I just want to be sure.'

'It's fine. No one followed us.' Even with his eyes closed, he could sense what she was thinking.

'Are you sure?'

'As sure as I can be.' He opened one eye and peered at her, before closing it again.

She turned to face him. 'You're not going to sleep are you?' Crystal wasn't sure if she felt anxious at the thought of meeting the others, or over the fear of being left on her own – vulnerable.

'Well, I was thinking of grabbing a few minutes of shut eye, before we got to Reading.' He opened his eyes and pulled himself to an upright seated position. 'But I guess, by the nervous tone in your voice, that you'd rather I didn't.'

'Don't care if you do or not.' The screwed up look on her face said otherwise. Her eyes flicked around the carriage again.

'Why don't you just relax? It's only twenty minutes until we reach Reading station.'

Crystal closed her eyes and rested her head against the seat headrest. 'I can't help it; I guess reading *that* book has made me a bit paranoid.'

'How's it going – with "the book" I mean?' He used his fingers to emphasis speech marks around "the book".'

She could feel how intense his gaze was, so she opened her eyes and met his stare. 'It's a bit heavy going in places.'

'I've heard that about it.'

She leant forward in her seat, and lowered her voice to ensure the other occupants couldn't hear their conversation. 'What I don't get though is why do these other half- bloods help The Others?'

'I guess they're scared of what would happen if they don't.'

'But if they know what we know, about the enlightened ones and the lives we all lead, why would they not want to put an end to it?'

Nathan ran a hand through his hair before putting his hand in his pocket, touching the cold metal of his empty silver flask. It was times like this that he really missed the drink. 'The Others have people all over the world, some of which hold very high – if not the highest – positions in government, churches, industry etc., so it's understandable that people may be scared.' The tone in his voice gave away his true feelings for these people.

Crystal's mouth turned up slightly at the corner. 'Now tell me what you really feel about them – not what my mother would rather you say.'

He grinned and relaxed his shoulders. 'Okay, I think they're cowards, sheep who would rather continue living under the pretence of a 'free' life instead of standing up and being counted. I think they should grow a pair and claim back what is rightfully theirs to take.'

She slowly nodded her head and smiled. 'Now, *there's* the real you. I know my mum is worried about me, but I am an adult and you don't have to protect me from the truth – regardless of what she says.' She looked up and met his gaze again. 'I'm a big girl you know, and if I'm supposed to play a part in all of this, the least I deserve is the truth.'

'Fair comment, I just don't want to get on the wrong side of your mother, so I won't tell her what I tell you, if you promise not to tell her either. I've grown quite attached to my testicles.'

She laughed. 'I don't want to know about them thanks, but I agree. You're not that bad you know, when you're sober I mean.'

Nathan slumped back against the window and closed his eyes. 'Yeah, well I'm working on that.'

Crystal started to look around at the other passengers again.

'Don't even think about doing that again.'

'What?' Her head swivelled back to Nathan, who had a wry grin on his face.

'Checking out the other passengers.' He raised an

eyebrow. 'You need to start trusting your instincts and senses. So stop acting and looking so paranoid.'

'Okay!' She held her hands up in resignation before folding her arms across her chest. 'I take it back; you're just as irritating sober as you are drunk.'

'Whatever.'

They both sat in silence until the train pulled into Reading station. They then both got off the train and walked along platform 2 and through the turnstiles to the main entrance.

'This way.' Nathan cocked his head to the left. They walked down Beckhurst Street, before crossing the busy bypass and heading to the industrial estate. It had started drizzling, the orange street lights illuminating each raindrop and adding to the heavy atmosphere emanating from the deserted estate. Nathan turned up the collar of his oilskin coat and shoved his hands into his coat pockets. Crystal followed behind, walking slightly faster every now and again, in an effort to keep up with his longer pace. They turned a corner and crossed the road. Nathan glanced behind them to check they weren't being followed, before heading towards a small ramshackle row of four outhouses, hidden behind a decrepit-looking abandoned paper mill.

Once inside, Crystal pulled down the hood of her coat and let her eyes adjust to the darkness. They were standing inside a cold brick room, with a door at the far end. She wrinkled her nose as the fusty smell assaulted her nostrils.

Nathan briskly rubbed his hands through his hair, sending tiny drops of water spraying in all directions before heading towards the door at the far end. Crystal followed him through, into another damp and dark room, identical to the first. This time though, a slight flickering glow could be seen through the cracks, under and between the planks of the wooden door at the far end of the room.

Nathan strode across the room and hesitated briefly, looking back at Crystal. 'It's fine, honest. They're through here.' He pulled open the door and gestured for Crystal to go through first.

There were five other people stood around a wooden crate. The candles burning on top of the crate sent exaggeratedly large shadows of them dancing around the walls of the room. They all turned to face her as she walked into the room.

'It's all right, she's with me.' Nathan closed the door behind him and unbuttoned his coat. 'Everyone, this is Crystal.' He placed a hand gently against her back, leading her towards the crate and the relative warmth from the candles.

Crystal glanced from one unfriendly face to another, before stopping at the last person, a stocky man who looked a bit older than Nathan. She held out her hand. 'Hi, I'm Crystal. It's nice to meet you.'

He wiped his hand on his jeans before taking hold of hers, shaking it firmly. The unfriendly look fell away as a smile spread across his ruddy face. 'It's good to finally meet you.' His voice boomed around the room. 'Let me introduce you to the others. He pointed to the blonde lady stood beside him. 'This is Tina, she's a healah. And this is Stephanie, she's a flyah.' Crystal nodded to the slim brunette, who appeared to be slightly older than her. 'This is our father and son contingent, Martin and Richard. They're both flyahs.' She smiled at the two men. They both nodded in response before walking over to Nathan and they took turns to hug and back-slap each other in greeting, obviously delighted to see him again.

Having introduced Crystal to everyone, he pointed to the last person in the room– a sullen, stocky lad in the corner. 'And this is our son, Jeremy.' The pride was evident in his voice as he walked over to Tina and put his arm around her. Jeremy glanced up at Crystal, his greeting nod barely evident. Crystal smiled at him, but there was no response from this lad who was younger than her as he quickly looked away.

Tina took a step towards the candlelight and held her hand out for Crystal. As Crystal took hold of Tina's hand she could feel the warmth radiating from both the candles and Tina. 'Sorry about the stony-looking faces that greeted you – we just weren't sure who you were.' She smiled at Crystal. 'And my husband, forgetful as ever, forgot to mention his own name.' She grinned back at him before returning her attention to Crystal. 'He's Patrick and in case you couldn't tell from his rather bull-like figure, he's a digah.'

Crystal shook Tina's hand and smiled in response. Martin walked back to the crate and held his arms up for silence. 'Okay, let's get this meeting started, as we only have limited time.' Everyone quietened down and congregated in a circle around the warmth of the candles standing on the crate.

'First of all, it's good to see you all and to know you're all safe.' He smiled around at them all before settling his eyes on Crystal. 'And it's good to finally get to meet Crystal.' A murmured 'yes' echoed around the room. 'We'll be keeping this meeting quite short, as usual, to minimize the risk of being found together. Especially now Crystal is here.'

All eyes fell on Crystal. She felt her skin flush red and she lowered her eyes, too embarrassed to meet anyone's gaze.

'It's imperative that we are all protecting ourselves and

our families now. So, practise using your abilities whenever you can, but ensure you are keeping those practice sessions to less than fifteen minutes a time. Also, make sure you are protecting yourself from detection at all other times, by whatever method you have found works for you.'

'We know all that, but why was it so important that we all got to meet *her*?' Richard pointed accusingly at Crystal. Crystal felt Nathan tense next to her.

'Son, we've been through this, but for the benefit of the others.' He turned back to address everyone in the room, his eyes going from one to the other, until they rested on Crystal. 'It's important for you to meet Crystal, the one remaining angel, the one who is going to bring enlightenment to all.' His eyes didn't flicker and Crystal did her best to meet his stare and not show the fear and embarrassment she felt inside. 'And it's important for Crystal to meet us, so she knows she isn't in this on her own.' He finally let his gaze move from her and back to the room in general. 'She has a huge task ahead of her, and it is our job to ensure she succeeds. And, my friends, that is much easier for everyone concerned, if we can put a face to the names of those involved.'

'I'm glad we did, as she isn't what I expected.' Stephanie stepped forward. 'I mean, she's younger than I thought she'd be, and prettier.' She grinned confidently at Crystal.

Crystal grinned back at her but stayed quiet.

'You're stupid, Stephanie. I mean we all knew she'd just turned twenty-one, so she's obviously gonna be young.' Richard chipped in sarcastically.

Martin held his hands up to quieten the youngsters. 'Okay, that's enough you two. We all know she's younger than you both, and to be fair, she does look even younger.' He turned to Crystal. 'No offence meant, Crystal.' She nodded her acceptance. 'But, regardless of her age, Crystal *is* unique and therefore the only person on the planet who can bring an end to The Others. The only person who can bring an end to this. So that we – and others like us and our families - don't have to hide our abilities and what we know to be true from the world. We should all be proud to be the limited few who have actually met her face-to-face, rather than just forming our own opinions of how she looks from the stories we've been told. We should all be proud to help her achieve her destiny so that we can live complete lives again. I know I, for one, am honoured to serve her.' Martin held his head high and turned to face Crystal.

Tina was the first to applaud, followed quickly by her husband. They all turned expectantly toward Crystal. Confused, Crystal looked up at Nathan. The silence stretched for what seemed like an eternity. Taking pity on her, he leant down and whispered in her ear.

'They're waiting for you to say something.'

'Like what?' she whispered, panic-stricken.

'Just tell them you're glad to be here and so on.' He laid his hand gently in the small of her back and gave her a slight shove forward.

Classy bird, Crystal thought, as she looked for all the world as if she'd just tripped forward over her own feet and into the middle of the circle.

'Um, I'm glad to be here.' She smiled at the faces around her – all filled with anticipation and hope – except for Nathan's. He was exaggeratedly rolling his eyes skywards in despair.

'I don't really know what you all want me to say.' She laughed nervously.

'Something useful would be good,' Richard mumbled.

Crystal glared at him and continued. 'Up until recently I

thought I was just a normal girl. It's a bit overwhelming to be honest, knowing I'm supposed to be so much more.' Her hand went to her mouth, but she quickly lowered it again – resisting the urge to bite her nails. 'I've started working on my flying...' she looked at the ground and let the sentence die, before perking up slightly and adding, 'and I'm reading The Account, so it shouldn't take me too long to finish it and be up to speed.' She was drowning – she knew it and so did they.

Nathan stepped forward, 'This girl has had a fun-filled couple of weeks. She's learnt she's an angel, realised she can fly, met with The Guardian, collected The Account,' he paused, then continued, 'and realised she's one of only a few who can *actually* read it.' A slight laugh rose from those around him. 'She also realising that there's a lot of things that can, and will, happen.' He looked around at the others in the room. 'Especially after The Guardian, Father Javier, has already been taken for his part in helping Crystal – oh, and of course, finding out there's others who can help,' he theatrically swept his arm around the room. 'and met you all – and heard, and probably met, some of those who are there to stop her. So, she's been through a lot, and for that reason you'll have to forgive her first attempt at public speaking.' The others smiled sympathetically in Crystal's direction. 'But I have no doubt that, contrary to how she looks and acts at the moment, she will be ready, willing and able to carry out whatever she has to do, when the time comes. Appearances can be deceptive and, I for one am standing with her one hundred percent and will be by her side until the end.' He met everyone's gaze. 'She *is* the one, she *is* unique – the last angel – and we *will* be ready.'

Spontaneous applause echoed around the room and Martin stepped forward, holding his arms up for silence.

'Okay everyone, we have to wrap this up.' He looked at his watch. 'You have about five more minutes before we should leave. Remember to actively seek out others who can join our cause and stay safe.'

The circle around the crate quickly dissolved as they all turned to grab their belongings and have a quick chat with each other. Stephanie, dragging Richard by the arm, headed straight over to Crystal.

'Crystal, we should swap numbers, in case you need us.' She pulled her mobile out of her coat pocket and frowned at Richard, signalling him to follow suit. He did as he was told and grudgingly added Crystal's number to his contact list.

'It's a bit overwhelming when you first meet others, isn't it?' Stephanie touched Crystal lightly on the arm, making her jump slightly.

'It is a bit. Thanks for being so friendly.'

'Anytime. Just give me a shout if you need to talk – or want to meet up – or need help. Anything, really.' Stephanie gave her an affectionate nudge.

Nathan finished saying his 'goodbyes' and walked over to Crystal. 'We should be going.' He nodded at Stephanie and Richard.

'Oh, okay.' She glanced at them apologetically. 'I'd better go. Maybe text you during the week?'

'Sure. Like I said, anytime. See you later.' Stephanie waved and casually took a few steps backwards. Crystal turned and walked with Nathan towards the door, but was close enough to hear Richard's parting remark.

'Stephanie, you're such a kiss-ass. I don't think Crystal's that way inclined.' As Crystal walked out of the door she chanced a glance back, her eyes meeting Richard's gaze, before the door swung closed behind her.

They'd made the right decision in not storming into the outhouses when it was first discovered as their meeting place. A stray black curl of hair fell forward over his forehead, dropping cold rainwater into his icy-blue eyes. He was glad he'd convinced them to let him come on his own – after all, they weren't exactly going to argue with him were they? And that meant he was the only person here to witness, first-hand, her first get together –that first ray of hope – and it made him feel connected to her somehow.

He pulled the collar of his black coat closer to his neck, to stop the rainwater dripping down inside and took a step back into the shadow of the derelict warehouse. It made him feel honoured to have shared this moment with her – and he'd feel even more connected to her when the time came for him to take her last breath – and to see that last ray of hope die in her eyes.

29

Even though it was a cold evening, Amy's blue silk skirt left little to the imagination. She looked admiringly at herself in the mirror, checking that her makeup was perfect. Satisfied that everything looked how it should, she bent down and fastened the buckle of her blue suede stilettos. Pulling on her black fitted suede jacket, Amy gave one last check in the mirror before heading downstairs.

'I'll see you later.' Amy thought it was only polite to let her mother know she was going out.

'Where do you think you're going at this time of night?' Mandy looked rather shocked. She was sitting on the chocolate coloured sofa.

'Out.' Amy answered, flippantly. 'I *will* be back later.'

'Come here when I'm talking to you.' Mandy demanded. Amy walked into the living room, chin held defiantly high. 'What an earth are you wearing? Do you not have any respect for yourself?'

'You'd know all about respect wouldn't you, Mother?'

'Don't talk to me like that!' Mandy bit back at her daughter.

'Well, look at you,' Amy sneered at her. 'You sat there in your beige baggy cardigan, hiding behind that Bible. You won't find any help in there you know.'

''Don't change the topic, my girl. I asked what you were wearing. You can't go out looking like *that*. You look like a common little tart.' Her eyes were narrowed slits, and her mouth turned down in distaste at the edges.

'I happen to think I look rather hot,' Amy smirked back at her.

'What's the matter with you? You're asking for trouble – dress like a whore, get treated like one. Is that what you want?'

'Maybe I like it. Nothing like using and abusing people. You should know – you did it to Dad.' Her green eyes glinted, cold and hard, back at her mother.

'I did nothing to your father! He was a nasty, vindictive bully.' Mandy got to her feet, hands on hips, mouth held so tightly closed that her lips almost disappeared.

'He was not nasty! He left because you let yourself go.' She cast an eye up and down her mother. 'Look at you, who'd want *you*? You could be good looking – hell, you were once good looking but you got all religious and decided that looking good was a sin. Like God gives a crap about what you look like.'

'Don't you blaspheme! I've a good mind to get your uncle Frank over here! He'll sort you out.' Mandy started to rummage around for her mobile phone.

'Save it, Mother. He's just as weak as you are. He's not my dad and never will be. My dad would still be here if you hadn't driven him away.' She turned to walk out of the room.

'Where do you think you're going?'

'I told you – out!' Amy walked out of the living room and headed for the front door. 'And if I'm really lucky, I might not even come back until the morning!' She slammed the door shut behind her.

It was only a ten-minute walk to the pub. She needed the time to calm down. Anger was never a pretty look to wear – and she didn't want her mother ruining her entire Wednesday evening. Crossing the road, Amy headed for the Duke of Earl pub to meet up with Chris. He had a drink already lined up for her when she walked in. Smiling suggestively at Russell, she walked up to Chris, leant over and gave him a kiss on the cheek.

'Hi handsome, you okay?'

Chris hugged and kissed her back. 'I'm fine, gorgeous. How are you? You're looking good.'

Amy undid her coat and sat down on a vacant stool. 'Just had another 'chat' with my mother. She can be such a bitch.' She picked up the drink and took a swig. 'God, I need this – thanks.'

'What was it about this time?'

'The usual. She thinks I'm a tart – I think she's pathetic.'

'Well, you do sleep with a lot of people.' He raised his hands to stop her objecting. 'But then again, so do I. And it's no fun unless you've got someone to compete with. I do believe I'm currently one ahead of you at the moment. The only difference is all of mine are still talking to me.'

'Maybe I am a tart.' She tucked a black lock of hair behind her ear. 'Besides, I can't help it – I just happen to like sex.' She smiled at Chris. 'That's why you and I get on so well.'

'Talking of getting on, how did you get on with the HR guy – Matthew wasn't it – well anyway, the guy from the other night? Is he another one to add to your score?'

'Of course!' Amy smiled. 'He was all right, nothing to

write home about though, but I do believe that makes us currently even.'

'Ah, but is he still talking to you? Remember, you only win if you beat my score *and* can still get the guy to be nice to you afterwards.'

She watched an attractive slender and petite blonde walk in towards them. She walked up to Chris and gave him a slow, seductive kiss on the lips.

'Hi sugar, haven't seen you for a while,' he said. The blonde smiled in response, before leaning forward and whispering in his ear. Chris's eyes lit up and a smile spread across his face. 'I'm sure you could if I let you! I'll bear it in mind – maybe I'll call you.'

'Anytime. You have my number.' She gave Amy the once over, before turning to leave. Chris leant forward and gave her butt a friendly slap as she walked off giggling.

'One of your exes I presume? Chris Cousins, I don't know how you do it.' Amy shook her head in disbelief. 'No matter how many women you sleep with; they go right on worshipping you.'

Chris grinned. 'You either have it or you don't. And I guess I have! You know baby girl, we could be so good together.'

'We could, I know, but we both love ourselves too much.' Amy emptied her glass. 'How about getting me another, to save me flirting another free drink out of Russell?' She gave Chris a suggestive look. 'I tell you what, if we're both single when we hit thirty-five, we'll make a pact to get together and see if the sex is as explosive as we both think it would be. What do you think?'

Chris picked up his drink and downed the contents. 'I'll drink to that!'

Amy laughed and grabbed his wallet. 'I'll guess you'll be wanting another too?'

Chris looked at his watch before answering. 'Yeah, as I'm paying. It doesn't look like Mark and Emily are joining us.'

'My poor naive cousin is probably too loved up at the moment,' she replied distastefully. 'I know Crystal isn't coming as she's too busy.' She turned round to face Chris. 'Actually, she seems to have gotten awfully busy, just lately.'

'Maybe she's avoiding us?' Chris answered.

'No, we're the only bunch of friends she has.' Amy replied before getting sidetracked by Russell and ordering the drinks.

Emily was sat on the sofa in the boys' den at Mark's house. Mark had his arm draped casually around her shoulders, as they sat watching TV. Mark and his older brothers had converted the upstairs room in the garage to a den, or games room, to use when they needed a bit of space from the rest of the family.

'It's quiet out here, isn't it? I guess that's why your mum sent us out here.' She leant her head against Mark's arm.

'My family can be a bit loud.' He grinned and leant back to close his eyes.

'I like your parents, they let you do whatever.' Emily sighed.

'Your parents are okay. Well, your mum is.'

'Mum's cool. But my dad would never let me and you be alone in our house together.'

'He's probably just worried about you.' Mark tried to be tactful. Emily loved that about him.

'Hmm, possibly. More likely though, he's worried about

what God and the church congregation would think about it.'

'Do you believe in God then?'

'Not really, but I'd never admit that in front of my dad!'

Mark gave her a reassuring squeeze. 'Your dad really bothers you, doesn't he?'

'He's just a bit overbearing sometimes.' She turned to face him. 'My mum is always so tense when my dad's around. The only time I can relax is when I'm round here with you and your family.'

'Well, you're welcome to come over anytime you like. My family like you as you are.' He leant forward and placed a tender kiss on her lips. 'I like having you round here too.' He turned slightly in his seat and put his other arm around her, bringing it forward to cup the side of her face. 'In fact, I like you, full stop.' He kissed her again, this time with more passion. Emily returned the kiss, opening her mouth slightly to let his tongue in. Closing her eyes, she revelled in the feelings currently exploding inside her body – the butterflies going berserk in her stomach, the rapid beating of her heart – even the feeling of her chest; desperate for her to stop holding her breath and let some much needed air into her lungs.

Mark finally let her go and took in a deep breath of air. 'Sorry, was that too much, too soon?' The tell-tale red flush of his cheeks relayed the embarrassment he felt. Emily smiled shyly at him. 'Kissing is fine. In fact, kissing is good.' She grinned at him before beckoning him forward and leaning in for another kiss. He leant closer this time, wrapping his arms around her, pulling her body closer to his and sliding her slightly down on the sofa and she could feel the full weight of his body on top of hers. His knee pressed slightly against her legs, enough to make her part them slightly and feel his weight shift slight as his groin pressed against hers. The buckle of his jeans belt was digging into her stomach slightly, but his kisses were doing their best to distract her from the pain her stomach was feeling.

Emily wrapped her arms around him, enabling her hands to wander up and down his back. She let an in an involuntary gasp as his hand found its way into her cotton shirt and she had her first experience of his skin against hers. He undid the rest of her shirt buttons – the whole time, his kisses were driving her to distraction. Her heart was thumping double time, her breath short and shallow. Mark's kisses made their way down to her neck and Emily arched her back, letting her head fall backwards, exposing every inch of her neck to his gentle nibbles. Emily pulled frantically at his shirt, untucking it from his jeans and allowing her hands to explore the bare flesh of his back and then, to finally feel his warm bare skin against her stomach. The atmosphere around them had become charged and heavy, his kisses making their way down to her throat, and only the occasional drawn out sighs from Emily and heavy breathing from them both, quelled the silence. Mark deftly undid her bra and his hand found its way to her breast, followed quickly by his mouth.

Emily took a double sharp intake of breath, his touch enough to send the butterflies into full flight mode. Her heart was positively drowning in the new sensations her body was feeling – but her head, alas was filled with the disappointed face of her dad.

'Stop.' She whispered, before repeating it again, louder this time.

Mark pushed himself off her body, taking the weight on his arms and knees – his face full of concern.

'Are you okay? Are we going too fast?' He sat back

against his heels and held his hands up reassuring her. 'We can stop, not a problem.' He shook his head. 'Damn, I know I should've stopped sooner. I bet I've spooked you now.' Emily finished doing up her bra and leant forward, cupping his face with her hands. She leant forward and kissed him slowly and tenderly on the lips. 'It's nothing you've done, honest. I just think years of living with a religious dad have rubbed off on me slightly.' She looked into his concerned eyes. 'Don't worry, it's fine.' She smiled at him and did up the buttons of her blouse. 'I liked everything you were doing – in fact I *really* liked everything you were doing! I could just feel the disappointment coming from my father.'

'It'll be okay; I don't mind waiting. I'd rather wait until you're ready than risk pushing you and losing you altogether.' Mark stood up and tucked his shirt back into his jeans. He held out his hand – Emily took hold of it, and he pulled her to her feet, before wrapping his arms around her and kissing her forehead. 'We have all the time in the world.'

'Thank you for being so understanding. I love you, Mark Curtis – and all of your family – and even your mad dog!' She kissed him fiercely before taking a step back, still holding onto his hand. 'Talking of your family, shall we go and spend some time with them before I have to go back into the religious confines of my home?' She led him downstairs and out of the garage.

Making their way into the house, Emily and Mark followed the sound of the TV and sat down on the spare sofa in the living room. Mark casually draped his arm around Emily's shoulders; she snuggled up against him, grateful that he wasn't mad at her. Kitty spotted the slight flush on Emily's face and glanced at Peter, her other half, giving him a slight grin and a knowing look.

'Would either of you like a cup of tea? You look slightly

flushed?' Kitty asked with a straight face, and immediately the colour rose up Emily's face.

Emily went to stand up, but Kitty held her hand up in protest. 'No, don't worry, I'll make you one. Anyone else?' She glanced around at her other three sons, all of whom shook their heads. 'Okey dokey, back in a minute.' Kitty returned a few minutes later with a tray containing three mugs of steaming hot tea and a plate of biscuits.

'Pull that side table forward, then shift up and I'll sit next to you.' She signalled for Mark to move closer to Emily, so he let his arm fall away from Emily's shoulders and they both budged up to one end of the sofa. Kitty sat down, putting the tray on the table and placing the mugs in front of them. She glanced across at them, both sitting with their arms by their sides. 'You don't have to be all prim and proper now I'm sat here! Put your arm back around her, you donut!' Her laughter broke through their awkwardness and they both relaxed back into their original positions. Satisfied, Kitty picked up her mug and returned her attention to the television.

Presently Emily glanced at her watch, horrified to see that an hour had already passed. 'I'd better make a move or my dad will be worried.' She rose to her feet, followed quickly by Mark and Kitty. 'I'll see you all soon.' Peter and the boys waved absentmindedly at her – their attention firmly on the TV programme.

'I'll walk out with you.' Mark took hold of her hand and led her from the room, followed by Kitty. They made their way down the corridor and through the kitchen, before Kitty spoke.

'Emily, come here and let me give you a hug. Mark will get your coat.' Emily dutifully walked back to Kitty and hugged her tightly.

'Thanks for having me over again.'

'You're most welcome darling. Now remember, you don't have to be anything but you in this house. So relax and just be yourself. No one here will judge you for *anything*.' Kitty took hold of Emily's shoulders and held her at arm's length. 'And you are more than welcome to come over her anytime you like. Even if Mark's not here – I will be. So don't be a stranger. Just think of this as your second home.' She pulled Emily back into an embrace and then let her go. 'Now, say 'Hi' to your mother for me and let her know I'll catch up with her in the week.'

'Thanks Kitty.' Emily hesitated slightly, before continuing. 'Do you really mean that? I mean, that I can come round anytime?'

'I wouldn't have said it if I didn't. You're a good girl Emily, I'd be glad to get to know you and help you come out of your shell a little bit. Now here's your lovely boyfriend with your coat.' She grinned lovingly at Mark before ruffling his hair – much to his annoyance.

'Get off Mum, I'm not a kid!' He batted at her hand before smoothing down his hair and rolling his eyes theatrically at Emily. 'I'll walk you half way, if you like?'

'That would be nice. Bye Kitty.' She gave her another quick hug before turning and walking out of the back door.

Mission accomplished, I do believe, Kitty thought, smiling slightly smugly.

30

The ringing of Crystal's mobile phone woke her abruptly. She sat up, trying to clear the fog from her mind and remember when exactly she'd fallen asleep. She glanced, first at the clock, then at the caller ID before answering.

'Hi Emily, everything okay?'

'Sorry, is it a bit late to ring you?' Emily sounded wired.

'No, it's never too late to get a phone call from my bestie.' Crystal yawned. 'I had a rather busy night, what with going out with Nathan and nipping out on the sly, to do a bit of healing. Thanks for the heads up on the sick old lady. I hope your dad doesn't cotton on that you're looking at his prayer list and passing those names onto me.'

'You're welcome.' Emily sounded more hyper than usual.

'Anyway, you sound super-excited, are you sure you're all right?'

'I couldn't be happier! I spent the day round Mark's.' Emily replied gleefully.

'You didn't do it! Did you?'

'No, of course I didn't.' Emily sighed. 'Not that I didn't

want to. But I'm certain I'd like to stay a virgin until I'm married' Crystal could hear Emily smiling, probably beaming away to herself and this, in turn, made Crystal smile.

'Bless, nice to see that only a few of your dads' beliefs are rubbing off on you. Let me guess, you made out though, right?'

'We did!' Emily shrieked down the phone.

'Good for you. I'm happy for you. Nice to see one of us is having a love life.' She threw herself back onto her pillows.

'Oh, what's up?' Emily lowered her tone and tried to restrain her happiness, for the sake of her friend.

'There's been so much going on at the moment, I don't even know where to begin. And on top of all of that, I haven't seen Tony outside of work for ages.'

'Has he not been at work?'

'Nope. Well, only twice. And then he keeps it firmly business-like. I think he might have gone off me.' Crystal sighed.

'Nah, he's probably just really busy. So what have you had happening then? You said you'd had lots going on.'

Crystal glanced across at the window sill. 'Oh, just the usual. Do you want to come over tomorrow? It'd be better if we could talk face-to-face.'

'Course I can. Would six thirty be okay, as I've got school reports to finish?'

'That'd be great. I'll fill you in on everything then. Oh, and I really am glad you and Mark are getting on so well.'

'I know you are. I'll see you tomorrow then. Take care.' Emily rang off and Crystal hauled herself back to a seated position, before deciding to go downstairs and get a can of cola from the fridge.

She crept past her mother's room, as she figured she

would already be in bed as it had gone eleven, but Nathan's door was still open and his room was in darkness. Crystal made her way downstairs, not bothering to turn on the kitchen light. She glanced out of the kitchen window and saw a light on in her mother's shop. She's working late, she thought, before opening the fridge door and letting the interior light illuminate her silhouette against the darkness of the kitchen. Crystal grabbed a can and closed the door, waiting a couple of seconds after it had swung shut to let her eyes adjust to the darkness again. Turning to go back upstairs, she noticed that the light in the flower shop had been turned off, so she flicked on the under-cabinet lighting, so her mother wouldn't have to fumble around in the darkened kitchen when she came back in.

Crystal made her way back upstairs and closed her bedroom door behind her. She vaguely remembered hearing the kitchen door open and gently close, before sleep claimed her.

She opened her eyes to blackness. Her eyes slowly adjusted to the darkness and she looked around. She was in a small, brick build room, similar to the outhouse where she'd met the other full and half-bloods – she could just about make out a door on the left-hand wall at the far end of the room. Her senses were pin-sharp; her nostrils taking in the familiar smell of the fusty room, whilst the hairs on her arms and back of her neck stood to attention, as a static charge of electricity tingled all over her body. She could also sense that someone was stood the other side of the door. She tried to move, but her limbs felt too heavy for her to lift – as if she'd had the energy drained out of her.

She tried to remember what had happened prior to waking in this room, but her mind was fuzzy. She lay on the floor, her head turned to face the door; cheek flat against the cold, solid stone flagstones.

The fog in her head slowly started to clear. Occasional snap-shots of prior events flickered through her mind – the room, the young girl in bed, the healing, then darkness. She pulled herself to a seated position, using the wall for support. Resting her head on her hands, she closed her eyes as the exertion of moving positions used the last few remnants of her energy. The static energy around her body moved slightly and she sensed the person on the other side of the door move closer. As the door handle was pushed downwards, she felt the electric static intensify and her vision seemed to switch to that of someone looking down a black tunnel. Not knowing who was on the other side of the door, an illogical feeling of dread filled every fibre of her being, and grew until the terror threatened to burst out of her very core. She fell back to the floor, exhausted, her breathing getting heavier and more labo-rious and as the door opened, the last thing she saw, before her eyes closed to black again, was the silhouette of a curly-haired man coming into the room...

The alarm on her bedside clock sprang into life at 6.15 am, startling Crystal awake. Falling back onto her bed, she reached her arm out and slapped the top of the clock to turn it off, before dragging herself out of bed. Going downstairs, Crystal mumbled, 'Morning,' to her mother and grabbed a bowl out of the cupboard.

'Morning. Take it you had another dream, judging by the bang I just heard.' Izzy stared over at Crystal, looking worried..

'Uh hmm,' was all Crystal could muster; her body felt wrung out – she couldn't decide if it was because of the fall onto her bed or the dream she'd just had.

'You look pale. Was it the same dream again?'

'No.' Crystal grabbed a Red Bull from the fridge and cracked it open, before sitting down at the table with her bowl of cornflakes. Izzy sat patiently, waiting for a more in-depth response. A few minutes passed before her enquiring stare prompted Crystal to finally start speaking in full sentences – between mouthfuls of cereal.

'It wasn't the same dream – I think it was after.' She closed her eyes momentarily, partly to calm herself and partly because she was so god-damn tired.

'I was in a dark room and someone was outside the door – a man with curly hair – and he terrified me.' She took a swig from her Red Bull can. 'I didn't recognise him, but I could feel the darkness oozing from his every pore. He made my skin crawl, the hairs on my neck and arms tingled with a static electricity and I felt so heavy and tired.' She rested her head on her hands, elbows on the table – cereal forgotten, eyes glazed – as she relived that moment.

'Did you speak to Nathan about your dreams?' Izzy's voice jarred Crystal back to the present.

'No, not yet. I don't think I was ready to know, but now I think I need to.' She looked up at her mother and smiled weakly.

'Make sure you do. I'm worried about you, hun.' Izzy reached across the table and took hold of Crystal's hand, giving it a gentle, reassuring squeeze. 'Promise me.'

'I'll speak to him tonight, I promise.' Crystal pushed the half eaten bowl of cereal away and stood up.' I'd better get ready for work.'

'Do you think you should go in? Maybe you can ring in sick?' Izzy held her hand against her chest, in an effort to stay calm. 'I mean, you look so tired.'

'I am, but I'll be fine.' Crystal replied. Besides, she wanted to see if Tony was going to turn up today.

'Well, if you don't feel any better by lunchtime, please come home. I can shut the shop up early if you want company.'

Crystal shook her head and smiled. 'I'll see how I get on. I'd better go.' She gestured towards the stairs, before rushing over to her mum and giving her an impromptu hug. 'I'll be fine, I'm sure of it. Don't worry. It's just a dream.' She turned to go, but turned back to face her mother. 'Talking of tired, how do you manage to look so wide awake? Especially after your late night working session.'

'I didn't have a late night last night.' Izzy looked confused. 'I was in bed by ten.'

'Oh. I saw the light on in your shop and assumed it was you.' They stared at each other; both looking as confused at the other, before Crystal suddenly recalled something. 'Nathan must've been in there. I remember walking past his bedroom door. It was open and his room was in darkness.'

'Maybe.' Izzy tried to keep her voice casual, but the hesitation was evident. She watched Crystal walk out of the kitchen and up the stairs.

~

'Hey sleepyhead, are you with us?' Amy prodded Crystal in the back, making her jump in her chair.

'Sorry, what were you saying?' Crystal rolled her head slightly to ease the tension in her shoulders and neck.

'I was telling you about... it doesn't matter. Are you okay?' For once, Amy actually sounded concerned.

'Yeah, I'm fine, just tired.'

'I'll get your phone when it rings, if you like?' Amy looked quite worried.

'I can manage.' Crystal smiled at her. 'You wanna be careful; you're actually showing you care.'

'Shut up, I just don't want to have to do all your work, as

well as mine, especially as I don't want to carry anything over to Friday's already busy workload.' Amy grinned. 'Anyway, lover boy's got his eye on you, so you'd better perk up. No man likes a girl to look like she's at death' door.' She spun her chair back around and tried to look busy.

Tony was staring out of his office window at her. Crystal smiled and waved slightly – he didn't respond. So much for keeping it all friendly at work, Crystal thought sarcastically, before turning back to her computer screen.

She spent the next half hour clearing the important things out of her inbox, looking up when she heard Tony's office door open. She could still see him in the office, so guessed that someone else had entered. Clearing out her junk folder in her email account, a message about YouTube caught her eye.

She didn't know why she hadn't thought of it before – or social media, for that matter. It was the perfect way to spread the word, if you had something important to say. And Crystal certainly did. Giving a quick glance around the office, to make sure no one was looking her way, she connected to the internet. A couple of minutes later, she'd opened accounts with several social media sites. She looked up when she heard Tony's door open again, and saw the IT guy walk out. He'd obviously gotten his ear bent, as he looked as pissed off as usual. Crystal casually glanced around the office again, before going to YouTube and opening an account there too. Satisfied to have finally done something constructive towards her task, she spent the rest of the morning getting some actual paid work done.

Lunchtime arrived and, as Crystal was making preparations to leave her desk, Amy prodded her in the back again.

'Hey, lover boy wants to see you.'

Crystal looked up and saw Tony beckon her to his office.

She stood up and made her way across the room and opened the office door.

'Hi, I wasn't sure if you were going to be in today, as you've been out most of the week.'

'Sit down Crystal.' She didn't like the tone in his voice, he sounded so... business-like. Shit, maybe he knows I've been using the internet, she thought.

'Is there anything you want to talk to me about?' He fiddled with the clip on his Parker pen, before looking up and staring at her.

Do I just admit what I've been doing, as the IT guy has obviously told him – and this isn't my first time either? She raised her hand to her mouth, ready to bite her nails, but then realised that would make her look guilty so lowered it quickly again.

'Crystal, are you okay? I've been keeping an eye on you all morning. You don't look very well. I did mean what I said the other day. You can talk to me about anything, you know.' He'd changed his tone – his voice was now full of concern.

She closed her eyes momentarily. 'To be honest, I don't feel that great. I thought you wanted to keep business and our relationship separate?'

'I do. Well, I did – but you look so pale.' He leant forward across the desk. 'I was worried about you.'

She smiled at him, glad he was so concerned. 'I'm fine. It's just these dreams I've been having.' She rubbed her temples. 'They're so real. There's just so much going on at the moment and...'

'Why don't you go home? Catch up with some sleep and I'll pop over and see you later.'

'I couldn't...'

'Go on. I'm asking as your boyfriend.

'Is that what you are now?' She glanced shyly up at him.

'I do believe I am. But hey, if you want me to ask as your boss – well, you don't look well and I don't want whatever you've got to spread around the office, so go home!' He grinned at her.

'Bad dreams are not contagious, you know.' She stood up, relieved to have been given a free pass.

'Dreams? The boss-side of me has no recollection of anyone saying anything about bad dreams – now scoot!' He waved her out of the office.

'Thanks Tony, I'll fill you in on the details later then.'

'Okay, I'll text you when I'm on my way.' He watched her walk out of his office and as she shut the door he added, 'I'd love to hear about your scary dreams and night terrors.'

Crystal went back to her desk and cleared her things away. Amy finished the phone conversation she was having, hung up the receiver and turned to face her.

'You off home then? Lucky cow.'

'Yeah, I'm under strict orders to get some sleep.'

'Fair enough. He probably wants you to save some energy for him.' Amy jerked her head towards Tony's office.

Crystal couldn't be bothered to retaliate. 'I'll see you tomorrow.'

Amy picked up her nail file and watched Crystal walk out of the office. She was still filing her nails when she noticed the creepy-looking IT guy skulk his way into Tony's office. She walked over to Crystal's desk, to get a better view. They'd left the office door slightly ajar so Amy walked casually to the photocopier, next to Tony's office. Hitting the 'copy' button, Amy photocopied blank sheets of paper whilst trying to hear what was being said.

She wondered if the guy was about to be sacked, as she heard the word 'trust' mentioned a couple of times, followed by 'accountable', but the photocopier noise was drowning out the rest of the conversation. It also reminded them that they'd left the door open, as Tony got up and closed it. Amy walked back over to Crystal's desk so she could watch them but, a couple of minutes later the IT guy came out of the office and walked towards her. He didn't say anything; he just stood there with his arms folded, tapping his foot and waiting.

'Oh, sorry. Am I in your way?' Amy slowly stood up and walked back to her desk. 'Crystal didn't say anything about her PC being broken again.' She swung her chair round to face him. The IT guy didn't respond, he just unplugged the base unit, picked it up and carried it from the office.

'Talkative, aren't you?' Amy sarcastically shouted at his receding figure, before returning to her nail file.

31

Crystal let herself in the back door, pausing only to wave back at her mother, who was standing in her flower shop, gathering flower stems. Walking over to the fridge, she grabbed a can of cola and put her bag down on the kitchen table, before leaning against the kitchen counter. Now she was home, she felt slightly better but, figuring that a short sleep wouldn't hurt her, she was just kicking off her shoes when she heard the floorboards creaking upstairs. She hesitated, just long enough to register that it was actually Nathan coming down the stairs, so she pulled a chair out and sat down.

'Hi, I didn't realise you were home.' Nathan quickly finished doing up his shirt buttons.

'Yeah, benefits of dating my boss. He sent me home as I wasn't looking too great.' She took a sip from her can.

'Why'd he send you home? Is everything okay?' He grabbed a mug and started to make himself a coffee.

'I'm just really tired. Been having dreams again.'

Nathan sat down with his mug of coffee. 'Are they all the same – these dreams?'

She shook her head. 'Originally, I'd dream about flying into a little girl's bedroom and healing her.' Crystal rested her head on her hand. 'But, as I'm healing her she starts getting greyer and greyer; her breathing gets louder and I can hear it wheezing and rasping around inside her chest. She opens her eyes. They're so black and I can feel them boring into me. I manage to break contact and take my hands away from her face, but the darkness that's spreading around the room engulfs me, making it difficult to walk. My limbs get heavier and just as the darkness consumes me, I wake up.'

'Nathan didn't take his eyes off her. 'Does the little girl say anything?'

'Yeah, she doesn't sound like a little girl though. Her voice is too deep and manly.' Crystal looked upwards, recollecting the words spoken by the girl, before lowering her eyes and making contact with Nathans stare. 'She say that I did this to her, but I don't know how I did or even what I did.' The confusion she felt was echoed in every word. 'Do you know what it means?'

Nathan didn't respond with an answer – he just asked another question. 'What about the other dreams?'

'There's only been one other, so far.'

'Tell me about that one.' He sounded concerned, and Crystal couldn't decide if that was because of the details of her dream, or the fact that he knew what it meant.

'Well, I think it continues on from the first, judging by the snapshots of memory I have whilst in the dream.' She took another swig from her can and placed it back on the table.

'I'm in a room, much like the one we met the other full and half-bloods in. It's dark and cold; I'm lying on the floor and feel as if the energy has been sucked out of every part of my body. There's someone the other side of the door –a man.' She looked across at Nathan, but his face stayed neutral. 'You know, I can feel them – their energy – it's dark and heavy; suffocating almost.'

'Do you see who it is? How do you know it's a man?' He swallowed nervously; Crystal watched his Adam's apple go up, then down. The vein on the right side of his forehead was prominent – throbbing as the blood rushed around his body.

'I see his silhouette – just before I wake up.' She shivered involuntarily. 'His presence makes my skin crawl; the hairs on my arms and neck react to some kind of static electricity. Do you know who he is?' She held his stare, willing him to back down first – certain that he would divulge some much needed insight into these dreams.

Nathan blinked and looked away. 'I might know who you're talking about.' He raised a hand briefly to prevent her speaking. 'I'm not saying I know his name – but I do know his type.'

'What type is that then?'

'Let's just say it's not a good type.' Nathan stared at his mug, contemplating his next response.

'Mum said to talk to you about the dreams; that you would know what they meant.' Crystal rubbed her temples, closing her eyes momentarily. God, I'm so tired, she thought.

'Maybe you should get some sleep?' Nathan went to stand up.

'Don't you dare! I think I deserve some real answers, don't you?' She glared at him as he went over and put his mug in the sink. 'You said you'd be honest with me. You said you'd treat me like an adult, as long as I didn't relay what you said back to my mum. If you won't be honest with me, maybe I'm better off talking to Tony! At least he's interested!'

Nathan sat abruptly back down. 'You haven't told him anything, have you?' She didn't answer, so he leant across the table and grabbed her arm tightly, shaking it and forcing her to look at him.

'Ouch, you're hurting me!' Crystal wrenched her arm away, rubbing where his fingers had dug in.

'Did you?'

She scowled back at him. 'Of course I didn't! Well, I didn't tell him the details, but he knows I've been having bad dreams.'

'God, you're so naive.' He shook his head slightly before resting it on his hand. 'I'm too tired for this shit. I need a drink.' He closed his eyes. 'You cannot trust *anyone* – especially people you have only known for a short time.'

'Well, if you will go rummaging around the shop at stupid hours of the night, you will be tired,' Crystal chipped in, to change the conversation. 'Anyway, what were you looking for?'

His eyes sprang back open again. 'When? What are you talking about?'

'You were in the shop last night. I came down to get a drink' Crystal pointed to the under cabinet lighting. 'I left those lights on for you. I thought it was Mum at first, but I asked her this morning.' Her voice had a slightly accusatory tone to it.' And you weren't in your room when I walked past... so where were you then, if you weren't in the shop?'

Nathan was fully alert now, sat bolt upright in his chair. 'I was out with Martin and Richard. We were chasing up a few leads on other full-bloods.'

Her accusatory tone changed to one of panic. 'But, it

must've been you. I heard the back door open and close shortly after I went to bed.' She turned around to look at the door, as if waiting for it to confirm her story.

'I didn't get home until after you left for work. I was out all night.'

The silence was deafening. They both stared at each other; Crystal full of panic, Nathan full of concern.

'We should speak to your mother. Find out if anything is missing.' He stood up and walked over to the back door, bending down to check the latch. 'There's no sign of a break-in, so it was either unlocked, or the person had a key.'

'You need to tell me who the man is – what type is he?' Crystal hollered after him, but he'd already walked out the door. She got up and followed him to the flower shop. Izzy was still tying hand-held bouquets, but stopped when she looked up and saw Nathan walking towards the shop with a look of thunder on his face. Crystal managed to catch up with Nathan, just as he was walking in through the main door.

'What's going on?' Izzy stood, one hand holding a half finished bouquet, the other holding a single stem.

'Does anyone else, apart from you, have a key to the shop?'

Izzy laid the bouquet down on the counter. 'No, well only Crystal – she has the spare key, in case I lose mine.' She glanced past Nathan and stared at Crystal's worried face.

'What's going on?'

'Crystal told you she saw a light on in the shop last night?'

Izzy nodded. 'But she said it was probably you, as you weren't in your room.'

'Well, it wasn't. Is anything missing?'

'The float is still in the cash register and the safe hasn't been touched.' She swept a hand around the room. 'So, unless they wanted to take any flowers – then no. Don't look so worried, there's no damage been done.' She smiled weakly at him, but the slight tremor in her voice gave her real thoughts away.

'You're no more convinced than I am.' Nathan folded his arms. 'You can't keep burying your head in the sand, Izzy. This is happening and it is happening now.'

'I'm not burying my head...' Izzy refused to look at him.

'Well, I know you're not stupid but, just in case there's a remote chance that you are. Crystal had her bag stolen, right after she was given The Account. It was found, with everything in it – including her keys and phone. The only thing missing was Father Javier's business card. He's now been taken. Your spare key was on that same key ring in Crystal's bag and now your shop has been searched. 'The sarcasm dripped off his tongue. Turning to Crystal, he continued. 'Did Crystal also tell you that she heard someone come in the back door?' He turned back to Izzy. 'I take it from the look on your face that she didn't.'

'I didn't because I assumed it was either you or Mum!' Crystal interjected indignantly.

Nathan continued, 'I changed the locks on the house doors, so either someone left it unlocked or got a key from somewhere else.' They stared in silence at each other for a couple of minutes. Each trying to remember who was actually the last person to come into the house that night.

Recollection flashed into Crystal's mind and her hand flew to her mouth. Horror, mixed with guilt flashed across her face. 'It was me. I left it unlocked.'

'But you went to bed early.' Izzy replied.

'I went back out – later, after you'd gone to sleep.' Crystal looked down and scuffed the flower stand with the toe of her shoe.

'But why? Where did you go?' Izzy looked totally confused.

'I think I know.' Nathan looked at Crystal and shook his head slightly. 'It was you, wasn't it?'

Crystal refused to look at him.

'Will someone fill me in on what you're talking about?' The frustration was evident in Izzy's voice. She stood there with her hands on her hips, the single stem flower still in her hand.

'She's been going out healing sick people in the district. Haven't you, Crystal?'

'Are you insane? What if someone had seen you?' Izzy was horrified. She walked over to her daughter and placed her hands on Crystal's shoulders, shaking her slightly. 'You could've been putting yourself in danger – do you realise that. The Others could've found you; the person you were healing could've seen you. Oh my God!' She let go of her daughter's shoulders and put her hands to her head. 'What were you thinking?'

'I just wanted to help – to do some good with my abilities.' Crystal mumbled into her sweater.

'You're too valuable to put yourself in those kinds of positions – especially on your own.' Izzy took a deep breath in to calm herself down. 'Crystal, I of all people know what you're trying to do. Don't you think I want to help others? I'd love to heal those that are sick. But it's not safe for us to use our abilities for too long.' She turned to face Nathan, turning her anger on him.

'And you knew? You knew she was going out on her own, and you didn't think to say anything?'

'Hey, I'm not her father! It's your job to keep an eye on

your daughter, not mine. I didn't sign up to babysitting duties! And anyway, I didn't know for sure.' He shrugged. 'Well, I knew she was going out, but for all I know, she could've been meeting up with a fella.'

'It's your job to protect her though, isn't it?'

'Fair point.' He held his hands up, showing he was defeated and lowered his voice to a whisper. 'So, if Crystal left the door unlocked, I don't need to change the door locks again. But, it does beg the question – who were they and were they actually looking for the book?'

'Well, nothing was taken, so maybe it was a random burglary?' Crystal chipped in, hesitantly.

'No, it wasn't random. If nothing was taken, then something might've been put in.' Nathan kept his voice as a whisper but started to scour the shop.

'What are you looking for?' Crystal asked.

'He thinks the shop's been bugged.' Izzy whispered, signalling Crystal to lower her voice too. 'You search that side of the room and I'll search over here.' She signalled for Crystal to take the wall with the main window and door in, whilst she made her way to the back wall.

'Mum!' Crystal whispered, trying to get her mother's attention.

'What?'

'What do they look like?'

'Just look for something small and made of plastic or metal – something that doesn't belong.' Izzy whispered in reply.

'Use your brain, Crystal!' Nathan whispered exasperatedly. He made his way around the shelves behind the counter, before moving to the cash register. 'Hey!' he whispered, also clicking his fingers to get their attention. 'I've found something here.' He pointed to the underneath of the cash register, before holding his finger to his mouth. Nathan carried on looking around the counter.

A couple of minutes later, Crystal clicked her fingers and signalled to the side of the door frame that was nearest to the wall. Izzy shrugged, showing that she hadn't found anything. After they'd searched the rest of the shop, Nathan stood up and rolled his head side to side, to ease the muscles in his neck and shoulders. He sighed and returned his voice to a normal level. 'Well, I guess it was just a random stranger. I can't find anything to suggest otherwise.' He held his hand up to signal them to stop any objections, before waving it upwards to show he wanted them to say something in reply.

'Umm, no, I haven't found anything either.' Crystal replied.

'Maybe I just left the shop unlocked? Panic over.' Izzy replied. 'I guess I'll be going back into the house and put the kettle on. I haven't had any lunch yet either.' She pushed the latch down on the main door lock to lock it, before they filed out of the back door and into the garden.

'Wait. Before we go into the house, I want to say something.' Nathan stopped them in the garden. 'The chances are, if they've bugged the shop, they might've bugged downstairs – they wouldn't have had time to do upstairs and besides, coming into our rooms would've woken us up. From now on, we only speak about The Account out here, or in the bedrooms. It'll only be for a few days, until I can get hold of someone who knows how to do something with the bugs. So, in the meantime, act normal and stay calm.'

'Okay.' Izzy replied. Crystal just nodded. 'By the way.' Izzy turned to Crystal. 'What are you doing home? Did you decide to follow my advice?'

'Tony actually sent me home, as I didn't look too great.'

She stopped Izzy interrupting. 'I told him I was having some bad dreams and they were making me really tired.'

'He doesn't know what they're about, does he?'

'No. And it'd better stay that way.' Nathan interrupted, glaring at Crystal.

'I know! I said I wouldn't tell him.' Crystal replied sarcastically, raising her eyebrows and glaring back at him. 'But he is coming over later, so I have to think of something to say to him.'

'I'd quite like to meet him, face-to-face.' Nathan was still glaring at her.

'Mmm, we'll see.' Crystal replied, whilst thinking 'Not a chance!'

They all walked back into the house and Izzy set about making herself some lunch. 'Do you want some?' she turned and asked both of them.

'No, I'm fine thanks. I'm making a coffee; do you want a cup?' He started to fill the kettle.

'I'm going upstairs for a lie-down, before Tony gets here.' Crystal smiled at her mother and made her way up the stairs to her bedroom. Once inside, she spent ten minutes checking for listening devices, before realising there was no way the person she heard enter the house would've had long enough to do the whole house. She pulled the blind down on her window and retrieved The Account from its hiding place. She had been genuinely tired when she'd got home, but the fiasco in the shop had given her her second wind. There was no way she was going to go to sleep now, so she opened The Account and flicked through the pages.

The Others have made it nigh on impossible for people with abilities to meet now. They have converts in the government and other places of power, including police, schools, large corporations and several religious institutions. We are fighting back as best we can, but enlightened ones are few and far between and others who have abilities are too scared to congregate. One of the enlightened ones managed to infiltrate the ring in government, but his career was halted when scandal about a non-existent affair with an underage girl was broadcast. His murder was made to look like suicide.

I don't know how The Others manage to find out about us, but they always do. My advice is to find somewhere to run – anywhere that is safe – and stay there until the uprising. May light be with you.

Crystal flicked to the last few pages, to see what Father Javier had written.

I've been watching her for days. My role as the parish priest makes it easier to be around without actually being seen. She is the one – of that I am certain. Her aura is pure, brighter and whiter than I have ever seen. There is a certain amount of naivety about her, but she is so strong and there is also an air of assurance about her; the knowledge of how to fulfil her destiny is buried inside her mind, ready to be released. She is capable of fulfilling everything that she is destined to do – and so much more as well – she just has to open herself up to her true potential. I am honoured to have been the guardian at this final stage of the rebellion – and to have been the one to pass on The Account to its rightful owner. After this, The Others can do whatever they want with me – I have fulfilled my role and handed the baton on to the final player. For so long we have prayed, 'may light to be with you' – and now it is finally here.

Crystal put the book down on her bed and sank back

against her pillows. He had so much faith in her – he believed she could really do it. But it was more than that – he had no doubts whatsoever. Crystal stared up at the ceiling of her bedroom, letting it all sink in. He really believed in me, she thought. She rested her hand on The Account, enjoying the feelings currently rushing around her body. She was sad that he was no longer here to talk to; to thank for his kind words. This was mixed with guilt – the guilt in not having that much belief in herself. But mostly she felt anger. Anger for the words she had been reading, how much the world at large was ignorant of, the loss of someone who obviously really looked up to – and believed – in her, and finally, anger for all those people who had suffered as a result of the knowledge contained within the pages of this book.

She got up and grabbed her laptop.

'It all changes now.'

She sat down in the chair, pulled the lid open and clicked on the audio recording software icon. Hitting 'record', she started to speak.

'I am Angel and I have a message for you all. You're all living your life whilst half asleep. Your day to day existence is allowed, as long as you stay in blissful ignorance to the truth. I'm here to wake you up and open your eyes. The truth will set you free.'

Crystal played the audio back. Satisfied, she looked for a picture that could be used as a screen shot. She grinned as she found a picture of a burning book. I do believe you'd be perfect, she thought. She purchased the royalty free version and used it to turn her audio into a video. She then logged into the domain name she'd purchased yesterday and posted the video, before going over to the YouTube site and loading it there too. Sitting back against her chair she smiled, satisfied that she had taken a positive first step. She glanced back to The Account, remembering the kind words of Father Javier. Father Javier, I'm ready to do whatever is needed, she thought, before lying down on her bed and closing her eyes.

32

A gentle tapping on her bedroom door woke her. Crystal opened her eyes and glanced over at the clock, before sitting bolt upright on her bed.

I slept through dinner, she thought, before the persistent knocking on her door reminded her that someone was there. 'I'm coming!' she called rather groggily and struggled to her feet. Opening the door, she stood in the doorway staring blankly at Emily.

'Hi sleepyhead. Did you forget you'd invited me over?' Emily's face changed from one of happiness to concern as she checked the time on her watch. 'You did say half past six didn't you?'

'Crystal rubbed her eyes and stood back to let Emily in. 'I did. Sorry Emily, I lost track of time.'

'That's okay.' Emily walked past her and across to her bed. 'I'll just sit here so you can't go back to sleep.' She flung herself down onto the bed. 'Writing reports is *so* boring! I'm glad to get a change of scenery. Ouch!' As Emily sprawled flat onto her back, her head just narrowly missed the metal bedstead, but not the book currently taking up residence in the corner. Emily retrieved it from under her head and held it up. 'What's this, anything interesting?' Her voice was full of intrigue as she waved the book in the air above her head. 'Ooh, is it your diary?' She laughed as Crystal tried to snatch it from her, so Emily turned it over and moved it closer to her face. 'The Account. What's that then?'

Crystal couldn't decide whether to be mortified over leaving it out whilst she slept, or relieved that it was her best friend who'd found it. She opted for the latter. Her eyes made contact with Emily's – she didn't need to say anything. Emily stopped laughing and sat up, whilst Crystal walked over, closed her bedroom door and sat down next to Emily on the bed.

'You have to promise not to tell *anyone*.'

'Of course I won't! What is it?' Emily smiled at her.

'No, you really have to promise Emily. This is life and death – literally.' She caught Emily's attention and refused to break eye contact. 'This is even bigger than what I told you last time.'

'Is this to do with those Others that you were talking about? You know you can trust me, Crystal. I promise I won't breathe a word of it to anyone,' Emily replied solemnly.

Crystal untied the string and handed it to Emily. 'It's called The Account. I have to protect it as it's the only copy. It's the real story of man's origins and existence.' Emily gently opened the cover and flicked through the pages.

'And you can read this? What language is it written in?' She looked at Crystal in awe.

'It's written in Hebrew – and yes, I can read it.'

'I didn't know you studied Hebrew.' Emily frowned. 'So it's like the Bible then?'

Crystal shook her head. 'No, it's actually the *real* Bible. The one that's used around the world is actually a cover-up for this one. And I didn't know I could read Hebrew – until I turned twenty-one, then everything kind of woke up inside me, including the ability to learn things really quickly.'

Emily sat looking stunned for a few minutes. Crystal gave her the time needed to let the words sink in. The atmosphere weighed heavy on them both and Crystal tried not to hold her breath – worried that Emily might just freak out.

'So, you're saying that the Bible that churches use – and people like my dad – is a fake?' she asked quietly in a shaky voice. 'What about the people who work for those churches – do they know?'

'I guess the best way to explain it is it's a book of half-facts and half-truths. The Others don't want the real story getting out there, so the stories written in the Bible are written in such a way to keep The Others – along with mans' natural curiosity – happy. And I don't know who does and doesn't know at the moment. I do know that Father Javier knew – he helped me – he gave me this book. That's why The Others took him.'

'Do The Others know you have this book?' Emily bit her bottom lip.

'I'm not sure.'

'What will they do to you if they do know?'

'Honestly?' Crystal paused. 'They'll kill me – and anyone else who gets in the way.'

'Oh.' Emily frowned and looked at the floor. 'Can't you just give the book to someone else? Someone who's older; a soldier or something?' She looked anxiously at Crystal. 'I don't mean it the wrong way, but someone who can protect it and themselves?'

Crystal closed her eyes momentarily and took in a deep slow breath. 'I wondered the same thing.' She turned slightly and took hold of her friend's hands. 'But I'm the only one of my kind left. It's complicated, but you know when I last confided in you we talked about me healing people?'

Emily nodded.

'And remember I joked about the fact that if they woke up, they'd think I was an angel?'

'Emily nodded.

'Well I am an angel. Not in the conventional way, but traditional angels are only a half truth. You see, angels are not angelic beings, they're human and like normal other people, well as normal as they can be.' She realised she was wittering now, so shrugged her shoulders and tried to get back on track. 'Basically like everything else that's mentioned in the Bible it's a half truth. Angels are a cross between two half-bloods that live hidden amongst normal humans – a flyah and a healah.'

'So, how do you know that you the only one then, if there are others that live among us?'

'Because The Others killed all of the other angels.'

'Why?'

'The really short version? In The Account an angel is destined to bring enlightenment to the rest of the population, so The Others ordered a purge on all half-bloods – especially angels. So, as I'm the only angel left – that means the destiny is for me alone.'

Emily sat there, staring at Crystal and looking positively stunned.

'But there is good news.' Crystal kept her voice upbeat. 'There are others who can help. Others with abilities like mine.'

'So you've met them? And they'll help you?' Emily raised her head, her eyes full of hope.

'Yes and yes. See, it'll be fine.' Crystal tried to sound convincing.

'But you might still get hurt.' Crystal could see the hope fading from Emily's eyes.

'Yes, but then I could go outside and get run over by a bus tomorrow.' She squeezed Emily's hand. 'You could too.'

'But I don't want you to die.' Emily's eyes filled with tears.

'You daft cow. I'm not going anywhere. Not if I have my way.' Crystal put her arm around her friend and hugged her tightly. 'If you can't handle it, I'll understand. But if you want me to keep you up-to-date, I will.'

Emily sniffed and dug a tissue out of her jeans pocket. 'I want to help. Just tell me what to do.'

Crystal let her shoulders relax and let the air she was holding in her lungs escape. 'I'm glad I have you as my friend, I really am.' She let go of her hand and got her laptop. 'Actually, there is something you can help me with.' Crystal pulled up the video file. 'I've decided, as it's my job to enlighten everyone, to set up a website, as well as social media accounts. I'm going to post video clips everywhere, so I know it's not much, but you could help me with that – and spreading the news about all of this.' Crystal pointed to The Account.

'I can do that, not a problem.' Emily smiled, before screwing her face up slightly. 'So if you're a cross between a healah and a flyah, I'm guessing your dad is a flyah then? I know your mum must be the healer, as she heals things, but I just put that down to the healing energy therapy, you know, the reiki that she learnt.'

'Yeah, my dad's a flyah. He can come back to be with us, if I complete what I'm supposed to do. At the moment he's staying away to try to help keep us safe.' She glanced across at Emily. 'He sent Nathan to protect us, as he's a flyah too.'

'Really? You mean he can really fly? Why hasn't he got wings?' Emily's eyes were like huge blue saucers.

'He has got wings. So have I, but The Others have blocked us from seeing them. I'm still slightly puzzled by it all, but I think it's along the lines of - you cannot easily believe in something you can't see. They figured that if you couldn't see your wings, you'd have to trust that they were there – and most people wouldn't have that much faith in themselves.'

'So, if you can't see them, how do you know you have them?'

'When I fly I can feel the weight on my back, can feel my shoulder muscles moving. It's kinda weird.'

Emily picked up The Account. 'Will you read some of this out to me?'

'Yeah, if you want.' Crystal opened the book at random and started to read.

Now the purge is complete, Interbreeding has been forbidden. Anyone breaking this rule is swiftly found and dealt with – usually taken to serve The Others in a work on other planets – or rounded up and kept somewhere until needed. The Others have ordered the flyahs to be ever watchful of the healahs, as they are the pivotal point – they have love at their very core. They are the only ones who can turn a flyah, or more rarely a digah, and open them up to persuasion and love. Once love enters their hearts, it is hard to turn off – their loyalty is then to that healah. The only way The Others can turn them back to their designated role is to swiftly deal with the healah. It's easier with flyahs, as their usual role is quite neutral-based. Digahs are harder, as they have heavy-based emotions at their core. As The Others have found out, kill their healah and, if their loyalty isn't quickly turned back to The Others, you run the risk of turning them into a dark, vengeance-filled monster. Full-bloods mate for life – The Others don't understand why, but we know it's because once you have love filling your heart, it can help you overcome, and become, anything you want.

'They're not really very nice, these Others, are they?'

'No, and that's why we have to let all of this be known to the world at large.' Crystal's phone lit up and vibrated. 'Shit! I forgot Tony was coming over.' She looked up guiltily at Emily before looking around at her slightly untidy room and remembering the possibility of listening devices downstairs. 'Maybe I'll meet him outside and we'll go to a pub.'

Emily dismissed Crystal's concern with a wave of her hand. 'Don't worry about me, and don't stay cooped up inside. Go out and have some fun – you really need it with everything you're dealing with at the moment. I'll go home.' She tried her best to hide her disappointment.

'If you're sure you're okay with that?' Crystal pleaded with her. 'I'm really sorry. I was looking forward to spending time catching up with you, but I don't get to see him that much.'

'Don't worry about it. We can catch up another time. I told mum I'd be out all evening, so I'll just see if Mark's home and go over there.' Emily took her phone out of her bag and started to type out a text, while Crystal rushed around getting changed and putting on some make-up.

Emily's phone pinged to indicate she'd received a reply to her text. 'It's fine. Mark's home, so I'll head over there. I'll walk out with you when Tony picks you up.'

'Okay.' Crystal nodded. 'So, rain-check on our girly catch

up? I'll text you when I've got some time free, if you're okay with that?'

'Yeah, no worries.' Emily pointed to The Account. 'Does that need to go somewhere safe?'

'It certainly does.' Crystal took a calming deep, slow breath. 'I need to get my act together.' She picked up the book and put it in the usual hiding place. 'You're the only one that knows where it is. If anything ever happens, and you need to get it...'

'I won't tell anyone where it is – and nothing's going to happen.' Emily placed a reassuring hand on her friend. 'I have faith in you.' She held a fist over her mouth as she fake-coughed. 'Well, I'll have more faith in you when you've learnt to kick some ass!'

Crystal gave her a quick hug. 'You're the best!' They both turned as the front door bell rang.

'I'll grab that for you, on my way out.' Emily volunteered. 'Text me when you get a second and I'll see you soon.' She walked out the bedroom, leaving Crystal to finish getting ready. Emily made her way downstairs, smiling as she opened the door to Tony. Looking up, her eyes met his.

'Oh, I was expecting Crystal.' He smiled at Emily, his blue eyes staring, his white teeth gleaming.

'She'll be down in a second. I'm Emily.' She held her hand out and Tony took hold of her hand. His grip was strong and he continued to lock eyes with her, until Emily broke both eye and hand contact. She glanced behind her, relieved that Crystal was coming down the stairs, before muttering 'I have to go.' She turned and walked quickly away, rubbing her hands together and shivering into her coat.

Tony watched her walk away then turned to smile at Crystal. 'Glad to see you're looking much better. Are you going to let me in?' He took a step forward, but Crystal stepped outside and pulled the door shut behind her.

'I thought we could go out. I've been cooped up all afternoon and could do with some fresh air.' Crystal smiled up at him, but let the smile drop from her face as she saw his jaw momentarily clench. She placed a hand on his arm, feeling the tension in his arm muscles. 'You don't mind, do you?'

Tony shook his head and patted the hand resting on his arm. 'No it's fine. I just thought I might get to meet your mum.'

Crystal was relieved to feel his arm muscle relax under her touch and her heart warmed. 'That's so sweet. You actually want to meet my mum. Maybe you can another time. I want you all to myself at the moment.' She squeezed his arm and smiled up at him. Tony stepped forward and opened the car door for her. 'Your carriage awaits.' He half-bowed as she stepped into the car and he closed the door gently behind her. Crystal couldn't see his face as he walked around to the other side of the car, but was relieved to see that he was still smiling when he got into the driver's seat.

'I know a really nice quiet pub we can go to. It's only half an hour's drive.' He turned the key and started the car. 'You can tell me all about your bad dreams over a drink and something to eat.' He didn't look at her as they pulled away. Crystal was relieved, as he didn't see the flash of guilt cross her face – and it also gave her time to think up something to say to him.

33

'Are you all right? You seem miles away.' Mark gave Emily a friendly nudge with the shoulder he had closest to her.

'Sorry.' She turned and smiled at him before sighing and looking around the den. 'I guess I am, slightly.'

'Anything you want to talk about?' Mark shifted round to face her on the sofa.

'Thanks, but no, it's fine.' She frowned slightly.

'Did you hurt yourself?' Mark took hold of her hand, examining it for cuts and bruises.

'No, why? What are you looking for?' She laughed and took her hand back from him.

'Just checking. You've been rubbing your right hand since you got here.'

'Have I? I didn't realise.' Shocked, Emily glanced down at her hand again, then shook her head and laughed. 'It's nothing really. I met Crystal's boss earlier. He was picking her up to go out.' She looked across at him. 'I didn't like him.'

'Why, what's he like?'

Emily frowned. 'He's blond, tall, good looking.' She shrugged. 'Your typical stereotypical American – white teeth, tan and square jaw.'

'Oh, so 'I don't like him' actually means 'I fancied him'.' Mark prodded her slightly in the ribs. Emily's head swung round to face him and she glared at him. 'No, it doesn't. I *really* didn't like him.'

'Okay. Calm down, I was only joking with you. What didn't you like about him?'

Emily shook her head, frowning to herself and absent-mindedly rubbing her hand while she tried to think of a rational explanation. 'I really don't know. He just didn't feel right. I mean, I didn't get a nice feeling from him. If you know what I mean.'

He put his hand over hers, catching her attention and making her realise she was rubbing her hand again. 'Sometimes people are like that. There are some you instantly like, others you don't. Don't worry about it.'

'You're probably right.' Emily ran her hand through her blonde curls. 'That's enough focusing on him, let's put the TV on and watch a film.' She picked his arm up and draped it around her neck, before wiggling down into the sofa and snuggling into his armpit.

Mark picked up the remote and turned the TV on, before selecting a film from the 'On Demand' section. They sat in mutual silence – Mark engrossed in the film, Emily occupied by her thoughts. Presently she sighed and sat up.

'Do you want a drink? I'm going to go and grab a cup of tea or something. I'm getting a slight headache.'

'I'll come with you if you want?' Mark paused the film and went to stand up, but Emily stopped him.

'No really, don't worry. I'm more than capable of getting a couple of drinks and some paracetamol, besides, you're enjoying the film.' She bent down and kissed him first on the forehead, then slowly on his lips. 'Don't worry about pausing it, carry on watching. I'll be back in a bit.'

Emily made her way down the stairs and out of the garage. She spent a couple of minutes just stood outside in the garden, breathing in the fresh air. The family dog, Oscar, a scruffy Norfolk terrier, came and sat at her feet, so Emily sat down next to him, absentmindedly stroking his ears, whilst he licked her arm. She closed her eyes and took several slow, deep breaths in. The night air felt good as she inhaled and, shortly she felt her headache easing slightly.

Finally, Emily opened her eyes and stood up, slightly embarrassed to realise that Kitty had been watching her from the kitchen window. She wiped the dust from her jeans and went to join Kitty inside.

Kitty was stood by the kettle, with her back to the door when Emily walked in. 'Do you want a cup?' she asked, without looking round.

Emily pulled a chair out and sat down at the kitchen table. 'Yes please.' Oscar swiftly jumped onto her lap, so she continued stroking his ears.

Kitty nodded. The only sound you could hear was the kettle. Kitty made them both a drink and placed Emily's in front of her, before sitting down in the opposite chair and taking a sip from her cup.

'Is everything okay, Emily?' Kitty peered at her from over the top of her cup.

'Yeah.' Emily looked down at Oscar. 'Thanks for the tea. I have a slight headache though; do you have any paracetamol?' Emily rubbed her temples, frowning slightly. Kitty got up and retrieved a couple of tablets from the medicine box in the corner cupboard. She filled a glass with water and handed them to Emily.

'Thank you.' Emily looked up at Kitty and took the glass and tablets. She swallowed them and downed the glass of water.

'You're welcome.' Kitty sat back down and took a sip of her tea. The silence stretched on for a few more minutes.

Emily finally looked up. 'Mark's watching a boring film, so I thought I'd come in and keep you company.'

'Thanks. I like having female company. The house is usually full of males.'

'You don't mind do you?' Emily looked up, slightly panicked.

'Of course not. You're always welcome here, whether Mark is here or not. I've told you that.' She smiled across at Emily.

Emily leant across the table, staring down at her cup. 'You've been friends with Izzy since you were little, haven't you?'

'I have. We've been friends since our very first day at nursery.' She continued sipping tea from her cup, her eyes focused on Emily. 'Your mum and Mandy were friends at school too. They were four years above us, but we all kind of blended together nicely.'

'So you're Izzy's best friend, like I am with Crystal?'

'I guess I am.' Kitty smiled to herself. 'Is there something you wanted to ask about her?'

Emily quickly shook her head. 'No, of course not. I just...' She paused to rephrase the question. 'I know everything about Crystal, that's what best friends do, don't you think?'

Kitty nodded but stayed silent.

'I tell her about me and Mark, she tells me about her and Tony, we know each other's favourite foods, colours and everything. I tell her secrets I wouldn't tell anyone else.' Emily paused, knowing she was rambling, but needing to vent her thoughts. 'I *know* all Crystal's secrets too.' She looked up to see if Kitty's' facial reactions gave anything away. Her expression stayed blank, so Emily continued – her eyes locked with Kitty's. 'I'd help her with *anything* she needed my help with – you could say we're *accountable* to each other.'

Kitty broke eye contact. 'That's good. She's lucky to have someone like you as her best friend.' She took another sip of her tea and stared straight at Emily, their eyes locked together again. 'As Izzy is with me. It's something we *don't* need to talk about – we just *know*. I'm sure you understand.'

Emily nodded. 'I think I do. There is one thing I haven't told Crystal though. She looked up at Kitty again. 'I don't like her boss, boyfriend, whatever you want to call him. I don't know why I don't like him, I just don't.'

Kitty leant forward. 'How many times have you met him?'

'Just the once.' She dropped her gaze, and then looked up with renewed determination. 'I know it sounds completely irrational, but he just doesn't *feel* right.'

'No, I get it. You should always go with your gut feeling, Emily. Remember that.'

Emily nodded and stood up. Oscar jumped off her lap and sat on the floor, whining at her. 'Thanks for the tea – and for listening. I'd better be getting back to Mark. He'll be wondering where I've got to.'

'You're welcome. I hope the headache eases.' She paused before continuing. 'And remember, Emily, you can talk to me anytime. About *anything*.' They both stared at each other for a few seconds. Realisation hitting both of them; knowing they were on the same wavelength.

'Thanks Kitty.' Emily turned to go before looking down

at Oscar. 'You coming, boy?' She smiled at Kitty, lightly tapped her leg and walked out of the kitchen.

Kitty watched her walk back into the garage before picking up her phone and dialling.

'Hi, it's me. I think we may have a problem.'

34

'So, now you're feeling a bit better, do you want to talk about it?' Tony asked.

'This place is really pretty.' Crystal looked around the interior of the pub. There was a huge fireplace at the far end of the room. The tub chairs were chocolate brown and the lighting was subdued. She stared at the light glowing from the bulb of the converted oil lamp on their table. 'It's nothing really.' Crystal leant back in her chair, hands cupped around a pint glass filled with vodka, Red Bull and orange juice. 'How'd you find out about this place? It's rather tucked away.' She glanced up at him, her head tilted slightly.

'You'll be amazed at some of the places I know about in this area.' He leant back into his seat, grinning slightly to himself and closed his eyes. 'This place is one of my favourites. I like the ambience.'

Crystal looked up to find his blue eyes staring right back at her.

'What?' she said, somewhat defensively.

He shook his head. 'Nothing. I just thought you were all set to tell me about your bad dreams.'

'I never said they were bad.' She looked down.

'Well, I assume they're not good – if they've been affecting your sleep.' He watched her trying her hardest not to bite her nails. 'I let you go home early as I was concerned about you. Maybe I don't like feeling used.' His voice was steady and even.

Crystal shot her head up. 'I haven't used you!'

'I didn't say you had. I just said it felt that way.' He tried to placate her. 'Maybe if you talked about what's bothering you, I could help.'

She realised he wasn't going to give up. Time to lie to him then, she thought. 'Well, I keep dreaming about clowns. They're chasing me and get me holed up in a tiny, dark, damp smelling room. It's dark and there's one the other side of the door.' She looked up from under her eyelashes to see if he believed her. His face was expressionless. 'One of them walks in the door and I know he's going to kill me.' She shook her head and looked up. 'See, I told you it was nothing really, just a couple of silly phobias that have been playing havoc with my mind. I can't help it, I've always been afraid of clowns and the dark.' She quickly took a swig of her drink and averted her eyes.

He stayed silent, staring at her. After a couple of minutes, she guessed he was satisfied with her answer, as he changed the subject.

'Well I'm glad you're feeling better.' He raised his glass and toasted her. 'Now, let's grab a table in the dining area and see what's on the menu. He got up and had a quick word with the waitress, before they were shown to a secluded table for two, in the corner of the dining area.

Crystal took her seat and looking at the menu, she

started to relax, knowing that Tony wasn't giving her any grief over her dreams.

The meal passed without incident, the conversation and wine free-flowing, the food exquisite – which was understandable, once Crystal realised they were actually being catered for by a Michelin Star chef. They ordered dessert and sat back in their respective chairs, staring at each other. Tony was the first to speak.

'Oh, I almost forgot.' He rummaged in the inside jacket pocket of his long, woollen outer coat, before his hand re-emerged with a square, flat, red cardboard box. He slid it across the table to Crystal.

'I wasn't planning on giving you this tonight, but maybe this will help take your mind off those nasty dreams.'

'Thank you.' Crystal sat forward in her chair, looking quite shocked. She untied the golden cloth ribbon that was holding the box closed, and lifted off the lid.

'It's beautiful, Tony!' she gasped as she lifted the red velvet cushion out of the box. Inside was an anklet comprising of a silver chain and several black stones. Crystal held it up to the light, moving the chain around in her hand to watch the light dancing off the stones.

'What are the stones?'

Tony sat back to let the waitress place their dessert plates down on the table. He watched her go, before answering.

'I'm not sure, but I was reliably informed that they would help 'guide and protect you through your dreams.' He opened his eyes wide and waved his fingers to illustrate the mystery of the stones. 'Well, that's what the shop assistant told me at any rate.'

Crystal got up and walked round the table to give him a

kiss. 'Thank you, it's beautiful.' She sat back down and put it back in the box.

'You're not going to put it on then?' He sounded slightly disappointed. 'Do you not like it?'

'I love it, honestly! But I'm wearing ankle boots at the moment. I promise to wear suitable footwear next time, so I can show it off.' She lifted her jean leg slightly, showing her boot to collaborate her reasoning.

'Just promise me you'll wear it.' he begged her, looking across the table – his eyes pleading with her. He reached across the table and touched her hand. 'Promise me.'

'I'll put it on tomorrow and never take it off.' She smiled back at him and placed her hand over his. Feeling his signet ring under her fingers, she examined it closely, before exclaiming, 'Look, you have one of the same stones in your ring!'

Tony looked surprised. 'I can't say I noticed. How observant of you.' He pulled his hand out from under hers and lifted his dessert fork, scooping up a piece of his lemon meringue pie. 'Good.' he mumbled through a mouthful of pie. 'I mean, this pie is good.' He swallowed and took a sip of his wine. 'How's yours?'

'It's lovely. And so is the pie.' She placed a hand on the red box. 'It's been a perfect evening.'

'I'm glad you approve, anything to keep you happy. So no more bad dreams about clowns then.' He looked at her from over the top of his wine glass.

∾

Izzy heard the car pull up outside and rushed up to the window. Peering from behind the curtain, she saw Crystal undo her seatbelt and lean across to kiss Tony. Izzy let the curtain go and hurried to the front door, opening it just as Crystal got out of the car.

'Evening hun.' She waved at Crystal and started to walk down the garden path.

Crystal waved back. 'Everything okay Mum?'

'Yes, fine thank you. Did you have a nice time? I was hoping to meet Tony this time, but was busy in the shop when you left earlier.' Izzy walked down the path towards Crystal whilst she talked. She reached the gate as Crystal shut the car door behind her. Izzy smiled at her daughter and leant her head to one side, trying to catch a glance of Tony through the side window, but the car had already started pulling away. She sighed. 'Maybe next time then?'

Crystal linked her arm through her mother's and walked with her back to the house. 'I had a lovely evening. We had a wonderful dinner, cooked by a Michelin chef and Tony bought me a beautiful silver anklet.' She closed the door behind them and took her coat off. 'Look.' She took the box out of her bag and showed the jewellery to her mother. 'He said the shop assistant said the stones would help me with my dreams.'

'It certainly is beautiful.' Izzy gently touched the black stones. 'Did he say what the stones are?'

'He didn't know. But isn't it pretty? He said the stones are meant to protect me during my sleep.' Crystal put the lid back on the box. 'He's so generous – and thoughtful.' Crystal shrugged her shoulders, a big beaming smile spread right across her face. She leant forward and kissed her mother on the cheek. 'I'm going to go straight to bed, as I'm knackered. Night, love you!'

Izzy watched her go up the stairs. The anklet certainly is pretty, she thought, It would be interesting to find out what the stones are though. She sighed and laughed slightly, shaking her head in disbelief. 'Stop worrying Izzy and let Crystal live her own life. She has a right to some fun, after all she's learning.' She was still shaking her head as she turned the lights out and headed up to her bed.

35

The imposing structure was lit up like a Christmas tree on Nathan's second visit. It was like a lighthouse on a rocky cliff edge on a dark night. But, rather than warning them to steer clear, it seemed to be begging them to come closer – inviting them inside. They used the shadows, created by the uplighters lighting up the Victorian house, as cover. The garden was in darkness, as it was when Nathan was last here.

Nathan, with Richard and Martin following behind, ducked under the large downstairs windows, making his way back round past the patio doors and to the set of steps he'd gone down on his last visit. The van was gone and no other vehicles were parked anywhere on the property – they'd checked prior to making their way towards the house. Pausing at the top of the steps, Nathan glanced up, checking to see if there was a hint that anyone might be watching them. Satisfied they weren't being watched, he retraced his steps down the five steps and through the plain, heavy wooden door. Richard and Martin followed silently behind and into the dimly lit corridor.

Nathan had previously warned them to be alert for any symptoms they might feel – including the electrical charge and heaviness of breath – symptoms they'd feel if the dark angel was there. Once Richard had closed the door quietly behind them, Nathan turned and silently asked the question by shrugging his shoulders. They both shook their heads to indicate that they didn't feel anything out of the ordinary. They walked past the unlit rooms along the corridor and followed the corridor around the left turn at its end. Nathan signalled to show that the two rooms at the far end were the ones they were headed for. He signalled again to show he wanted them to stay put and crept his way towards the room on the right first. He was glad to see that it was empty this time. He realised he'd been holding his breath, so he let out a sigh before making his way to the first one – the one that had previously housed Father Javier.

The digahs that had previously been guarding Father Javier had long gone. Unfortunately, Father Javier hadn't. His body lay in a heap on the floor, surrounded by a pool of his own blood. His arm was bent at a right-angle to his body. Where his face should've been there was just a bloody mess – his skin beaten until it resembled raw hamburger. Nathan closed his eyes and held his hand over his mouth in an effort to stop himself being sick. He backed out of the room and closed the door quietly behind him. He turned and met Martin's enquiring gaze before slowly shaking his head.

'He's dead. There's no one else in there.' He kept his voice neutral and at a normal speaking level.

Richard took a step forward but Martin, taking note of how pale Nathan looked, stopped him. 'Son, I don't think you want to go in there.'

Richard shrugged him off. 'Dad, I'm not a child; I'm twenty-four years old. I can handle it.' He glared furiously at his father and took a step forwards. Martin lifted his hand to restrain his son, but Nathan blocked him, letting Richard carry on walking into the room. 'Martin, he's gonna have to get used to seeing dead bodies,' he said quietly.

'I know, but it's bad in there, isn't it.' He looked at Nathan, not really needing confirmation on that statement, then shook his head in disappointment when he heard his son retching on the other side of the door. Nathan let go of Martin's arm and let him go to comfort him.

'I'm all right Dad!' Nathan could hear Richard protest furiously, followed by Nathan's calming voice. 'It's ok son, come with me - let's get you out of here.'. As they came out of the room Richard glared at Nathan, whilst he wiped his mouth clean.

'You could've warned me, you bastard!' His head was lowered, but Nathan could see his eyes boring holes into him from under his fringe.

'Oi, watch your language!' Martin cuffed his son swiftly round the head.

Nathan shrugged. 'You wouldn't have listened even if I had.'

Richard grunted and rubbed his head, before grudgingly replying. 'Yeah, I suppose you're right.'

Nathan laughed. 'You're quite the awkward little gobshite aren't you?'

'Yeah, I suppose I am.' He puffed his chest out slightly and relaxed his shoulders – the tense atmosphere broken.

'So, do we just leave – or take it with us?' Martin looked back towards the room.

'We'll have to leave it or they'll know we've been here.' Nathan rubbed his chin, thinking through their options. 'Hang on a minute.' He disappeared back into the room and returned with Father Javier's' cross hanging from his finger.

'If any of his family are still alive, they deserve to have something of his returned to them.' He used his shirt to wipe it clean then gently let it fall into the palm of his hand before placing it in his jeans pocket. Looking back up he added, 'It's the least we can do.'

He turned and walked back along the corridor, retracing their steps. When they got to the door he pushed it open and walked back into the darkened garden, giving his eyes a second or two to adjust to the darkness.

It took him a further couple of seconds to realise it was actually in total darkness. The uplighters that were lighting up the house when they went into the basement had been turned off.

'We're not alone. There's someone here.' He scanned the garden in front of them. He couldn't see anyone – but he could smell them. The earthy smell of digahs assaulted his heightened senses. He glanced back and noticed that Richard and Martin had come to the same conclusion. All three of them broke into a run, away from the house and towards the tree line at the edge of the grounds. Martin managed a quick glance backwards.

'We've got four digahs on our tail!' he shouted.

'Do we stop and fight them?' Richard replied breathlessly.

'Shut up and run!' was Martin's reply.

'We could fly.' Richard suggested.

Nathan glanced back to see how much of a head start they had. To make flying possible they needed a couple of seconds lead to enable them to focus their attention. They didn't have enough time for that. Ah shit! Man I'm out of practice, he thought, as he slowed his pace to a trot, giving himself time to catch his breath.

He stopped and turned to face the stocky guys currently

charging at them. 'It's a bit early, but fuck it – let's get this party started.' He clenched and unclenched his fists. 'I may be out of practice, but I sure know how to fight.'

Richard and Martin stopped running and walked back to stand by Nathan's side – Martin rolled his head from side to side and Richard cracked his knuckles. All three were standing with legs slightly apart, bodies crouched – coiled springs ready for action.

The four digahs stopped running and let their arms drop to their sides. The one in front let a slow grin spread across his face whilst the other three fanned out. They liked nothing more than a good punch-up –it was in their nature.

They stood, battle lines drawn, eyeing each other up. The three flyahs might have the height advantage – but the digahs had brute strength. Nathan and the digah directly in front of him eyeballed each other for a couple of seconds before the digah lowered his head and charged. Nathan landed on the cold grass, completely winded but he'd managed to draw back his fist and make contact with the digahs ribs just before he landed, so they both took valuable seconds recovering. Nathan jabbed the digah under the ribs again – knocking him to the side and off Nathan. Springing to his feet, Nathan managed to give him a hefty kick in the stomach – followed by another swift kick into his groin. The digah curled up in the foetal position; hands nursing his privates.

Nathan looked over and saw Richard kicking the downed digah that had been assigned to him. He gave a brief nod of appreciation for how the younger flyah was handling himself. The remaining two digahs had mistak-enly honed in on Martin – one held onto his arms whilst the other one pummelled his stomach. Nathan ran over and grabbed the restrainee by the neck, using his arm muscle to dig into his windpipe. He let go of Martin focused on getting Nathan of off his back – flailing his arms wildly around in an effort to grab him – but giving Martin a chance to retaliate to the one punching his stomach.

Unbeknown to Nathan, the original digah on the ground had recovered enough to get up. He pounced on Nathan, dragging him – and the digah Nathan was hanging on to – to the ground, before swinging back his boot and aiming a hefty kick towards Nathan's side. He managed to move out of the way, but in doing so, he let go of the digah's neck, enabling him to turn around and punch Nathan in the jaw. Nathan's teeth clattered together and his head ricocheted off the ground. He momentarily closed his eyes in pain, but managed to swing his fist, and it made a satisfying crunch on his opponent's chin. The digah roared in pain and lunged at Nathan. He opened his eyes in time to see the digah's furious face, before he sank his teeth into Nathan's right shoulder.

Nathan shrieked as the digah's teeth went through his t-shirt and grazed his skin. Nathan tried to aim a punch with his slightly less effective left arm, but completely missed his target. The digah sank his teeth in for a second time. This time he succeeded in ripping Nathan's flesh – he shrieked in agony and tightly closed his eyes against the pain, when suddenly he felt the weight of the digah ease on his chest. He opened his eyes and was relieved to see that Martin had hold of the digah by his hair – Richard was kicking the shit out of the other one. Martin let the digah go and he scurried off, back towards the house, collecting his comrades on the way. Richard watched them go as he wiped his hand against his bloody mouth and spat on the ground. 'And don't fucking come back!' he hollered after them, raising his fist in the air – full of youthful victory and bravado.

Martin helped Nathan to his feet – Martin wincing over the exertion. 'We're getting a bit too old for all this shit, aren't we?' He let go of Nathan's hand and held his arm gingerly around his sore ribs.

Nathan pulled himself to a seated position and hung his head between his knees. 'You might just be right.' He spat some blood out of his mouth, wiped it with the back of his hand and struggled to his feet. Richard walked over to join them, and all three of them stood staring back at the house. It was still in darkness with no visible signs of anyone ever being there – the digahs had disappeared into the night.

Martin placed his arm on Nathan's shoulder. 'It's a long way to walk back, although we can if you need to – but are you capable of flying?'

Nathan rolled his head from side to side. His neck made a few quiet cracks and he proceeded to roll his shoulders, testing how painful it was. He winced. It hurt like hell, but he'd live. 'I think I can manage a short flight.'

They stood grouped together for a couple of minutes while they gathered their thoughts and focused their minds. Richard, being the youngest and quickest to recover, was first to leave the ground – followed by his father – who glanced down to make sure Nathan could manage to leave the ground. Nathan checked his pockets, making sure he still had Father Javier's metal cross, before he placed his hands parallel with the ground and gently rose into the air.

Crystal woke early after a particularly refreshing night's sleep – which she thankfully attributed to the shiny black stones evenly spaced around her anklet. Reaching down to the floor, she dragged her laptop up onto her lap. Sitting upright in bed, she set about recording another few short audio clips. She listened to the end result, checking for clarity.

'I am Angel and I have a message for you all. You're being fed lies on a daily basis. These lies are told by those in positions of authority – people in government, religion and even in the companies you work for. You are capable of *so* much, more than you *ever* thought possible. But *they* want to keep you in blissful ignorance – and totally submissive. Remember your potential. The truth will set you free. '

Satisfied with the results, she emailed them to Emily for editing – she would also be able to add the fixed picture and upload them to both the website and YouTube.

She glanced across at the clock at the bottom of her laptop screen, before spending another ten minutes working on the website layout. When the clock reached

7am, she grudgingly closed the lid and swung her legs out of bed.

By seven-forty Crystal was downstairs eating her breakfast cereal. She looked up as the back door opened and Nathan walked in.

'Don't you ever sleep?' She frowned at him. Nathan ran his hand through his hair, making it look even messier than usual.

'In the words of Bon Jovi, I'll sleep when I'm dead.' He walked over and flicked the kettle switch on.

'Spent the night anywhere interesting?' She continued eating her cereal, her eyes focusing on his bruised knuckles.

'The usual. I was with Richard and Martin, scouting around the neighbourhood.' He poured the boiling water into a mug and the smell of coffee filled the room.

'What are you scouting for?'

Nathan sat down at the table. He looked shattered. His skin was pale and taut, highlighting the dark circles under his eyes. He rubbed the stubble on his chin.

'We're keeping the area safe, that's all you need to worry about.' He shrugged his coat off, wincing slightly as he moved his arms.

'You're hurt!' Crystal got to her feet. 'Let me have a look.'

Nathan held his hand up. 'Don't worry about it. You need to go to work.'

She hesitated. 'But I can help.'

'No offence meant, but I'd rather wait for your mother. You need to save your energy.'

Crystal roughly pushed her chair back under the table before clattering her bowl into a slot in the dishwasher. 'Fine. Suit yourself.' she replied and stomped out of the room.

Nathan waited until she'd gone upstairs before he

gingerly undid a couple of his shirt buttons and peeled it back from his right shoulder, revealing a wad of white gauze to the right of his collar bone. He peeled the tape away and inspected the wound. The skin around the bite had gone an angry pinkish-red colour, the edges of the wound jagged and angry – the teeth marks were clearly evident.

He stood up and, holding his arm around his bruised ribs, he reached to get the medicine box out of the cupboard. He wasn't sure how long it would be before he saw Izzy, so he swallowed a couple of painkillers and redressed the wound. He was doing up his shirt buttons when Crystal walked back into the kitchen.

'Are you sure you don't want me to look at that?' She nodded in the direction of his shoulder.

'No, I expect I'll see your mother at some stage today – I'll last until then.'

Crystal pulled on her coat and wrapped a purple scarf around her neck. 'Oh, I almost forgot. Mum's gone to get her flowers from the market – she always does on Fridays – she'll be back in about an hour or so. See you later.' Crystal walked out of the back door and disappeared off to work.

'Okay – bye.' Nathan called after her sarcastically. He got up and went to the living room. Lying down on the sofa, he gingerly made himself comfortable and closed his eyes. God, I'm so tired! Maybe I can catch an hours sleep or so, before Izzy gets home, he thought wistfully. He opened one eye briefly, just to check what the time was, before letting sleep take over his battered body.

He didn't know how long he'd been asleep for, but as he was coming round he realised he wasn't alone. He opened his eyes and shot to his feet in one swift movement – fists raised at the ready.

'Woah there!' Izzy held her hands in front of her, partly

to protect herself and partly to try and placate Nathan. 'It's only me, Nathan.'

He fell back onto the sofa, groaning. The exertion had not only hurt his already bruised body, but had also caused the gash on his shoulder to start bleeding again.

'You're hurt – take your shirt off and let me have a look at the damage.' Nathan undid the buttons and Izzy helped him remove his upper garments. 'Lie down on the sofa and let me look. Is this the only wound?' She knelt down next to him and peeled back the gauze, sitting back on her heels she looked at him, noting the bruises on his ribs and knuckles, the worry evident in her voice. 'What the hell have you been up to?'

'I went out with Richard and Martin, back to the house where they were keeping Father Javier.' He closed his eyes as Izzy placed her hands on his ribcage. Her hands warmed and shortly the orange glow changed to yellow. It was the calmest he'd felt for months. The euphoria of her healing energy coursed through his body, soothing every cell, reaching his very core. His mind exploded into a myriad of colours – blue, green, purple and white – like bolts of coloured lightning flashing against the darkness of his closed eyelids. Finally, the glow from Izzy's hands turned to white and the adrenaline high he got from the pure energy and love racing around his body caused him to feel invincible.

Nathan lay there with his eyes closed for several minutes after Izzy had finished. He let the feelings invading his body naturally subside to a manageable level before opening his eyes and turning to thank her.

'You always were an amazing healer.' He smiled slowly at her, before letting the smile drop slightly. 'We found Father Javier – but we were too late.' He stood up and stretched, checking that he was in full working order again. 'I thought his family should have this.' He pulled the metal cross and chain out of his pocket. 'Maybe it will help them find some closure – when we can finally find them to give it to them, that is.'

'That's a really nice gesture.' Izzy sat on the chair, waiting for her energy levels to return to normal. 'You might want to ground yourself. I had to give you quite a blast.' She closed her eyes and visualised closing off her energy before imagining the lower half of her body being tethered to the centre of the earth with lots of tiny red strands; Strands that were weaving and burying themselves into the ground like the roots of a tree, grounding and stabilising her.

Nathan sat back down and placed his feet flat on the floor, doing the same visualisation. After a couple of minutes, he opened his eyes, as did Izzy. She turned to face him. 'So, who were you fighting?'

'Digahs. They jumped out on us as we were leaving the building.' He looked down, deciding whether or not to tell her the rest of the story. He looked up, straight across at Izzy. 'I didn't tell you the other day, but last time I was at the house I felt the presence of a dark angel.'

Izzy's face paled slightly. 'Here in Thatcham?' She held her hand to her mouth. 'That can only mean one thing, right?'

'I don't know if it's a coincidence or not, but it doesn't necessarily mean that he's looking for Crystal.' He kept his voice even and calm. 'Besides, I won't let any harm come to her, you know that. I swore my allegiance to you and Samuel the day she was born – I'm not going to go back on that now. He'd have to kill me first.'

'Did he kill Father Javier?'

Nathan shook his head. 'He was beaten to a pulp by the digahs. I don't think they needed any extra help.'

'Poor Father Javier. I hope he's at peace now. When this has all calmed down, we must make an effort to find his family and give them his necklace and some closure. They knew his fate was marked the minute he was old enough to take on the role of the Guardian, but at the very least, they'd want to mourn him.' She pointed to the cross. 'And that can be passed to the next in line.'

Nathan put the cross back into his jeans pocket. 'It'll be interesting to see who the next Father of the parish will be. We were lucky to have someone inside that'd infiltrated the religious community – it will be difficult, if not impossible, to hope that his replacement will be sympathetic to our cause.'

Izzy nodded slowly. 'It also makes you wonder how they're going to smooth over Father Javier's death. I mean, they've sullied his reputation by implying he was inappropriate with the young girls in his congregation – maybe they'll rule his death as a suicide? That would certainly seal his fate in the religious community – after all, as far as they're all concerned that would then mean he would forever be condemned. Suicide deaths are considered a sin and he'd be forbidden from ever entering heaven.'

'For someone who had so much belief and faith in his cause and the truth, I'm sure his soul will be laughing its ass off over that one,' Nathan replied dryly.

37

It was dark when Crystal left work. Winter had truly taken hold, and the only remaining signs of autumn were the occasional dried up leaf whistling past her head. Crystal pulled her coat tight around her neck, to stop the cold northern chill from getting onto her body and, head down, she hurried along the pavement. As the cold wind bit into her hand, she wished she'd had the sense to bring her gloves with her this morning – or at least a scarf - so she could've kept her hand in the warmth of her pocket, rather than holding the collar of her coat shut.

She scurried along the pavement and turned right into the alleyway, looking up only briefly to ensure there was no one in front of her on the isolated pathway. The wind rustled the bushes and trees with its occasional gusts, causing Crystal to jump every now and again at imaginary attackers. The only other noises she could hear were her own rhythmic heartbeat and the occasional train in the distance. She stopped briefly to swap hands and wipe her ice cold nose, before hurrying along the alleyway and towards the promise of warmth at home.

The alleyway wound around several corners before it opened out onto a playing field. Crystal walked past the deserted swings and slide, before turning left and into a narrower walkway with high-sided fences on either side that shielded the adjoining houses from prying eyes. Presently Crystal became aware of an echo to her footsteps – someone who was walking slightly out of step to herself. As the alleyway bent round to the left she chanced a look behind and could just make out the figure of a person walking roughly fifteen metres behind her. Detouring slightly, Crystal turned right into another alleyway, going in the opposite direction to her house. She took a quick glance behind. The person was still there but now, lit by the dull orange of the streetlight, she knew it was a man.

Speeding up slightly, Crystal turned left and came out onto the pavement alongside the main road. She crossed to the middle island and waited for the flow of cars to abate before crossing to the other side of the road. Looking back, she held her breath as she waited for the man to appear by the side of the road. He didn't. Breathing a huge sigh of relief and cursing herself for being so paranoid, Crystal continued to follow the pavement along the main road, grateful it was well lit by the newly fitted, modern white lights.

As she neared her house, she saw that the florist shop was closed and in darkness. The house however, was lit up like a Christmas tree. Crystal put her key in the back door and let herself into the kitchen. It was in total disarray. All the cupboards and drawers were open, the contents were strewn across the floor. Crystal crunched her way over broken glass, along with sugar and coffee granules, to the other side of the room and into the hallway. Walking through the doorway into the living room, Crystal was horrified to see that this was in chaos too. Her mother was sat on the only upright chair, a cup of tea in her hand and Nathan by her side. He looked up as she entered the room and nodded in greeting.

'Your mum's okay, just a bit shocked.' He gave Izzy's shoulder a slight squeeze.

'When did this happen?' Crystal looked slowly around the room. She spied a few photo frames laying face down on the floor, but noted that there wasn't any broken glass around them.

'Luckily your mother was delivering some bridal bouquets when they must have got in. They broke one of the windows in the kitchen.'

'The kitchen's a lot worse. Everything that was hidden away in cupboards and drawers seems to have been chucked on the floor.' Crystal walked forward and picked up one of the photo frames. She wiped it on her coat and placed it back on the shelf next to a gap where the TV had once stood. It was now in pieces on the floor.

Izzy let out a slight whimper and a single tear ran slowly down her face. 'It's such a mess, Crystal.' She held her hand out and Crystal rushed over to take hold of it.

'It'll be okay, Mum. I'll help tidy it all up and the insurance will cover the damaged items. The main thing is that no one was here to get hurt.' She glanced around at the ripped underside of the sofa. 'Let me just go and hang my coat up.' She gestured for Nathan to follow her. She walked over to the coat rack at the bottom of the stairs and undid her coat before turning to whisper to Nathan.

'How bad is upstairs?'

He shook his head. 'The bastards did an even better job up there.' His eyes glinted cold blue daggers in the direction of the stairs. 'You'd better go and check that you still have

The Account – that is, after all, what they were probably after. I'll go and keep your mother calm.'

Heart racing, Crystal ran up the stairs and past the spare room and her mother's room – noting that each were in total disarray. Every drawer and door had been flung open, their contents scattered all over the floor. She continued into her room and wasn't surprised to see that it looked exactly the same as the others. Crystal's attention turned to the window sill. All the wood was still in its original place so, firstly pulling down the blind, she checked underneath the corner piece of wood. The Account was still there, safely hidden in its hiding place. She replaced the wood and leant back against the wall, closed her eyes and breathed a huge sigh of relief.

Opening her eyes again, she looked towards her bed. Her laptop was still there, confirming that this really hadn't been a normal burglary. Crystal went back downstairs and let Nathan and her mother know that The Account was still safe.

'Mum, have you called the police?'

'I don't think that would be a good idea, Crystal.' Nathan interjected. 'After all, nothing was taken and we don't know who we can and can't trust.'

Crystal looked at her mother for confirmation. She nodded and continued picking up items off the floor.

'Well if we're not involving the police, then there's no point leaving this mess around. I'll make a start on the kitchen.' Crystal went to leave the room, but stopped when her mother spoke.

'I've let Kitty and Mel know what's happened here. I thought it'd be wise, as they will know to be on their guard – just in case someone's watching them or gotten a copy of their spare house keys – as I keep their spares in the kitchen drawer.'

'Umm, okay.' Crystal looked a bit confused.

'I'm just letting you know in case Mark or Emily call you. I know Emily knows what this is *really* about, just as Kitty and Mel do. Let's not pretend otherwise.'

Crystal looked embarrassed – Nathan extremely pissed off.

'I thought I told you both to keep it quiet. It's for your own protection.' Nathan scowled at them both.

'You're an idiot if you *really* believed that was going to happen. It's what females do – talk to their close friends.' Izzy bit back.

'But...'

'Don't use that tone with me! Now is not the time, or the place, to be having this conversation, Nathan.' Izzy looked up at him, daring him to try and push this conversation on a course she didn't want it to go at the moment.

He stared at her for a couple of minutes – the tension in the room already at breaking point – Izzy's stony face making it crystal-clear she wasn't going to change her mind. Finally, Nathan nodded and he grabbed the sofa, returning it up the right way.

'See? You can't see the knife slashes once they're upright, so maybe you won't need to replace them.' His mouth flicked into a brief smile. The atmosphere and tension in the room discharged.

Crystal hovered in the doorway, unsure whether to leave them in the same room together. 'If you're both okay, I'll make a start on the kitchen now.' Uncertainty echoed in her voice.

Izzy looked up, nodded and smiled wearily at her daughter before continuing with the task at hand.

An hour later Crystal stepped back, leant against the broom and wiped her arm across her brow. By her side sat a rubbish sack full of broken glass and crockery. Anything left unbroken had been returned to the relevant cabinets. The plants sat on the draining board, minus their pots as they'd also been smashed, however the plants themselves had remained intact. They just needed repotting. Crystal boiled the kettle and made a pot of tea before calling through to Nathan and her mother.

They came and joined her in the kitchen, all three of them sitting at the table in silence – all three looking worn out. Nathan took a sip of his tea and pulled a face.

'Sorry, we didn't have any coffee left.' Crystal answered his unspoken question. 'I'll go out and get some after I've drunk this, as we also need some other bits and pieces.'

Nathan put his mug down. 'I'll go with you.' He glanced across at Izzy. 'You'll be okay here on your own won't you? I'm sure they won't be back again. As far as they know there's nothing here to come back for.'

Izzy held her mug tightly in both hands, staring at the warm steaming liquid inside. 'It's just going to get worse now, isn't it?' She turned her gaze to Nathan. 'First the increase in disappearances and now this.'

'We'll all get through this.' Nathan's voice was quiet.

'Will we? You can't guarantee we all will, can you?' Izzy replied angrily.

'Hang on a minute, what do you mean about the increase in disappearances? Do you mean the ones that have been on the news?' Crystal looked firstly at her mother, then at Nathan.

Izzy looked guiltily towards Nathan. He shook his head slightly.

'Come on, you guys must think I'm stupid! If you know

something about those disappearances, you have to say something.' She stared in shock at her mother, before repeating her question. 'Mum, what does our break in have to do with those disappearances?'

Izzy momentarily closed her eyes, summoning up the energy to respond. 'The Others need them to fulfil jobs. They're usually wanting them to build things for them.'

Nathan continued. 'But now they know the last angel has The Account, they'll want to increase their allies, so to speak.'

'Presumably to get the angel – namely me. Great!' Crystal responded bitterly. 'So is that what you've been doing, when you said you were scouring the neighbourhood? You were actually trying to prevent others being taken?'

'My job has always been to protect you and your mother – not everyone else. I was making sure there were no stray flyahs and digahs near you.'

'But he did go back to the house to see if anything could be done for Father Javier, didn't you?' Izzy interjected, noting the red flush working up Crystal's face and trying to soothe over that mounting anger. 'But he was too late.'

Crystal turned in her chair to face Nathan. In a calm voice she asked. 'So you knew why those people were being taken, you were even witness to some, and you did nothing?'

Nathan looked confused. 'But I thought we all knew why they were taken.' He looked firstly at Izzy, then at Crystal. 'I mean, you've read about it in The Account, haven't you?'

'I've read about them taking people to fulfil a job, but I didn't realise that was what *these* disappearances were. You knew, but didn't do anything to help?'

'Well, you can't get angry with *me* for not helping them.

I'm not bothered about anyone else. I'm doing my job – and that's protecting *you*!'

'Can you please not have this argument now?' Izzy slammed her mug down on the table. 'I'm just about hanging on to my sanity, what with everything that's been happening with Crystal, The Account and now *this*.' She pointed at the bin bag full of broken glass and crockery. 'I'd really appreciate just having a quiet hour or two, to process everything that's been happening. Is that too much to ask?' She rested her elbow on the table and slowly rubbed her hand across her forehead.

Crystal leant across and touched her mother's arm. 'Sorry Mum, we'll get through this you know.'

Izzy nodded. 'I know we have to. It's the right thing to do. I just hoped we wouldn't have to.'

'Not just that – we're doing it for Dad too.'

Izzy nodded and remained silent.

'Will you be okay on your own? Do you want me to get Mel or Kitty to come over?'

'No. I'll be fine. You go.' Izzy managed to smile at her daughter and patted her hand. 'Just ignore me, I'm being silly. I suppose it's the shock of finding my house a mess – and knowing that someone has been rifling through our things.' Her eyes welled up and she waved her hand to stop Crystal coming over to give her a cuddle.

Nathan pushed his chair back and stood up. 'Let's make a move and get that stuff, Crystal, and give your mother some space.'

'Umm, okay.' She got up and followed Nathan down the hallway and to the coat rack, grabbing her boots and black woollen coat. She took them back to the kitchen and sat down to put her boots on.

'Shall I grab something for dinner? I'm guessing none of

us are in the mood for cooking.' She glanced up through her black fringe.

'That would be good. Thanks hun.' Izzy smiled and leant her elbows on the table, placed her head on her hands and watched them both walk out the back door.

38

The dog didn't stand a chance. The silver Audi came tearing round the corner – its headlights lighting up the poor animal, frozen in fear and surprise in the middle of the quiet road. The girl watched from her vantage point behind the privet hedge. As if in slow motion, the car bore down on the dog, quickly made contact with a dull thud and continued driving away. A single yelp on impact was followed by a whimper, as the dog tried to get up and drag itself to safety.

She rushed across the pavement and into the road, to see if there she could help the wounded animal. The retriever lay still on the floor, his eyes full of pain, his pale yellow coat showered in bits of gravel – his front legs lying limp and still. Looking around to see if they were alone, she slowly fell to her knees. The road grit dug into her bright pink tights, but she ignored the discomfort and lent forward to place her hands on the dog, all the while talking soothingly to him in a slight Welsh lilt.

'It's all right my darling. I just want to help you.' He tried to move in pain as her hands touched his damaged legs, but his eyes stared back at her full of hope and trust. She rubbed his neck, using smooth even strokes, noticing his leather collar.

'Someone's going to be missing you.' She turned the silver disc to the light, enabling her to see the name etched on it. 'Marmalade? Well, I'm guessing some young child would be heartbroken if I didn't help you.'

She slowly moved her hand back towards his shoulders.

'Marmalade, I'm just going to make you feel better. I'm not here to hurt you. There's a good brave boy.'

She bowed her head, letting her brown curly hair fall forward, slightly obscuring her face. Closing her eyes, she focused her thoughts on all the positive things she could think of – her younger sister Felicity, the love she felt for her mother and father, beautiful black and jade butterflies and the warmth of the sunlight on her skin. Her hands let off a luminous orange light, before turning yellow through white. The retriever got up and gratefully licked her face, nearly knocking her over.

'You're welcome love.' She laughed and cuddled him tightly before getting to her feet and smoothing down her pleated denim skirt. 'Now Marmalade, go home – and stay away from the road!'

She watched him trot away, his fluffy yellow tail wagging furiously back and forth before walking to the edge of the road and sitting on the kerbside to wait for her energy levels to return to normal.

After a couple of minutes, she stood up and went back to the privet hedge to retrieve her bags. She slung the rucksack onto her back before bending to lift the large holdall over her left shoulder. The neatly rolled sleeping bag strapped to the top of the rucksack nestled into her neck, protecting it from the cold winter breeze. She dug the road map out of her coat pocket to check which direction to take, before stepping back onto the pavement and heading west – towards the church.

As she walked she glanced at the big houses and gardens on either side of her. They looked huge compared to the one her parents owned back home. Her heart skipped a beat as she remembered the cosiness she had left behind, and her eyes filled with tears.

'Now Serena, stop that you cry baby!' she reprimanded herself out loud. After all, there wasn't anyone else around to hear her – and even if there were, they'd take one look at her attire and baggage and assume she was homeless and probably drunk.

She walked slowly, without purpose and in no particular hurry. She stopped to admire various things that took her fancy – a deep red leaved ivy that grew over an old stone wall, a baby hedgehog curled up in a tiny ball, laying on top of the remnants of autumn leaves that had been swept to the side of the pavement, and a fluffy black and white cat that had walked out of the house she had just passed to wind around her legs, purring in delight as she stroked its soft head. The street was abandoned, apart from the couple who were currently walking towards her. She smiled at the dark haired girl as they drew level – she looked a bit friendlier than the blonde haired man with the stony face who walked beside her. The dark haired girl smiled back, but Serena noticed that there was an aura of sadness about her – she could sense it as they walked past her. She turned and watched them walk away down the road and disappear in the direction she had just come from – grateful they hadn't been around to witness her healing Marmalade.

Serena stopped and sat on an empty wooden bench, overlooking an area of green, swinging her rucksack off her back and placing it next to the holdall. The darkness didn't bother her and her thick green duffle coat kept her warm. Digging into her holdall she pulled out a packet of crisps. As she crunched mouthfuls of crisps, she watched the birds nestling in the bare branches. Their old nests were clearly evident, now the leaves previously shielding them had disappeared. A female blackbird hopped around on the ground a short distance in front of her. She gently threw the remnants of her cheese and onion crisps onto the ground for the bird to investigate.

Throwing the rucksack back onto her back, she pulled her cream woollen scarf tighter around her neck and continued her leisurely pace along the path. Walking between the dull orange glow of the street lights, she felt slightly uneasy, feeling as if someone was watching her. She looked around but there was no one there.

'Come on Serena, stop being paranoid.' She shrugged the rucksack slightly, getting it to sit better on her back, before continuing along the path, hesitatingly singing her favourite Destiny's Child song quietly to herself, amending the lyrics to suit. 'Do you know what? I AM a survivor; I WILL make it...'

She'd reached a dark point, between two orange street lights, when she had the feeling of being watched again. She looked round but, again there was no one there. Looking ahead, she hastened her speed slightly to reach the next dull orange spotlight – unsure whether that would make her feel better – or highlight her to whoever was watching. Serena felt a breeze above her, a split second before she heard something behind her and felt movement above her head.

The rucksack on her back suddenly got heavy, the straps digging into her shoulder joints and Serena felt it being tugged upwards. She batted her arm behind her to hit off whatever had landed on it. Her hand made contact with someone's head. She screamed and swiftly managed to shrug her way out of the shoulder straps, whilst simultaneously dropping the holdall to the ground, freeing herself to escape. She should've run, but instead, she turned to face whoever it was behind her. Except they weren't behind her – they were above her.

Her eyes widened in shock, her mouth fell slightly open and Serena took precious seconds staring at the man hovering above her. Taking a few steps backwards, she continued staring. He launched the rucksack at her, knocking her to the ground.

'Oi, What the hell do you think you're doing!' She sprang to her feet indignantly. She stood looking up at him, hands resting on her hips. 'More to the point, what the frigging hell are you?'

He landed on the ground a few steps in front of her. His head dropped slightly and he glared at her menacingly. 'I'm here to collect you. You have a job to do.'

'You're not bloody taking me anywhere! Now bugger off!' She continued looking at him, whilst she picked up her rucksack and holdall. He grabbed her rucksack, pulling it – and her – closer to him

'It's my job to collect you and it's yours to fill the role waiting for you.'

Serena continued hanging onto the rucksack, using the weight of her body as a counter-weight to his, whilst hollering the same two sentences over and over again, as loudly as she could.

'Get off me! Somebody help!'

She glanced around to see if there was anyone in earshot and was relieved to see a couple come out of the alleyway at the far side of the green.

Crystal and Nathan rounded the last corner of the alley, before it opened onto the green. They saw the girl they'd passed earlier whilst on their way to the shop, the one who looked homeless. She was the other side of the green, fighting with a man.

'We have to go over and help her.' Crystal looked up at Nathan.

He'd stopped walking and stood, just on the edge of the green. 'I told you, I'm not interested in others, my only job is to protect you.'

'How can you say that? She's only young and obviously on her own here. We need to go and help!'

'We need to stay out of it.' Nathan responded stubbornly, his jaw clamped shut.

Crystal handed him the carrier bag of shopping she was carrying. 'Well, if you won't help, I will.' She closed her eyes to concentrate, holding her arms out slightly she tried to leave the ground – nothing happened.

'Are you okay?' She opened her eyes to see Nathan staring at her.

'Course I am, just tired – but she isn't!' Crystal pointed across the green and started to jog along the path towards the girl. 'She's screaming for help.' She looked back at Nathan. 'And if your job is to protect me, then you'd better come too, because I'm going to help her.'

Nathan shook his head and rolled his eyes. 'Fine, I'll go help. Just let me deal with the flyah.' He took a few swift, long strides to overtake Crystal. He didn't want to frighten the girl by taking to the air, or she may think he was in cahoots with the other guy.

She grinned. 'Okay, whatever you say.' And she followed him towards the confrontation going on in front of them.

Serena had seen them approaching. If I can just hold him off until they get a bit nearer, she thought. She continued hollering and took a couple of steps closer to her attacker, enabling her to swing her right foot and kick him deftly on the right shin with her sturdy walking boot. He lifted his leg briefly in surprise, so she swiftly wrenched at the rucksack and took a few more steps back.

'There's no way on this planet I'm going to let you take me or my bloody rucksack!' She shouted up in his general direction.

He suddenly let go of the rucksack, sending Serena sprawling to the floor, enabling him to gain back the advantage. He threw the rucksack onto the floor at his side, as he took the last few steps towards her. He was leaning over her, arms reaching to grab her, when he was launched sideways, knocked over by the man who had come to her aid by ramming him with his left shoulder. He walked over to him and kicked him swiftly in the ribs.

'You're not taking anybody. Now get lost – your lot are not welcome around here.' He aimed well-aimed shot with his boot and the man lying on the floor grunted slightly, before getting slowly to his feet and, holding his arm around his ribs, he limped away.

Nathan turned to head back to the girls and, as he did so, he felt a slight breeze as the flyah left the ground and disappeared into the night.

Crystal stepped forward, picked up the carrier bags of

shopping that Nathan had dropped and helped the girl to her feet.

'Are you okay?' Crystal bent down to pick up the rucksack and handed it to the young brunette stood in front of her.

'Thanks to you both.' She took the rucksack, swinging it onto her back and wincing as it bashed against her elbow. 'Ouch!' She bent her arm to look at the damage. She gingerly pulled her sleeve back down over the graze and picked up her holdall.

'Are you hurt?' Crystal took a step forward, but the girl stepped back slightly.

'I'm not going to hurt you – I could take a look at that wound if you like?' Crystal volunteered, but the girl shook her head.

'It's fine, I'll deal with it later. What did he mean by 'your lot?'' She looked around, clearly wanting to make a move to somewhere safe.

'Where are you headed?' Crystal asked, ignoring the question. 'It's just we could walk with you, if you're going our way.' She pointed in the direction of the housing estate the other side of the green.

The girl hesitated before answering. 'Um, okay then. I'm heading to St Barnabas's church. I heard there's a church run hostel there.'

Crystal glanced at Nathan. He nodded his head, already knowing where this conversation was going.

'The Father that run it is no longer there, so they shut it down last week.'

'Oh.' The girl's face fell slightly.

'Look, I know you don't know us from Adam, but you're more than welcome to crash in our spare room – we only live a couple of minutes from here.'

'I'm not sure...' Serena thought they seemed genuine enough, but you can never tell.

'Look, my name is Crystal and this is Nathan. I live with my mum, she's a florist and Nathan is a family friend.'

'I'm Serena.' She was still unsure about giving too much information to these strangers. She looked from one to the other.

'Hi Serena. You look like you're on your own, and judging by your accent, you're not from around here.' Crystal stepped forward and placed her hands on Serena's shoulders. 'But I do know you're different, otherwise that man wouldn't have just tried to take you.' She felt Serena tense and try to move away from her. Crystal held onto her shoulders and stared straight into her eyes, letting her hands glow slightly orange, sending her healing energy down Serena's' arms and towards her graze. 'I know, because I'm different too – see? And besides, you have a tell-tale slight glow about you that only those with healing abilities have.'

Serena relaxed her shoulders and closed her eyes, momentarily enjoying the soothing light travelling down her body and calming every cell. She opened her eyes and stared back into Crystal's eyes.

'Okay, I'll take you up on your offer – but if I don't like what you're saying, I'll be leaving.'

'It's a deal.' Crystal let Nathan take one of the carrier bags from her and he reached over and took Serena's holdall with his other hand, before falling into step slightly behind the girls. He let them talk, getting to know each other, grateful he didn't have to reveal his ability – as Serena would probably think he was in cahoots with the guy who'd attacked her.

A couple of minutes later, they walked across the back

garden and into the newly tidied house. Izzy looked up from her seat at the table, surprised to see they had someone with them.

'Mum, this is Serena, we just rescued her from a flyah and I said she could stay in our other spare room.' Crystal spoke all matter of fact, swinging the carrier bag she was carrying onto the table before beginning to unpack the contents within.

Izzy stood up and stared at Serena for a few seconds, before stepping forward and taking hold of her hand in a double handshake. 'It's lovely to meet a fellow healah, Serena. I'm Isobel, but please, call me Izzy.' She pulled a seat out from under the table. 'Please, have a seat. Would you like a cup of tea?' She turned and walked over to the kettle, talking as she prepared the mugs. 'You'll have to excuse the slight untidiness of the house. We had a break in earlier today.'

'Good one Mum, make her feel even safer, why don't you!' Crystal binned the carrier bag and sat down next to Serena.

'It's fine, they won't be coming back. You'll be perfectly safe here. We've got Nathan to protect us.'

Serena accepted the mug of tea Izzy handed her and placed it gently onto the coaster on the table. Finally, she spoke.

'Thanks for the tea. But what's a flyah?' She looked totally confused.

Nathan took a step forward and stopped Crystal from replying. 'Look, you've had an eventful evening – in fact, we have too – so why don't we all just get a decent night's sleep? Crystal can give you the crash course in the morning and answer any questions you're bound to have.'

Izzy looked around at the three of them. Her hands were

cupped around her mug, but her eyes looked fully alert again, now the shock of the break-in had worn off. 'I'm fine with that Nathan, but first I need to show Serena how to close off her energy, because you both may not be mentioning it but someone has to.'

Serena looked shocked and immediately suspicious, but Izzy quickly continued. 'Serena, you're a healah, the same as me. We healahs have a slight yellow glow around us and, if we don't close it off, other people, like the flyah who attacked you earlier, can find us. It doesn't hurt you and it will only take a couple of minutes. I promise it's nothing to be scared of. It's just a simple visualisation.

'Okay, what do I have to do?' Serena put her mug down and placed her hands on her lap.

Izzy talked her through the visualisation she had taught Crystal to do, involving the red energy threads being tethered to the Earth's core. She watched Serena as she visualised and was relieved to see the yellow aura around the girl fade and disappear.

'You can open your eyes now, Serena.' Izzy touched her gently on the arm. 'You'll feel slightly heavier now – less head in the clouds kind of feeling.'

Serena nodded. 'I do. That's weird!' She blinked a couple of times, as if awaking from a deep sleep. 'It's kind of cool though.'

'Glad you feel that way, because tomorrow you'll be getting the crash course in all the other bits that you need to know about having your ability. Think you can handle that?' Nathan looked at her from over his mug of coffee.

'I think so.' Serena nodded. 'Maybe I'll stay around a bit longer.' She undid her coat buttons and let her coat fall from her shoulders and back against the chair.

39

As he landed outside the Victorian house, the flyah let out a grunt in pain. He let himself in through the study doors, nodded a greeting as he made his way past the digahs, who were playing cards in the corner of the room, and he carried on up the stairs.

He walked into his makeshift bedroom and shut the door behind him, before leaning back against it and closing his eyes. He really should go downstairs to see the healah, but he had to report his latest failing first. The Others wouldn't be happy. He opened his eyes and looked longingly at the camp bed against the far wall – it had never looked as appealing as it did now, even if it did look rather lonely in the otherwise empty, cream painted room. He held his right arm protectively around his ribcage. What he wouldn't do for some sleep right now!

He gingerly made his way down to the floor. He crossed his legs, closed his eyes and concentrated. Letting his mind open, he focused his attentions on contacting The Others. He kept it short and to the point.

'I failed. I met with resistance from the healah. She had

help from another flyah and a half-blood. There are more of them. Send reinforcements. It has begun.'

He opened his eyes and spent a couple of minutes visualising his third eye and mind closing. Getting up off the floor he walked back out of the bedroom and down the stairs. The digahs looked up inquiringly from their card game.

'There are others coming to help.' He picked up the cards and started to pile them together. He stared at them, his expression neutral. 'Playtime is over. Make the other rooms ready.' He walked back out of the study and made his way down to the basement rooms where the healah was kept.

40

Emily was sat in her bedroom, reading the latest James Patterson novel, when her dad knocked on the door and let himself in.

'Are you okay? I just thought I'd come up to check on you, as you were very quiet at dinner.' Frank asked.

'Yeah, I'm fine thanks Dad, just a bit tired – I've had a lot going on at the moment.'

Frank sat down on the edge of Emily's bed. 'I've noticed that I haven't seen much of you. Is there anything you'd like to talk about?'

Emily closed her book, laying it gently on top of her laptop that was sitting on her bedside cabinet, before turned to face him. 'Sorry, I've just been busy.' She gave her dad a hug. 'You haven't been up to my room to see me for years. It's nice to spend time talking to you.'

Frank leant back to break the embrace and coughed to hide his embarrassment. 'Well, I guess we've all been busy, as your mother's been out more and more, you've been over at Mark's house and I've had church and everything that's been going on there. It's a shame you didn't feel like coming to Sunday Service today.'

'Sorry.' She tried to sound remorseful. 'But I heard about Father Javier. It's awful isn't it? It must've really upset the congregation.' She glanced across at him, her eyes full of compassion.

He lifted his head slightly, sticking his nose up in the air. 'Well, if he'd read more of his Bible, and respected the words within, maybe he wouldn't have been removed for acting inappropriately.'

Emily twiddled a blonde curl that had fallen forward out of her hair band. 'Dad, do you honestly think that all the answers are in the Bible?'

He spun his head round to face her. 'Of course I do. If you're a good Catholic you'd know that!'

'I know Dad; I was just asking.' She looked down.

'Maybe you've been spending too much time with Mark's family.' He let the sentence hang in the air for a couple of seconds. 'When your mother told me you were seeing Mark, I did have my doubts. Maybe I was right?'

Emily shook her head. 'No Dad, it's not anything to do with Mark. I'll try and spend some more time at home.'

He continued, as if he hadn't heard her. 'I mean, his family don't even go to church.' He touched her hand. 'Why couldn't you find a nice Catholic boy to hang around with? I'd know then that he wasn't leading you astray.'

'Mark isn't leading me astray, Dad. We're behaving ourselves, honestly.' She tried not to sound as if she was pleading with her dad as after all, she was a fully grown adult.

'Maybe spending some more time at home is a good idea. I can keep more of an eye on you then.' He stood up and kissed her head. 'I don't want you getting into trouble, especially at your age. I love you sweet pea, and so does God. Don't you forget that – we both want what's best for you.'

Emily nodded and smiled, but stayed silent. She knew arguing with her father was pointless.

She waited until he closed the bedroom door and she could hear his footsteps on the wooden steps as he made his way downstairs, before she picked the laptop up and opened it. Her screen had two windows open – one was Crystal's latest audio clips, now complete with pictures, and the other was Emily's diary. She logged into YouTube and scheduled the release of the latest batch of audio videos before switching to her diary screen and completing her latest entry of notes.

41

'I'm going out,' Crystal shouted as she walked down the stairs. She sat at the bottom of the stairs and pulled on her boots. She'd put on an extra thick pair of socks to protect the gorgeous anklet that Tony had bought her. As she did up her boots she smiled to herself. She was so grateful that Tony had had the foresight to buy it for her, as she'd been sleeping so much better now she'd been wearing it. She still felt really tired, but that was understandable, considering how much stress she was currently under.

'Where are you going?' Izzy walked along the hallway, wiping her hands on a tea towel.

'I'm going to do something nice.' Crystal replied as she stood up and pulled her coat on.

'You're going to heal another person, aren't you? I wish you wouldn't.' Izzy frowned at her daughter. 'It's a big risk, you may get seen.'

Crystal leant forward and kissed her mother on the forehead. 'I'll be careful, I promise. I have to do this Mum; it makes me feel useful.' She turned and opened the front door. 'I know you understand that.'

Izzy nodded. 'Just be careful.'

'I will.' Crystal smiled before closing the door behind her.

Winter had really taken hold now. The frost covered trees looked beautiful, as if Mother Nature had covered them in delicate white ice tinsel. As Crystal walked across the green the grass crunched beneath her feet, her breath creating her very own white cloud every time she breathed out. Crystal pulled her knitted hat down over her ears in an attempt to stop the cold biting into them and kept her eyes open for any late-night dog walkers. There was no one else around, the cold keeping them tucked up safe and warm inside their homes.

At the other side of the green Crystal turned right and walked past the children's playgroup, onto the main road. She followed this for five minutes before crossing over and heading down a quiet cul-de-sac. She stopped under the orange glow of the streetlight to check she had the right road. Satisfied she had, she continued to the last house on the right hand side. Walking quietly down their path, she was glad to see the house was secluded, hidden behind the aromatic, yellow evergreen hedge.

Creeping round to the side of the house, she picked her steps carefully to avoid treading on the various saucers of water and food left out for the stray cats. Crystal quietly unlatched the black metal side gate and stepped through into the back garden. The floodlight sensor tripped to light on, illuminating the centre of the garden, but leaving the part nearest to the house in darkness. Focusing her attention, Crystal rose quietly to the upstairs window.

'Damn, they've locked it,' she cursed quietly to herself, annoyed that there wasn't an easy way into the house. She sank back to the ground and gave herself a couple of minutes to think. She really wanted to heal this old lady as her heart may be very weak but it was full of kindness – the saucers left out were evidence of that. Crystal focused her attention and rose quietly to the upstairs windows again. She tried the frosted panel of the bathroom window, before coming back down to the ground, frustrated.

She tried the back door. It was locked, but the key was still in the door. She looked at the cat flap.

Don't be stupid, you'll never fit through there, she thought, but it did give her another idea. The handle and lock of the door were quite low down. She lay on the floor and put her arm through the cat flap. If I can just reach the key, she thought. Stretching as far as she could, her armpit wedged up against the cat flap, Crystal could just about reach the door. She didn't have enough leeway to turn the key, but she could manage to pull if from the keyhole. It clattered onto the tiled floor. She froze, watching and listening for any telltale signs that the lady inside may have heard her. A couple of minutes stretched past before Crystal grabbed the key and pulled it back through the cat flap. She unlocked the door and crept inside.

She made her way up the stairs, the carpet muffling her steps. The house only had one bedroom, so it was easy to find the old lady's room. Crystal crept over to the bed and stood with her hands over the sleeping body. The glow emanating from her hands cast a faint orange glow around the room. Crystal stayed there for ten minutes before her mind started to wander. She was so tired. She bent her head slowly to the left, then right, to ease her aching neck muscles. She forced herself to complete another ten minutes and to ignore the ache working its way down through her neck and into her arms. Finally, she stopped and turned to go.

'Are you an angel?' the timid voice quietly asked. Crystal froze, unsure whether to turn and face the lady, or run from the room. She turned slightly, just enough for her to see the woman in the bed.

'I am. You're quite safe so go back to sleep.' Her heart was beating somewhere in her throat.

'Thank you. May God be with you.' The old lady sighed and closed her eyes.

Crystal walked out of the room and back down the stairs. Locking the back door and pushing the key back in through the cat flap, she collapsed on the patio. Leaning back against the back door, she waited for her breathing to return to normal. Her limbs felt so heavy, her head as if it was too heavy for her neck. It would be so easy to close her eyes, just for a second, but she pulled herself to her feet and walked slowly down the path.

How could I have been so stupid? she thought, shaking her head slightly, annoyed and disappointed with herself. Not only did she see you, she heard your voice too. The cold air hitting her face made her feel a bit more alert and less tired. Reaching the green, Crystal opted for walking along the hilly mounds on the dark side, rather than the long, but illuminated, way around the path. Feeling a slight tingle around her head, Crystal looked up in surprise.

'Well now, who do we have here?' He landed in front of her and folded his arms.

Crystal's heart sank as she recognised the flyah that had attacked Serena.

'You got me into trouble the other day, for not collecting. Maybe *you'd* be a better peace offering.'

She knew she wouldn't be able to outrun him, but they would be equally paired in the air. Crystal focused her attention and felt her feet leave the ground. She managed a metre or so, before falling back to the ground, exhausted.

His laugh echoed around the empty field. 'Oh, so you're a wannabe! Is that all you've got? This *is* going to be fun.' He grabbed her by the arm and pulled her into the air. Crystal reached up to his hand and prised his thumb backwards.

'You bitch!' He let go of her and she fell awkwardly onto the cold ground with her foot twisted beneath her. She reached to rub her sore ankle, as the stones from the anklet dug into her skin. He landed next to her and swiftly slapped her with the back of his hand.

'Think you're clever do you?' His hand made contact with her face again, her icy cold cheek smarting. He grabbed a handful of her hair and dragged her to her feet.

'You're coming with me. See what The Others make of you.' He tried to restrain her by wrapping his arms around her, his breath hot against her forehead. Crystal raised her right knee, ramming it as hard as she could into his testicles. He let go of her, his hands falling down to cup and protect his genitals as he doubled over in agony, a high pitched 'ahh' escaping from his lips.

Crystal got to her feet and started to run, but her ankle hurt too much. She tried to fly, but she had no energy and couldn't manage to leave the ground. She looked back and her heart jumped to her mouth as she spotted another flyah heading towards them. She turned back to see in front of her, put her head down, gritted her teeth against the pain of her ankle and ran as best as she could. She risked a second glance back to see how close they both were to her.

Except they weren't chasing her. She slowed to a stop and turned fully around. It took a few moments for her to realise that the second flyah had been Nathan, and he was currently rolling around on the floor with her attacker. She gave herself a few moments to catch her breath before hobbling back to help him.

Nathan may have the strength and experience, but the younger flyah had youth on his side. He managed to duck out of the way of most of Nathans targeted punches, whilst swinging his own fists wildly in the direction of Nathan's face. A swift right hook knocked Nathan to the ground and the younger flyah threw himself on top of him, raining punches at his face. Nathan managed to get a hefty few jabs into the youngster's sides, but he seemed ignorant to the pain Nathan was causing him, driven by adrenaline and fury. Crystal raised her walking boot and kicked him off Nathan. It made her ankle hurt like hell – but it felt good everywhere else, especially when her boot made contact with his ribs. He fell to his side but managed to get back to his feet quicker than Nathan, this time turning his rage in Crystal's direction.

As his fist made contact with Crystal's shoulder, she felt something snap. A red mist of pain exploded and she fell to the ground. As her eyes closed, she saw Nathan homing in on the youngster, before she was swallowed up by blackness.

Crystal opened her eyes slowly. She was lying on the sofa in her living room and her mother and Serena were staring worriedly back at her. Struggling to a half seated, half slouched position, she groggily rubbed her head.

'You're awake! You scared the frigging hell out of us.' Serena sat back on her heels and relaxed her shoulders.

'How do you feel hun?' Izzy asked gently.

'What happened?' Crystal asked. 'The last thing I remember was a fight between Nathan and another flyah.' She pulled herself fully upright and, with panic evident in her voice asked. 'Is Nathan all right?'

Izzy put a hand on Crystal's shoulder and pushed her gently back against the sofa. 'He's fine. He'll be down in a minute. You may feel a bit tired, as I had to give you a hefty bit of healing for your shoulder.'

'I was tired before I got hurt.' Crystal muttered bitterly.

Serena sat forward. 'Your mum was brilliant,' she said, 'her Welsh lilt rolling and exaggerating the 'br' at the beginning of the word. 'Her healing is so much stronger than mine – *and* she healed Nathan!' The amazement and pride was evident in her voice. 'But I did heal your cheek – you had a nasty bruise coming up – and your ankle.'

Crystal raised her hand to gingerly touch her cheekbone. It felt fine – and so did her shoulder. 'Thanks Mum.' She smiled at her mother. 'And thanks to you too, Serena. You did great.' The younger girl's chin rose slightly as she lapped up the praise.

'Maybe now you'll listen to me and stop going out on your own little mercy missions.' Nathan uttered as he walked into the room. Crystal moved her head to watch him walk in and sit down in the chair opposite her.

'How did you know what I was doing?'

He rolled his eyes. 'Because I'm not stupid. I knew you wouldn't do as you're told, so I followed you.'

'Oh I didn't see you.' She hung her head slightly.

'Yeah, 'oh'. You didn't see me because I didn't want to be seen. But you're lucky it *was* just me watching you break into that old lady's house.' He looked at her, his eyebrow raised, mouth turned up at one side. 'You're lucky I was there to save your ass too.'

She managed a slight grin back at him. 'Well you do keep telling me it's your job.' She lowered her head before looking back up again. 'But thanks anyway.'

Nathan nodded.

'So how did I get back here?' Crystal asked

'I carried you back after you passed out.'

Serena, all wide-eyed on the floor, chipped in. 'Your shoulder was broken. We had to put it back in. And you'd twisted your ankle. It was gross! And Nathan had broken ribs and was covered in blood. His nose was broken too!'

Izzy frowned down at Serena. 'I don't think we need to give her *all* the details, do we?'

'Sorry. It's just I haven't seen actual people with broken bones, only animals.' Serena was still wide-eyed and hyper-active, but tried to calm down and sit still. She suddenly remembered something, stood up and retrieved the anklet from her pocket. 'I took this off when I was healing your ankle.' She handed it back to Crystal. 'I wasn't nicking it or anything; I just put it in my pocket to keep it safe – until you woke up.'

'Thanks Serena, you're a star.' She closed her hand around the anklet. 'I don't think for a second that you aren't trustworthy, so don't worry. Thanks for looking after it.'

'You're welcome.' Serena sat back down and relaxed. 'Are you going to put it back on?'

Crystal shook her head. 'Not at the moment. I'll wear it at bedtime though, as it's helping with my dreams.'

Izzy nudged Crystal's legs to get her to move them so she could sit down on the end of the sofa. 'Hopefully it will continue to help, as you need to shake off your constant tiredness.' She looked down at her hands briefly, before looking back up. 'What all this did demonstrate to me was how much you both need me. So, as much as I tried to stay out of it, I can see now that it would be impossible.' She looked at her daughter, then to Nathan. 'So, as of this moment, I am in. I'll do anything I can to help you fulfil whatever it is you need to do.'

'Your mum's going to train me up too!' Serena added, before going silent again when Izzy looked at her.

'Yes, I am going to train you too.' She looked back to Nathan. 'Besides, judging by today, you're both going to need all the healahs you can get!'

42

Afer the break-in Izzy was being extra cautious about having her friends over, in case the house had been bugged. Nathan had got his friend, the one that was 'in the know', to sweep for bugs and, although he'd found none, Izzy wasn't taking any more chances. That is why on a rainy Monday morning, she was currently sat in one of the booths at the local coffee shop, waiting for Mel and Kitty to join her.

Each time the main entrance door swung open, Izzy looked up to see who was entering, before looking back down to her newspaper crossword. The coffee shop had floor to ceiling glass panels on two sides, making it perfect for keeping an eye out for the girls – even though the panels currently had ribbons of raindrops streaming down them. It also had an impressive display of cakes and sandwiches to keep them nourished once they eventually got here but, unfortunately for Izzy, it had two entrances – one to the front and one to the side. From her vantage point in the booth, she could only keep her eye on the main door, and those shoppers that were hurrying past the frontage, a mass of colour and umbrellas protecting them from the rain.

Taking a break from the crossword, Izzy looked up to watch the shoppers – one of whom was wearing a green knee length coat and black boots – and Izzy smiled as she watched Mel put her brolly down and shake the water off it, before entering the coffee shop. She placed her order, pointing over to where Izzy was sitting before coming over to the table.

'I thought I'd save her the task of coming over to take my order. So Izzy, what's with all the cloak and dagger stuff?' Mel sat down on the brown suede chair opposite her.

'I'm sorry, I just thought it would be better meeting somewhere public. Since the break-in I've been a little jumpy about my house being bugged and everything.'

'That's understandable. Is Kitty on her way too?'

Izzy nodded. 'She is, she's just running a little late, due to the bad weather.'

Mel thanked the waitress for her coffee and watched her walk to the booth behind them before turning back to Izzy. 'So it all starts now, does it?' She turned as they heard the door open and smiled as they saw Kitty enter. Mel dragged a chair over to their table ready for her.

'How you doing, lovely?' Mel asked.

'I'm fine thanks. Are you okay though Izzy? What about Nathan and Crystal?' Kitty sat down to catch her breath whilst rummaging in her oversized shoulder bag.

'We're all fine thanks. The book's safe too.' Izzy replied.

Kitty pulled the local newspaper out of her bag and placed it on the table. 'Did either of you see this?' She pointed at a small article at the bottom of page fifteen. 'It's about an old lady who's saying an angel healed her of her cancer. Her doctor is, understandably, flabbergasted. Is this anything to do with you?'

Izzy groaned and put her head in her hands. 'Crystal really needs to be a bit more careful.'

'Well you can't blame her for wanting to help,' Mel laughed.

'So this is the beginning then?' Kitty looked at them both before pointing to another small article, next to the healing one. 'I'm guessing this has got something to do with it too, as have the other disappearances.' There was roughly a single inch long article devoted to the latest disappearance. This time it was a twenty-three-year-old man. 'They're happening so frequently now; they're not even making the front page anymore.' She turned to face Izzy.

Izzy slowly nodded her head. 'We believe The Others are involved, yes.'

Kitty sighed deeply and replied, 'Well, on a happier note, Emily and Mark are getting on like a house on fire and you were right about her knowing you and Crystal have abilities. I think I made it clear that I knew too.'

Izzy nodded. 'That's good and yes, this is probably where it all begins.'

Mel grimaced slightly. 'Why do I feel that I'm pimping my daughter out? I hate the thought of arranging her life for her.'

Kitty reached over the table. 'We all know that she needs Mark to relax her enough for the visions. We need those visions to guide others and spread the word. They genuinely *do* like each other, you know. He adores her.'

'I know, it's just that Frank is giving her grief about being out so much, especially as I'm out more now too.' She smoothed a strand of hair behind her ear. 'I know what it's like to be in a marriage of convenience, that's all.'

Izzy put her cup of tea down. 'Mel, we're not asking her to marry him. She was already attracted to him before we started pushing them together, so we've just hastened things along.'

'I know, it will help her in the long run, especially with her unique insight and intuition into what's coming. We'll need her to help Crystal in her quest. I just don't want Frank to find out about her – or me for that matter. If he finds out I have visions, he'll think I've been possessed! We didn't all marry the people we love, you know. You two are lucky.'

Kitty coughed and took a bite of her cake. Through a mouthful of crumbs, she replied 'I didn't.'

The other two turned to face her, eyes full of shock. 'But you love Peter!'

Kitty looked at them, all innocently. 'Oh, I *do* love him. I mean we never actually got married.'

Mel spluttered her coffee back into her mug. 'But you ran away to Gretna Green!'

'We did. But we realised that we were only getting married to keep everyone else happy, because I was pregnant – and it was considered scandalous – the running away and the pregnancy.'

'You little rebel!' Izzy clapped her hands in delight. 'So, why didn't you get married after you'd had Dave?'

'And what about your anniversary, you celebrate it every year,' Mel chipped in.

'That's what makes it even more special for us. It makes us feel like the rebellious teenagers we were back then – and that secret we both privately share, is what keeps our relationship very much alive.' She grinned back at them.

Izzy sat back against her chair, stunned. 'Well, I never! I don't really know what to say to that.'

'Don't say anything then. We're happy and we love the life we have. That's all that matters.'

Mel raised her glass. 'I'll drink to that!'

They chinked mugs together and laughed.

~

S ick of the rain, Mandy had stopped for an impromptu cup of tea to warm her. She walked in through the side door and was glad to see the booth nearest the door was empty. She sat down, grateful to get out of the rain but a bit annoyed at the cold draft whistling through the doorway. She picked up her handbag, ready to move to a table further inside, when she recognised the voices coming from the next booth. Sitting back down, she watched the waitress walk towards the next booth, before she came over to take Mandy's order.

'I'll take a pot of tea please,' she ordered quietly, as she didn't want them to know she was there. Ever eager for a bit of gossip, especially when it concerned her sister-in-law, she shimmied round the booth until she was directly behind them and settled back with a cup of tea – her ears tuned into the conversation they were having in the next booth.

Sipping her tea, she perked up when she heard mention of Frank. Listening with renewed enthusiasm, she eaves-dropped intently.

Well, well, well. That *is* interesting, she thought, as she listened.

Resisting the urge to run straight to Frank with details of what she'd heard, she beckoned the waitress over and ordered a congratulatory slice of lemon cake. She relished every forkful, grateful for God creating the bad weather that had ensured she entered the coffee shop at the right time, and had led her to this impromptu goldmine of informa-tion. She sat and waited, hidden from sight, silently offering up a prayer of thanks, until the other women had left the cafe.

After all, it wasn't every day you found the perfect tool to destroy your competition.

43

The pews were half empty in the nave. Of those who were present, Father Thomas guessed that at least half of them were only there out of a morbid curiosity to see who was replacing the disgraced Father Javier.

He let them wait, the buzz of quiet whispering– the atmosphere tense with expectation. He took his time getting ready, tying the cord sash slowly and precisely around the white linen alb he was wearing. He adjusted the stole around his neck before placing the green chasuble over the top. He smoothed down the robe before following the three servers, who carried the cross, candle and incense out of the sacristy, into the sanctuary and up to the lectern.

Standing in front of them, he waited for the room to fall silent. He led them through the Penitential Rites, otherwise known as the group confession, before completing the other introductory rites. As this was his first time in front of the congregation, and knowing about the departure of Father Abitu, he decided to precede the Bible readings with a brief introduction.

'I am Father William Thomas. Unlike the previous

Father, I expect to be addressed appropriately as Father Thomas. I do fear that his choice of address was the first of many wrongdoings committed by Father Javier Abitu. I will *not* be making the same errors.'

He glanced around to make sure his words were being heeded.

'It is not our place to judge, it is God's – and God's alone. As it says in Matthew chapter 7, verse 1:

'Judge not, that you be not judged.''

He banged his fist on the edge of the lectern, emphasising each word. 'Verse 2 continues:

'for with the judgement you pronounce you will be judged, and with the measure you use it will be measured to you.'

'God is merciful and he will show mercy on Father Abitu, for he is young and inexperienced. He has now been shown the error of his ways and, hopefully, he will continue his good works, as well as learning new things in his new placement.'

He looked down to check his notes before continuing. 'Today's lesson is about false prophets. There are those around us whose sole ambition is to disregard the word of God. They blaspheme his image and drag His word through the mud. If we read further into Matthew chapter 7 verse 15:

'Beware of false prophets, who come to you in sheep's clothing, but inwardly are ravenous wolves.'

'These false prophets are amongst us, mark my words.' He looked around, making eye contact with as many people as he could whilst speaking the next couple of sentences. 'Matthew chapter 24 verse 24 warns us that these people will perform great signs and miracles to deceive us – the elect ones – if we let them. Let me repeat that.'

Raising his voice, he banged on the lectern. 'If. We. Let. Them. Jeremiah warns us in chapter 23 verse 16,

'The Lord Almighty says Do not listen, they fill you with false hope."

He made eye contact with one of the men in the audience, holding his gaze, letting him drink in every word.

'These people will get your hopes up and lead you to believe there is another way for salvation.'

He held the Bible up. 'This is the only true word. The Bible is the only true book for you to follow. These people could be members of your family, our nearest and dearest, their friends and relatives, *anybody*. Evil is amongst us and we need to be diligent.'

Father Thomas smoothed back his greased hair and straightened his robe. 'If any of you have any concerns about anything I've said, or anything you have witnessed, please come and share those concerns with me. I can help you, with God's help of course. Lighten your hearts and ensure you are absolved of all sins, whether you have committed them or witnessed them.'

Frank watched Father Thomas with pride. Father Thomas had caught his attention, both with his words and the way he had selected Frank as one of those he made eye contact with. Frank felt as though he had been specially selected and was ecstatic that they finally had a Father who could lead them, who wasn't afraid to strike right at the core of the problem. He glanced slowly round, catching Mandy's stare, before nodding slowly and smiling.

Sitting back in his seat, Frank straightened his tie and puffed his chest out slightly. Finally, someone is in charge who can take control of my immediate problems, he thought.

44

Emily lay in bed, listening to the hustle and bustle downstairs. She should really get up and say 'hi' to her mum, before she left for work – but she was enjoying her lay-in too much to move. She heard the door shut and another open and close, as her mother always threw her briefcase onto the back seat, before getting in. Her mum's car sprung into life, followed by the crunch of gravel beneath wheels, as it reversed off the drive, before the engine sound slowly disappeared.

She lay there, thinking over everything that had happened lately – Crystal's revelations, The Others, Izzy's healing – before she relaxed slightly, knowing that Kitty and her mother knew too, so she had others to talk to and fill in the gaps.

Swinging her legs out of bed, Emily pulled on her dressing gown and pushed on the door handle to open the door. Except it didn't. She pushed the handle down again and pulled the door – it still didn't open.

'Dad!' She hoped her dad hadn't gone off to church early again this morning. 'Dad!'

There was no response, but she heard someone walking up the stairs. She rattled the door handle.

'Dad, is that you? I can't open my door.'

'I know.' He replied from the other side of her door.

Emily stopped rattling the handle, her heart beating rapidly in her chest.

'Dad, can you open it please?'

'I can't do that sweet pea. I'm sorry.'

Emily leant her forehead against one of the wooden inlaid panels. 'Dad, stop it. It's not funny. Please open the door.' The panic was rising in her voice.

'I know it's not a joke. It's for your own good sweet pea, until I can get you some help.'

'Help for what?' Her hands trembled against the cold metal of the handle. She rattled it again, hoping it would finally open.

'Your affliction.'

'I don't have an affliction, Dad.' She walked away from the door and started rummaging around for her mobile phone.

Where is it? she thought, I had it on the bedside cabinet when I went to sleep. Thinking it may have fallen onto her bed she threw the pillows on the floor and tossed the bedcovers back. The phone wasn't there. Emily stood upright and closed her eyes, giving herself a minute to calm down.

This is ridiculous. I'm a grown adult, she thought.

Walking back to the door she knocked hard against it with her knuckles.

'Dad, you have to let me out. I've got to get to work.'

There was only silence on the other side of the door.

'Dad!' she hollered as loud as she could.

'I'm here for you, my baby. It'll all be better soon.' His soothing voice just irritated her more.

'This is stupid. Now let me out!' She banged hard against the door again before turning back to look for her phone.

Think goddamnit, she thought, if it's not on your bedside cabinet, where would it be? She sat on her bed, massaging her eyelids with her finger and thumb.

My bag! Her eyes flew open and she started looking for her handbag. It wasn't anywhere to be found. The fear started radiating from her stomach. The sick feeling worked its way up to her head, making her feel slightly dizzy. She walked back to the door.

'Dad? You've got my phone and bag, haven't you?' She tried to keep her voice level and calm.

'I have. I used your phone to text school to let them know their number one teaching assistant was ill. They were very grateful and hope you get better soon. Sweet pea, I just want to make you better, so you are better soon. That's why I've let Father Thomas know your ailment – he'll be over to see you soon.'

Emily felt the door move slightly as her father sat down on the floor and leant against the door. She mirrored his actions, leaning against the other side of it.

'Dad, what are you doing? I really don't know what you're on about.'

'I heard about your visions. The Bible warns about false prophets – I'm concerned you may be one. Especially after Father Thomas's sermon on Sunday.'

'Dad, I don't have visions. I'm not a false prophet or anything else. I'm just Emily, your daughter.'

'But you will have visions, if your mother and her friends have anything to do with it.'

'What have they got to do with anything?'

'They're leading you astray – them, Crystal and Mark. Mandy overheard them talking and thankfully filled me in on the details. Both you and I are just pawns in their wicked, evil game. I knew it was wrong for you to spend so much time with them,' he replied bitterly. 'I'll be dealing with *them* later.'

'What are you going to do?' Emily held her breath.

'I'm going to help you, with Father Thomas's help. He's cleared his afternoon schedule tomorrow to come and see you. In fact, he was most insistent.

45

The hotel that housed the restaurant was beautiful, all candlelight and chandeliers. The diamonds in both the chandeliers and the table lamps bounced rainbow coloured prisms of light around the room. The men were all dressed in suit and tie, as the elegant establishment demanded. Ladies in beautiful cocktail dresses sipped from martini or wine glasses, their lipstick leaving the latest fashion colour on the delicate glasses. Amy walked into the eating area at 6.30 pm, bold as brass, down the middle of the room towards her table, head held high – green silk skimming the contours of her body, ending just beneath her pert, well-toned derriere. Taking her seat, she smiled at the man opposite her.

'Well, this is all rather fancy. I feel positively under-dressed.' She made light of the comment, but this was one of the few occasions where she really did feel that her favourite low cut dress didn't possess enough material. She straightened her diamante drop earring and picked up the wine list.

The black-haired gentleman sat opposite her leaned

forward. 'You look absolutely beautiful. I am so glad you decided to accept my invitation.' He raised his glass to her before sipping the deep red liquid inside.

'Thank you. I figured you deserve a break, Robert, as you have been bombarding me with phone calls.' Amy looked around at the other diners. Those that had been staring at her rapidly returned their attention to their food – the wives throwing a final scowl disapprovingly at her, before staring intently at their respective husbands. Amy crossed her legs, letting her skirt ride further up her thigh, to give them something else to be cross about.

Robert gestured for the waiter and annoyingly, ordered food for both of them. Amy bit her lip and said nothing though. He was the one paying, after all.

'You do like steak I presume?' His blue eyes didn't register the concern in his voice.

'I do, but it would have been nice to have been given a menu to choose for myself.' She handed him the wine list. 'I expect you to order a *very* expensive bottle of champagne as an apology. It's not like you can't afford it.'

Robert dutifully did as he was told, ordering a £170 bottle of 2002 Dom Perignon and then proceeded to tell her all about life in the London Stock Exchange, as he was a senior analyst at Goldman Sachs. Amy watched his mouth moving before letting her eyes wander, taking the opportunity to study him now they were in close proximity.

He's not my usual type of guy – definitely older – but with a lot more money, Amy thought as she smirked to herself. You've got to aim where you want to be–and you certainly want, no, *need* money!

The candlelight did a good job of smoothing out his skin, especially the crows feet around his eyes – the only thing that gave away his age and the twenty-year age gap between them.. His black curly hair was either dyed or else he'd escaped the greying associated with an older man. His hands were well preserved; his finger nails neatly manicured.

Amy nodded every now and again, letting him think she was interested in the boring banking conversation he was currently throwing in her direction. She silently cursed Chris for egging her on – she'd never given the man currently sharing her table a second glance, if Chris hadn't ridiculed her for not being able to go on a date without dropping her knickers at the end of the evening.

Their food turned up and it was exquisite. The pepper sauce was just a bit on the hot side for her, but the meat just melted on her tongue. The champagne was beautiful and the chocolate Chambord truffle cake, with raspberry compote and whipped cream was rich, smooth and velvety. It was just a shame the person sat opposite her was so boring.

The dinner over, Robert walked round and pulled her chair back. Amy stood up and linked her arm through his, letting him escort her from the restaurant. He escorted her through to the hotel bar, ordering another bottle of Dom Perignon. Amy laughed at his jokes and occasionally touched his knee or arm to let him think she was interested. But in reality, she was bored out of her brains.

Ever since Amy was little, there was nothing she liked better than being the centre of attention. Robert obviously appreciated her good looks, his eyes kept wandering to her cleavage and thighs, but all he wanted to talk about was himself and his job. When there was a lull in the conversation, Amy reached across and kissed him gently on the cheek.

'I've had a lovely evening, Robert.'

He turned his face to her and kissed her on the lips. Amy pulled back and tried to keep the look of disgust from her face. He looked so pathetic, sat there with a puppy-dog look of eagerness on his face.

'I was hoping we could continue our conversation upstairs. I've booked a room.' A room key hung from his index finger. He beckoned the waiter and ordered another bottle of champagne.

Amy stood up and emptied her glass.

'Robert, it was a lovely evening and I may be needy – but I'm not desperate.'

His face dropped. 'But... but... I thought you liked me?'

'I gave you a chance – the benefit of the doubt. I had a nice meal and you got to have the pleasure of my company for a few hours. I gave you a glimpse of what it would be like to be with someone like me.' She ran her hands over the curve of her thighs, just to emphasis her point.

'But I really like you.' He jingled the key, as if to make his point.

'Point made, darling. But unfortunately for you, a pity shag isn't on the cards, as I promised someone I wouldn't tonight.'

He grabbed her arm. 'But I spent loads of money on you. I expect you to show you're grateful.'

Amy rolled her eyes and looked sarcastically down at the hand restraining her. 'I did show my gratitude. I listened to you as you wittered and whined your way through a boring conversation. I laughed at your unfunny jokes and...' She wrenched her arm away. 'I let you grope my ass, my thigh and stare at my tits all night. You've got *way* more than your money's-worth.' Picking up her oversized handbag, she grabbed the unopened bottle of champagne and shoved it into her handbag before walking away from Robert without a backward glance.

~

She walked in the front door and closed it quietly behind her. Kicking off her stilettos, Amy walked barefoot into the kitchen, grabbing herself a glass and popped the cork from the bottle of champagne. Holding up the glass, she toasted the empty room.

'Thanks to the boring fucker, otherwise known as Robert,' she said out loud, then giggled and sipped a mouthful of champagne. Picking up the bottle with her free hand Amy tiptoed into the living room. She came face to face with her mother.

'What time do you call this?' Mandy looked at her wrist watch.

'Early,' Amy replied giggling. 'It's only nine, don't be so boring.'

'Look at the state of you.' Her lip curled up in disdain. 'What did I ever do to have a daughter like you?' She sat down on the sofa.

'I'm just following in mummy's footsteps. Remember, you used to be quite a floozy didn't you?' Amy saluted sarcastically.

'And look where it got me. Haven't you learnt anything from my mistakes?'

'Yeah, not to have kids. We Radcliffes obviously aren't the maternal type.' She sneered back at her mother. 'That's why I always use a condom.'

'It's not just about all the sex, you know.' Mandy could feel her temper flaring.

'I like the sex. Anyway, I didn't sleep with the guy I went

out with tonight.' She took a sip from her glass. 'I would've done if he wasn't so boring.'

Mandy closed her eyes and tried to calm herself. Opening them again, she tried a different tack.

'I just want you to have a better life than I did. Maybe with God's help you can find that.'

'What was so awful about your life, huh mother?' She raised her arms, spilling champagne over the carpet and sending drops of it running down her arm. 'Oh yes, *I forgot*. You had *me!*' Amy jabbed her index finger to her chest. 'Then you let yourself go and Dad got mad at you. He hit you a few times and, like a weak pathetic person, you let him. *I'd* never let someone hit me. *That's* because I'm stronger than you.'

'Your father was a bully.' Mandy got to her feet. 'He hit me more than a few times and over stupid little things.'

'He raised me, not you. You were a pathetic heap in the corner, drinking to drown your sorrows. No wonder he hit you. Have you not realised yet?' she sneered at her mother. 'Even God can't be arsed to save you.'

The slapping sound ricocheted around the living room. Amy's hand flew to her mouth as she watched her daughter's eyes well up and her cheek glow from a fresh hand print.

'I'm sorry. I...' Mandy sat back down on the sofa.

Amy raised her hand to her cheek and blinked back the tears. 'Now *there's* the real you. Dad only hit you to stop you hitting me in your drunken state. You drove the only person who really loved me away. I'll *never* forgive you for that.'

'I do love you – you're my daughter. God's forgiven me, Frank is forgiving me so why can't you?'

'If there really was a God he'd have taken you away, not my father.' Amy got up to leave the room.

'I blame the people you hang around with. They've dragged you down.' Mandy raised her voice slightly. 'Especially after what I heard the other day.'

Amy stopped and turned slowly around. 'What did you hear?'

'I told Frank, especially as it involved Emily. He was most appreciative.' Mandy had her head down and was fiddling with the edge of her cardigan.

Her attention piqued at the mention of her cousin, Amy sat down on the arm of the sofa, furthest away from her mother and near to the door.

'What did you hear about Emily?'

Mandy leant towards her daughter and whispered. 'I heard Izzy, Kitty and Mel talking about her being special.'

Amy stood up. 'Yeah, yeah, we all know *she's* special. Everybody loves Emily.'

Mandy gestured for her to sit back down. 'No, not like that. They reckon she can see things – like visions and that. Frank thinks she's a false prophet or possessed or something.' She looked down and fiddled with the edge of her cardigan again. 'He said he was going to sort it.'

'Did you hear anything else?'

Mandy nodded. 'I did. Mel doesn't love him, she married him out of convenience, to hide the fact she sees things too. Oh, and they said something about Crystal and a quest – but they didn't go into any more details, so I don't know what that was about.'

She looked up to see if her daughter was showing any interest, and was relieved to see she was indeed interested.

'Well, let's hope that Emily gets what she deserves. See, not everyone who seems all sweetness and light *is* actually a good person.'

'I know. I'm sorry I hit you.' Mandy looked apologetically at her daughter.

Amy shrugged. 'It isn't the first time. I'm used to it.' She got up and walked out of the room – her bottle of champagne and half empty glass forgotten. Two minutes later the heavy thudding of her stereo vibrated throughout the house. Mandy sat on the sofa, held her head in her hands and cried.

46

The clock on the kitchen wall chimed eight. Crystal got up and pulled the curtain back slightly, peering into the darkness outside. She sat back down and checked her phone. The screen was blank – still no texts received.

Crystal walked into the living room, placing the phone on the side table next to her, within easy reach, just in case Emily rang or texted her. She was worried. Emily usually ran a couple of minutes late, but never more than ten – she was now an hour late and wasn't picking up her calls. She sat on the sofa biting her nails and staring at the mobile phone, willing it to ring. Picking it up, she debated whether to ring the house phone or Mel's mobile. Putting it back down Crystal chewed on her thumb nail, indecision and worry racking her mind. She couldn't shake the nagging fear she was feeling, deep inside at the pit of her stomach.

What if The Others have taken her, like they tried to do with Serena, and the others that they were successful with? Crystal thought, as she tried to reason with herself, but the same question kept running through her mind. Finally, she decided to go with her gut feeling and picked up her mobile.

She really didn't want to interrupt their girl's night round Kitty's, but needs must. She dialled Mel's mobile number and waited.

Mel answered after the fourth ring. Crystal explained that Emily hadn't arrived and shared her concerns. There was a long pause on the other end of the line, as Mel repeated Crystal's concerns to the others present.

'I think you need to come over here, Crystal. Your mum's calling Nathan and he'll be with you shortly. Wait for him to get there and he'll walk with you.'

'I'll be fine to come over on my own; it'll only take me ten minutes.'

'No. Wait for Nathan, just to be on the safe side,' Mel insisted.

Crystal agreed and hung up. A couple of minutes later, a slightly hot and breathless Nathan walked into the house.

'Let's go.' He handed Crystal her coat.

'Don't you want a couple of minutes to get your breath back? You look like you ran all the way here.' Crystal obediently pulled on her coat and tied her boot laces.

'Flying half cut is not only difficult, it's an experience.' He leant against the door frame, his breath coming out in short, alcohol scented puffs.

'Do you think she's been taken?' Crystal looked up as she finished tying her laces.

'We can't be sure. But if she has, they may well be coming for you. So let's go.'

Locking the door behind them, they walked along the main road through the estate, avoiding the shorter, secluded route through the alleyways and past the green. After all, if anyone was coming for them it was unlikely they'd be using the roads.

Now Crystal had had a decent night's sleep her body was

rejuvenated. She felt great. Her skin was hypersensitive to any change in temperature and, although the winter chill was biting, her body felt as if it was buzzing with electricity and heat – alert to any potential attackers that might be coming from above or behind them. She knew Nathan was feeling the same, as his head was continually turning left and right, scanning the area around them for potential threats. The cold breeze was sobering him up quicker than a strong cup of coffee. He walked beside Crystal, hands braving the cold and hanging half clenched by his sides, ready for action.

They arrived at Kitty's house to find everyone was there. Kitty and Izzy were watching Mel's facial expressions as she called some of Emily's friends. As Crystal sat down next to her mother, Izzy leant over and spoke quietly to her and Nathan.

'Mel rang Frank to check whether Emily was home as Mel had come here straight from work at the textile company.' She added for Nathan's benefit. 'He was a bit preoccupied, but confirmed that she wasn't there. Could you help Mel by calling some of her friends? Judging by her face, she's getting a bit stressed.'

'Does Mark know what's going on?' Crystal whispered back.

Izzy shook her head. 'We didn't want to get him or Peter involved just yet. They're out in the garage, tinkering with the car engine.' She glanced across at Kitty before continuing. 'Kitty wants to keep her family out of it for as long as possible.'

Mel ended her phone call and shook her head. 'Well, that's another dead end.' She picked up her mug of coffee and took a swig, before dialling another number.

Nathan crouched on the floor between them. 'I've called

Richard and Martin. We'll go rattle a few cages and find out if anyone knows anything.'

'Okay I'm not going to ask whose cages you'll be rattling – just find out if they know anything.' Izzy patted his arm in silent appreciation whilst Crystal picked up her phone and called Chris. Izzy watched her as she spoke to Chris, hopeful of a positive outcome – but then feeling slightly disappointed as her daughter shook her head to confirm he hadn't seen Emily. Crystal ended the phone call then dialled another number. Getting no answer, she turned to her mother.

'Amy's not answering either.'

Izzy shook her head. 'We drew a blank with Mandy's mobile too. Maybe I should go round there?' She glanced worriedly at Mel.

Crystal stood up and put her coat back on. 'I'll go round there and see if they've seen her. You stay here with Mel.'

Izzy placed a hand on Crystal's arm and opened her mouth to speak, but Crystal cut her off before she could utter a word.

'Don't worry Mum, I'll be fine. I won't be long.' She kissed her mother's forehead and walked out the back door.

C rystal banged the door knocker of the white, glass panelled door in an effort to be heard over the music. She waited for a couple of minutes for someone to answer the door, but it remained unopened. Peering through the letterbox, Crystal could see the flicker of a television screen shining from the direction of the living room. She gently stepped onto the front border directly under the living room window and put her face up against the glass. Mandy was fast asleep on the sofa, oblivious to the loudness of the music, a bottle of champagne and a half empty glass on the floor below her.

Crystal stepped back to the front door and tried Amy's mobile number again. Looking back through the letterbox, she could see the offending mobile light up from where it sat on the hallway table. She grabbed the door knocker and hammered it against its metal base, as hard as she could, whilst hollering for Amy to answer the door.

The upstairs front window finally opened and the heavy beat of the R'n'B music instantly flooded out, louder than ever.

'What do you want?' Amy shouted over the music.

'Open the door, we need to talk.' Crystal gestured towards the front door, to get her message across.

'We've got nothing to talk about.' Amy disappeared back inside.

'Amy! It's important – have you seen Emily?' Crystal stepped back and shouted louder, straining her vocal cords to almost breaking point. 'Amy!'

The music stopped and Amy poked her head back out of the window. 'For God's sake, what do you want?'

'Open the door. We need to talk.'

After a couple of minutes, the front door finally opened and a red-eyed Amy stood there, arms folded, barring Crystal from entering.

'You been crying?' Crystal asked.

'No,' came the sullen reply.

Crystal reached out to comfort her, but Amy flinched and backed away.

'It's understandable that you'd be upset about Emily. You may not get on, but she is your cousin.'

'What about her?' Amy unfolded her arms and began inspecting the purple nail varnish covering each nail.

Crystal hastily backtracked, realising that no-one else actually knew. 'I'm just a bit worried about her. We arranged to meet and she didn't turn up.'

'Maybe she had something better to do – though who'd want to spend time with her is beyond me.' Amy's mouth turned up slightly at the corners – her left eyebrow raised slightly.

'I haven't got time for this, Amy. Have you seen her?'

Amy continued, 'Even Mark's only seeing her because he has to.'

'What's that supposed to mean? He likes her.'

'Yeah, with a little push from mummy number one and two,' Amy replied dryly.

'I have no idea what you're on about.' Crystal crossly folded her arms. 'You can't bear her having someone, can you? Especially when you can't keep a boy for more than one night.'

'How's your love life, little Miss Perfect? Surprised you've got time for anyone, especially when you have a top secret quest to fulfil.' Amy leant forward. 'We're supposed to be friends and you tell me fuck all. Wouldn't surprise me if Tony felt left out in the cold too. Did you know he's getting the IT guy to monitor your computer activity? I heard them talking about it. He probably thinks he'll learn more about you from that computer, than talking to you. You don't deserve someone like him – he's too good for you.'

'He's monitoring my computer?' Crystal looked up in surprise. 'What else did you...?' She shook her head. 'No. Do you know what? I really don't have time for this. I need to find Emily.' Crystal turned and started to walk away.

'Whatever's happening to her, she probably deserves it.' Amy shouted defiantly behind her.

Crystal turned and walked back to Amy, stopping when she was less than twelve inches in front of her. She could smell alcohol on Amy's breath and realised her red eyes weren't crying related.

'What's your problem with Emily? She's done nothing to hurt you.' Crystal looked up, her eyes narrow slits. 'She's always nice to you and your mother and she just wants to have a relationship with you both. What is so wrong with that?'

Well, she's not having a relationship with either. My mum may not be perfect, but she's the only one I've got. I won't be sharing her with anyone.' She stuck her face right up against Crystal's. 'So when you see her, tell her to back the fuck off.'

Crystal took a step back and her eyes opened wide in shock. 'Oh my God, you're jealous of her. What's up? Worried your mother will leave you too?'

'My dad didn't leave me! He left my mother, *not* me! She's got a mum and a dad who thinks the sun shines out of her arse. My mum may think we can all get together and play happy families, but I won't have it!'

'You are such a bitch.' Crystal shook her head. 'It isn't Emily's fault your father left.'

'Maybe not, but she may be about to find out what it's like to lose him. And it couldn't happen to a nicer person,' Amy replied bitterly before laughing slightly.

Crystal's face dropped. 'Why would she be about to lose him?'

'He knows about you all.' Her eyes were full of anger. 'Including Emily. My mum heard them talking about it in the coffee shop. She told him everything. He knows Mel doesn't love him too. So, whatever he's going to do to punish them – well, it's obviously long overdue.'

'Oh God!' Panicked, Crystal wrestled her mobile out of her pocket and fumbled with the keypad.

'You didn't know? Shame. Maybe you should all have stopped judging me and looked a bit closer to home. Now you know what it feels like to be left out of the loop,' Amy ended triumphantly.

'What have you both done?' A horrified Crystal looked up, just in time to have the door shut in her face.

47

Mel parked the car at the end of the road and they all got out. All four of them walked towards her house and the three women waited for Nathan to disappear round the back before they stepped onto the gravel. Mel squeezed Izzy and Kitty's hands for reassurance, before letting them fall and making her way to the front door alone.

She put her key in the keyhole and tried to turn it to unlock the door, but Frank had obviously left his key in the keyhole the other side, preventing her from entering. She rapped her knuckles against the solid wood and called out his name through the letterbox.

'Frank?' She saw him appear in the hallway from the direction of the kitchen.

'What do you want?'

'Why have you locked me out, Frank?' She kept her voice level and calm.

'You're a temptress and a heathen. I know you're not on God's side – and anyone not on his side is on the wrong side.'

She glanced back at Izzy and Kitty – they both beckoned her on.

'Frank, I've been married to you for twenty years. Don't you think you'd know if I didn't believe in God?'

He lowered himself so just his eyes were visible through the slot of the letter box. 'You married me for convenience. That's what Mandy heard you say.'

Mel kept her facial expression neutral, so as not to confirm or deny what he was saying. 'Frank, I love you. I always have. You know Mandy's lusted after you for years – even before Kevin disappeared. You can't trust anything she says.'

Frank turned, as a noise inside distracted him. Mel quickly started talking again.

'Is Emily in there Frank? I don't understand what any of this has to do with her.'

His eyes appeared back at the letterbox, his voice angry. 'Yes you do. You're trying to get her set up with Mark so she can connect with the devil! Probably the very same one that's giving you your so –called visions. I won't let that happen to my Sweet Pea. I'm keeping her here until Father Thomas can exorcise her, or something. He's going to help me.'

Mel looked back in panic at Kitty and Izzy. 'Ask when,' Izzy mouthed back at her.

'Frank, that's not my intention. I know you want what's best for Emily – so do I. When did Father Thomas say he was coming? I want to be there to see him too.'

'You just want to stop him!' Frank replied.

'I don't, Frank. I want him to help me too,' she pleaded with him through the letterbox.

He hesitated. 'You do?'

'Of course I do, Frank. I just want to be with you and

Emily. One happy family, like you always wanted.' She saw Nathan appear in the shadows, from round the side of the house, holding hands with Emily as he led her quietly along the hedge and towards the road. She watched as Kitty led her away and Nathan came back to stand with Izzy, before she realised Frank was talking and returned her attention to him.

'Father Thomas couldn't make it until tomorrow. He really wants to help.'

'I'll bet he does,' Mel replied dryly.

'Do you want to come in? I'll be happy to let you in – but they're not coming with you.' He looked past her to Izzy and Nathan. 'I know *her* and her daughter are not on God's side.'

'It's okay, Frank. I'll come in on my own.' She took a step back as she heard the door being unlocked. Frank peered round the door, looking at her.

'Come in.' He swung the door open wide enough to let her in.

'Can I see Emily?' Mel asked as she stepped over the threshold. It was a mistake to ask. Frank immediately got suspicious. He held his hand out and stopped her coming in any further.

'That's all you wanted to do, isn't it?' He looked so hurt.

Mel tried to deny it. Shaking her head vehemently, she replied. 'No, of course not!'

The reality of the situation hit him – she saw it register on his face. He pushed her back outside, before turning and running upstairs – leaving the door open. Mel stepped inside and ran up after him. He was frantically unlocking Emily's door as she reached him. He was walking into Emily's room as Izzy and Nathan crept up the stairs and into Mel's bedroom. Mel stood on the landing, waiting for the response.

'No!' Frank screamed. He backed out of Emily's bedroom, knocking a glass vase over in the process. The glass shards shattered around his feet.

'How did you get her?' He turned to Mel, his face red with rage. He walked towards her and grabbed hold of her shoulders, shaking her.

'How did you get her out? I locked that door!'

Mel looked into his eyes. All she could see was anger and hate. Tiny globules of spit landed on her face as he shouted at her.

'I just wanted to help her, can't you see that?' He hung onto Mel, in an effort to prevent his world from collapsing.

Mel reached up and gently took hold of his arms, removing his hands from her shoulders. Stepping back, she looked at him pityingly.

'Frank, I loved you the first time I met you. But since your brother disappeared, your religious aspirations have become an obsession. Now look at what you've done – you've locked up your own daughter, for crying out loud – driven by your religious beliefs. I will not have my daughter physically or mentally tied up so tightly by those religious rules and regulations.'

He took a step forward when he realised Izzy and Nathan were in their bedroom, but Mel held her arm out to prevent him from passing. 'I believe everyone has a right to live their own lives – whether they are young, old, black or white. And especially if they have special talents and abilities that the religious community consider 'evil', if and when it suits them.'

He looked at her, his eyes full of confusion and sadness – his anger subsiding.

'Tell me, Frank. If a person in your church community had visions, you'd consider it a miracle, wouldn't you?'

Frank nodded. 'Of course I would. There are plenty of examples in the Bible. Daniel Chapter eight and eleven both say Daniel and King Belshazzar had visions. Even in...'

Mel cut him off. 'But the thought of me and Emily having visions is so abhorrent? It's considered 'evil' or we're labelled as false prophets. I don't see what the difference is. I can quote Bible chapter and verses too, Frank. In Acts Chapter two, verse 17, it states

'And in the last days it shall be, God declares, that I will pour out my spirit on all flesh, and your sons and daughters shall prophesy, and your young men shall see visions, and your old men shall dream dreams.'

So you see, anyone can find a Bible reference to back up whatever they wish to believe.'

She watched Nathan and Izzy leave her room and walk down the stairs, both carrying bags containing her personal possessions. Frank watched them too, finally realising what was going on.

'You're leaving me, aren't you?' His arms dropped to his sides, his head hung in defeat.

Mel kissed the top of his head. 'I can't live with you while you care more about the church than us.'

'But I don't. I...'

Mel placed her index finger under his chin and raised his head. Looking straight into his eyes, she responded, 'Seriously Frank, are you more hurt about me leaving you – or what the religious community will say?'

He let his gaze fall to the floor. Mel let go of his face and walked past him.

'That's just what I thought, Frank.'

48

T he sunlight streamed through the crack in the curtains, waking Mel from her sleep. She yawned and stretched, before wiggling back into the warmth of the duvet cover. Even after three weeks of sleeping in Kitty's spare room, Mel was still surprised over the amount of space a single person had, when sleeping in a double bed. It was also a pleasant change to wake up refreshed and relaxed.

Mel fiddled with the gold bands on her left ring finger. Watching the light dancing off her engagement ring, she realised that she didn't miss him. In fact, the light dancing off her ring was the only thing that had managed to dance in pure joy since they were married.

Hearing the noisy voices echoing around the kitchen, she threw back the covers and grabbed her dressing gown. Mel placed her arms in the sleeves and tied the belt, before her temples started to throb slightly. Recognising the symptoms, she sat back down on the edge of the bed and calmly waited for the flash of light.

It only took a minute for the brief flash of white light, followed by the vision. She'd gotten used to the feeling of being pulled swiftly backwards down a light tunnel, when she was younger – in the years before she'd met Frank, so Mel closed her eyes and breathed calmly through the whole process. The tunnel was followed by the inevitable movie of picture and sound – a brief one-minute snap of a moment yet to happen.

Then, just as swiftly as it started she was racing back down the light tunnel and her eyes flew back open. She'd seen more this time, and she needed a couple of minutes to process what she'd seen. Mel sat gripping the edge of the bed, her knuckles white, heart racing, and tried to breathe through the fear she'd been shown. Knowing that the vision was only one interpretation of a future moment, Mel hoped she could manipulate the upcoming events to ensure this particular version didn't happen.

Mel stood up and placed her hand on her chest, feeling the reassuring beat of her heart through her rib cage – calming her, soothing her – until she felt ready to smile and go downstairs.

'Morning – sleep okay?' Peter was sat at the table finishing his boiled egg and toast.

'Fine, thanks.' Mel smiled and poured a glass of orange juice from the jug on the table. Peter was a sweetheart, he had absolutely no idea what was going on, but had let her and Emily stay without any questions being asked.

'Do you want any cereal?' Kitty stood there, apron on and dirty frying pan in hand. 'I could cook you an English breakfast if you want? The boys popped in before work for theirs, so adding another one would make no difference to me.'

'Honestly, I'm fine with just the juice.' Mel sat down and sipped from her glass. 'Has Emily been down yet?'

Kitty reached over and pinched a piece of Peter's toast.

'She went out for a run with Mark. The fresh air and space seems to be doing her the world of good.'

Mel nodded, understanding what Kitty was saying. 'She certainly seems a lot happier lately – without the stress from our house.'

Peter stood up and put his plate in the dishwasher, then leant forward to kiss his wife. 'We've always found the fresh air and space rejuvenating, haven't we Kitty?' He kissed Kitty again on the lips, giving her bottom a gentle slap as he walked past. 'You're more than welcome to stay as long as you like Mel. I'm off to work, so I'll see you later.' He opened the back door then hesitated. Turning around he continued. 'Besides, I'm sure Kitty loves having female company – she's been surrounded by testosterone for far too long!'

Kitty waved as he walked down the path and out the back gate. 'He's a diamond, isn't he?' She turned away from the window and wiped her hand on her apron.

'You're lucky to have someone so understanding,' Mel replied quietly.

Kitty took off her apron, placing it on the edge of the table before pouring herself a mug of tea. 'Are you okay hun? Is it making you uncomfortable seeing me and Peter together?' She reached over and touched Mel's hand.

Mel sighed. 'I'm fine.' She shook her head and smiled at Kitty. 'Of course it doesn't bother me – you're like a couple of love-struck teenagers!' She laughed and looked down at the rings on her wedding finger. 'Besides, I don't miss him you know.' She looked back up at Kitty. 'I know I should, but I just feel so relieved.' She let out a deep sigh. 'I'm relieved I don't have to pretend anymore. I'm relieved I don't have to carry that stress around with me. I just hope you and Peter can withstand anything that comes your way.'

'We're fine...' Kitty kept her tone upbeat. 'We can...'

Mel interrupted her. 'You say that now, but what happens when he finds out everything that's been going on? What about when he finds out we've all been hiding secrets from him?'

Kitty put her mug down and rested her chin on her hands. 'Don't you worry about us. It'll sort itself out – you'll see.'

Mel squeezed her friends' hand. 'I hope so. I'd hate to see our secrets affect your happiness.'

49

E mily loved Sunday evenings as she had her routine down to a fine art – especially since they'd moved into Kitty and Peter Curtis' house. She loved the freedom and the space; it was as if a huge rain cloud of stress had been removed from above her head. Her room was really pretty – cream and pink floral wallpaper adorned the walls and all the furniture was a white shaker style. The light was a gold and white mini chandelier, matching the colours in the soft pile carpet on the floor.

She'd spent the evening in the room above the garage, as this had turned into her and Mark's chill-out place. They'd snuggled up on the sofa together watching a film, before passionately kissing each other and coming back into the house. Then they'd join his parents and her mother in the living room for an hour or so, before going their separate ways to their bedrooms.

As Emily lay on her bed, she twiddled a curly strand of blonde hair around her finger. A smile of anticipation crept across her face. Since moving into his parents' house, her relationship with Mark had gotten quite intense, and she believed it wouldn't be long before her wish to remain a virgin until she was married might just fall by the wayside. Just the thought of being with Mark made her heart expand and her pulse quicken. Even when he was in another room, she could sense he was around – the hairs on the back of her neck would prickle as a paperclip would dance between two magnets – and Emily firmly believed they were both meant to be together.

Focus, Emily, she thought, as she let her breath rush out of her lungs, whilst letting the mental images she had of the two of them together go from her mind. She still had work to do before she went to bed. Reaching under her white and gold metal bedstead, she pulled her laptop onto her lap and logged in.

Firstly, Emily uploaded a new set of audio video clips to YouTube and the website. This was followed by a quick check and answer for incoming comments and finally, a check of the viewer statistics. Their audience was growing steadily and she was pleased to see other half and full bloods were answering their calls, as well as interested humans who wanted more information. She'd organised a guerrilla marketing campaign via social media for Thursday night, and was pleased to see they had people from all over the world taking part and offering to anonymously leave her specially designed 'Account' leaflets at random places and organisations.

Pleased with how things were turning out, Emily logged off her computer and got into bed. She briefly updated her diary before returning it to its hiding place under her bedside cabinet. She then picked up her mobile phone and dialled Crystal's number.

'Hey hun, how's it going?' The phone had barely rung when Crystal answered.

'I've just uploaded the latest audio clips. You'd be amazed at the viewing figures, Crystal – people are really starting to listen now!'

'That's great. I have a meeting with the others next week; I'll let them know about our progress. '

'I really want to meet them all.' Emily sighed down the phone.

'I know you do, but I don't want you getting too heavily involved.' Crystal paused. 'It's my fight; I'd never forgive myself if an innocent got hurt – especially if that innocent was you.'

'I know.' Emily rubbed her temples as she could feel a tension headache coming on. 'Just let me know how it goes.'

'I will. Have a good night and I'll catch up with you tomorrow.'

Emily said goodbye and ended the call. Her head was starting to ache now, so she turned her bedroom light off and lay in the darkness until she fell asleep.

50

Crystal stood on an old upturned tea chest surveying the thirty-strong crowd in front of her. They were all crammed into the small frowsty outhouse, where she'd met some of the regulars over a month ago. Nathan was stood to her left, protecting her like a faithful guard dog would and Izzy, Serena, Stephanie and Richard were smiling encouragingly up at her from their positions in the front row. She held her hands up for silence.

She was prepared this time. She lifted her notes so she could see them in the candlelight. Her voice was loud, confident and clear.

'The Account is the only surviving record of what really happened in the past – our past, and that of our parents and family before them. You can compare it to the Bible that is universally used throughout the religious community now, and see the deceptions – and warnings – provided to us.' She glanced down at her notes and continued. There are plenty of them to choose from, some of which are as follows:

Adam and Eve were used as an example to us all. They lived happily in the place provided for them, until their eyes were opened and they discovered knowledge. The Others realised they were suddenly full of the same knowledge they had – they could tell the difference between good and evil for themselves. This scared The Others as they were worried that man would realise how vast that knowledge was and, as a result, they would realise they could live forever, so they were sent away and punished.'

She looked around the room, making eye contact with as many as she could.

'Another person has rewritten the accurate account of Noah and the flood. This person states:

'Noah was saved from the flood and anyone who's been to church knows the story. He built an ark to save two of everything. But what the bible doesn't make clear is that the wooden ark is a metaphor for the barrier in your mind – the one that The Others put there. The flood he was saved from was a flood of knowledge – not water. He and the others in the ark were happy to stay in blissful ignorance, as long as they kept their lives. They chose to take the side of The Others.'

Crystal put her notes down and took a deep, slow breath before continuing.

'I am happy you have all been able to make it here tonight and that fear has not stopped you. I understand how scared you must feel – I felt that way too, at first – but we have the right to live our lives freely. We should not have to hide. Some of you have abilities that you are currently aware of – others have yet to have theirs awoken. The Account contains details of how best to look after and protect your-selves and your abilities and I will be sharing that information with you all. We are *all* able to do amazing things that are naturally part of our genetic make-up. We are *all* made from the same energy that The Others are made from. We *all* have unlimited potential. We just have to learn to manage it and to harness it. No one has the right to block us from our abilities, strength and personal power. Religion and governments are trying to pigeonhole us to fit a mould that suits them and keeps us ignorant and fearful. I say we should fight for what is rightfully ours!'

The applause was spontaneous. Nathan winked at Crystal and he leant over and whispered in her ear.

'Your public speaking has really come along, hasn't it?'

'I've been practicing – and I'm prepared this time – now I know they're all expecting me to say something.'

She held her hands up for silence again.

'There is a battle coming and my job in this battle is to bring enlightenment to the world, regardless of what they throw at me. Some of you are here because you have seen our audio visuals on YouTube; others are here because you have a deep need to find out who you are and what you are capable of. We all have to practise and harness our abilities and be ready to fight for what we believe is right. So, spread the word and let's increase our numbers, so we are ready for whatever's coming.'

51

Frank sat proudly on the front pew on Sunday. He was mesmerised by Father Thomas' sermon – the man never failed to inspire him. Frank smoothed down his already immaculate tie, tucking it into his dark grey waistcoat. Since Mel had left he felt free to voice his beliefs openly and honestly – and being here, at the front of the church for every service, was his way of showing how strong that belief was.

'We as a congregation must stand by our principles and beliefs.' Father Thomas was magnificent, his voice boomed around the room, filling every corner of the church with his words. 'We will be tested on our beliefs. In the book of Judges Chapter 16, Samson was betrayed by his own wife, Delilah.'

I know how that feels, Frank thought bitterly to himself. He glanced behind him, his eyes making contact with Mandy's. She reddened slightly and grinned, before lowering her eyes again.

'In Genesis Chapter 19, Lot's wife didn't do as was commanded and she was turned to a pillar of salt.' Father

Thomas banged his fist against the lectern. 'Even the angels were tested. In Jude I verse six, it states:

'And the angels who did not stay within their own position of authority, but left their proper dwelling – he kept in darkness until the judgement of the great day'.

'It – is – our – duty' his fist banged out every word on the solid wood beneath it. 'It is our duty to test those spirits, as is dictated in the first book of John Chapter four, verse I:

'Beloved, do not believe every spirit, but test the spirits to see whether they are from God, for many false prophets have gone into the world.'

'The book of Revelations warns us that the great dragon was thrown down and Satan *and his angels* were thrown to earth!' He paused to let his words sink in and lowered his voice, so Frank and the rest of the congregation were holding their breaths and craning their necks to catch his next words.

'My brethren, the world is full of false prophets and they hide amongst you. They won't all be wearing the face of evil, the face of Satan.' He leant forward against the lectern. 'As is stated in the book of Corinthians – even Satan disguises himself as an angel of light. My friends, these cowards of evil not only disguise themselves; some of them are too scared of rebuttal and ridicule to even show their faces! Some of these so-called-prophets actually teach their false doctrines, over the internet, via the written word and with recordings. '

The congregation jumped as he hit the lectern and raised his voice to shout the next words.

'Do not be fooled! The truth doesn't hide! God doesn't hide! He has always been there for you! If you want to be amongst those mentioned in the book of Revelations – those that are kept safe – then keep your faith strong! As he states in Revelations 7:

'Do not harm the earth or the sea or the trees, until we have sealed the servants of our God on their foreheads.'

'He will protect you, if you just keep the faith. In Chapter three, verse 10 it states:

'Because you have kept my word about patient endurance, I will keep you from the hour of trial that is coming on the whole world, to try those who dwell on the earth. I am coming soon. Hold fast what you have, so that no one may seize your crown.'

'My brethren, do not be afraid. Spread the word and be ready to fight for what you believe, for you will be tested. Some of you may even lose your life, but we all know this is only temporary, for God will resurrect those who believe, and you will walk the earth again. So be not afraid to fight for the time is nigh!' Father Thomas held his arms above his head, the victory evident in his face.

52

Getting out of bed, Emily put on her dressing gown and made her way to the bedroom door. As she made her way down the stairs, her temples started to throb slightly, so she rubbed them in small circular movements.

The others were already having their breakfast, even the boys, who had popped in for their usual home cooked English breakfast of sausage, egg, bacon, beans, plum tomatoes and toast. She smiled at Kitty and laughed slightly, as seeing her stood in her apron at the stove was a becoming a regular morning feature.

Reaching across the table for the orange juice, she carefully lifted the glass jug towards her to fill her empty glass. A sudden bright white flash of light blinded her and she fell to the floor. The glass shards fell over her body like fresh snow on inert paving stones.

Kitty dropped the frying pan back onto the stove and hurried to her side. At the same time five chairs were scraped back, as Peter and his sons all leapt to the feet and rushed over to the now orange soaked body.

'Give her some room!' Kitty shooed them all back. 'She'll

be fine in a minute. Move back!' She held her hand, patting it reassuringly. There was really nothing else she could do until she woke up.

'Tell me what's going on!' Peter raised his voice to be heard above the noise of his sons – all voicing their concerns.

'Oh my God!' Mel had heard the noise and came rushing down the stairs. She rushed over to her daughter's side. Sinking to her knees, she took hold of Emily's other hand. 'Honey, it will be fine. You're safe, just let it happen.'

'Boys, sit down and be quiet! Kitty, Mel, what's happening to her?' Peter stood above them, his voice angry, his face concerned.

Mel and Kitty exchanged looks. 'She'll be fine in a minute,' Mel replied. She glanced back at Kitty. 'I'm sorry. I should've told her what symptoms to watch for.' She closed her eyes briefly before looking back at her friend. 'It shouldn't have been like this, in front of others.' Her eyes welled up.

Kitty took hold of Mel's hand. 'It's fine. She'll be okay.'

'Will someone please tell me what the hell is going on?' Peter demanded. Mark got to his feet and stood next to his father. They looked identical, both five foot seven, curly brown hair and big brown cow eyes, full of concern. Mark put his hand gently on his mother's shoulder. 'Mum, what's happening to her? Is she having a fit?'

Kitty looked across at Mel. She was shaking her head, her eyes wide, willing Kitty not to say anything. She wasn't ready for them all to know just yet. Kitty closed her eyes and nodded slowly. She couldn't keep it from her family any longer.

'She's not having a fit; she's having her first vision.' She squeezed Mel's hand.

'Look at me, Mel.' She drowned out the noise of the men behind her and spoke quietly and calmly to her long-term friend. 'Remember when this first happened to you? Me and Izzy held your hand and let you come round in your own time. She's fine. Look, she's moving.'

The silence spread as everyone stopped talking and watched Emily. She pulled her knees up slowly, moving her into the foetal position. Then she let go of their hands. Mel and Kitty sat back, giving Emily room. Instantaneously her eyes flew open and she took in great gasps of oxygen, as if she'd be holding her breath the entire time she was unconscious. Her skin was pale, her eyes widened in panic. Finally, her eyes focused on her mother and Emily copied her in slow, deep breaths until her heart rate returned to normal. Eventually she spoke.

'He's here. Tell Crystal he's coming for her.'

ANGEL UPRISING

THE ACCOUNT TRILOGY: BOOK TWO

Read on for a sneak preview of Book Two ...

CHAPTER 1

They came slowly at first. Those that had read the leaflets, watched the YouTube videos or heard through word of mouth. They'd been practising their abilities for the past month, honing their skills and getting ready for the physical – and mental – battle ahead.

Crystal stood on an upturned tea chest in the last of four outhouses, watching those around her practising their healing energies. Clad in dark denim skinny jeans and a crop vest top, her toned, trim body showed the benefits of her heavy training regime.

They weren't short of healahs, Crystal thought. There were twenty in all, eager to explore their abilities and help the cause. Crystal understood that they were mainly alternative therapists – probably as they were more open to the subtle changes in energy in and around them. She loved watching her mother Izzy, as she taught them – aided by her more than capable assistant, Serena. She always spoke softly to them each individually, as she worked around the room. The energy in this room was amazing, it lifted your spirit until you felt drunk on the euphoria of the orange and white glowing energy emitting from their healing hands. It mingled with the flickering light of the candles placed in metal stands in each corner of the room.

They'd been using the same set of four outhouses for months – although they'd tidied them up a bit since Crystal first saw them. They were tucked down the back of a derelict paper mill factory in Reading, just a short train ride from her home in Thatcham. Judging by the rate the group were growing though, Crystal figured she'd better start looking for somewhere bigger – maybe they'd use the actual paper mill – she wasn't sure, so made a mental note to get Nathan to look into it later.

'Do you think they're ready?' Crystal jumped down off the tea chest and stood next to her mother.

Izzy nodded. 'I think so... I hope so.'

'Good. You're both doing a great job.' Satisfied, Crystal nodded. 'I'm just nipping outside to check the others. She let her mother go back to her teaching and Crystal walked through the small wooden rear door and into the yard out the back. She stood for a couple of minutes watching the thirteen flyahs – mainly men being taught by Nathan and Martin – but Stephanie was also there with two other new girls. They were being taught how to quickly focus their thoughts, enabling them all to levitate off the ground within a couple of seconds, as all flight was mind enabled as they had no physical wings to use. Stephanie noticed Crystal watching from the sidelines and waved frantically at her, a big beaming smile spread across her face.

'Bless her!' Crystal thought. 'She's adorable.' She turned to walk back inside, glancing up to check the skies. The familiar static electric caused the hairs on the back of her neck to stand on end, as if someone was blowing gently on her neck. She swung her head round to look behind her and, mixed in with the dark evening sky and grey clouds, she saw dark shadows appearing from the direction of the paper mill.

'Incoming!' She yelled as loud as she could, turning to run back towards the outhouses.

A large section of the wall, behind the rear of the outhouses, crashed to the ground, showering the flyahs with dust and debris. Several digahs came spilling through the wreckage, heads down charging at the main doors to the outhouses.

'Mum!' Crystal ran towards the building, frantic to get to her mother and Serena. She dodged the first flyah as he landed in front of her, but the second went to grab her. Raising her elbow, Crystal swiftly slammed it into his throat, briefly cutting off his air supply. He fell backwards, gasping for air, giving her precious seconds to get nearer to the building and her mother.

The chaos was everywhere. The banging and crashing of fighting mixed with the screams from inside the outhouses. Flyahs fighting flyahs as well as those digahs that had stayed outside. Healahs running from the outhouses and into the path of those fighting outside.

Nathan grabbed Crystal by the waist and left the ground, flying away from the scene.

'Put me down! I want to help my mum!' Crystal struggled in his arms, but he had both height and strength as his advantage.

'Keep still, you pain.' He clenched his teeth as he hung onto her. 'We agreed. You know the rules – you cannot be here now it's kicked off. You're too valuable – and you know it. Do I have to remind you that you're the only angel left?'

Unfortunately, he made sense, so she grudgingly relaxed

into his arms. 'Okay! Just give me the dignity of flying myself. It's not too far for me, you know.'

He hesitated. 'You won't go back?'

Crystal rolled her eyes. 'I promise. Now let me go!'

Nathan let her go and she dropped momentarily before rising slowly to his side.

'You're going straight to Kitty's house. I'll go back and find your mother and Serena, promise.' Nathan glanced across at her to make sure she was taking note.

She looked back at him, her eyes full of fear. 'Just you make sure you find them.'

CHAPTER 2

I t had been a week since the incident at the derelict paper mill. Crystal had been staying at Kitty's, sharing her best friend Emily's bed. Both Emily and her mother, Mel, had moved in two months before, after Mel had separated from her husband.

'Are you ready?' Emily stood behind the tripod; hand on the camcorder record button.

'Do you really want to do this?' She bit her bottom lip nervously. 'Would it not be safer to continue with the audios?'

Crystal shook her head. 'They're telling everyone we're false prophets, hiding behind anonymity. After their attack on us at the outhouses, we're not really safe anywhere.' She flicked a red and black strand of hair behind her shoulders. 'Let's do this.'

Emily hit the record button and focused the lens on Crystal, a full length shot of her sat on a plain white painted chair.

'I am an Angel and this is an important announcement for the world at large. Those of you who have been listening to our messages know what lies ahead for you. I'm not saying the road ahead will be easy, but you will be free to be whoever you truly are, at the core of you.

I also have a message for those in government, politics and religion – especially people like Father Thomas and his disciples.' She leant forward and rested her elbows on her legs, her chin on the knuckles of her cupped hands.

'You attacked us the other day. You threw the first stone and then ran away. You say we hide behind anonymity; well I'm not going to hide anymore. And I'm not afraid, for I *am* ready. Are you?' Crystal stood up and walked slowly and purposefully, closer to the camcorder, until her face filled the screen.

Staring directly into the camera lens, she slowly and menacingly uttered the next eight words. 'I – am – *that* – angel – and – I – am – here.'

ENJOYED THIS NOVEL? YOU CAN MAKE A BIG DIFFERENCE

If you enjoyed this novel, please spend a couple of minutes showing your appreciation by writing a quick review – reviews make all the difference to an author!

Reviews are the most powerful tools in my arsenal when it comes to getting attention for my books. Much as I'd like to, I don't have the financial muscle of a New York publisher. I can't take out full page ads in the newspaper or put posters on the subway.

(Not yet, anyway).

But I do have something more powerful and effective than that, and it's something that those publishers would kill to get their hands on.

A committed and loyal bunch of readers.

Honest reviews of my books help bring them to the attention of other readers.

If you've enjoyed this book I would be very grateful if you could spend just five minutes leaving a review (it can be as short as you like) - simply head on over to the site where you purchased your copy to leave your review.

Thank you very much.

ABOUT THE AUTHOR

Fiction author Sarah PJ White's approach to writing is to go with the flow, wherever the characters take her. She takes readers on a magical, mystery tour that leaves them enlightened, inspired and wanting more. In her earlier life, Sarah was a life coach and alternative therapist, founding 'Self Confidence Workshops', a self-help website for adults. She now combines the skills she's learnt to also write self-help books and mentor other writers.

Sarah lives in Cornwall, England, with her husband, daughter and hyperactive rescue dog, Danny.

For further information and updates:

sarahpjwhite.com

facebook.com/sarahpjwhite

twitter.com/sarahpjwhite

amazon.com/author/sarahpjwhite

pinterest.com/sarahpjwhite